NEBULOUS DECEPTION

Brent Hensley

To my wife Kay

I thank you for over thirty years of help, love and support making our marriage a wonderful trip of a lifetime.

With all my Love

List of Characters

Main Character—Connie Sue Womack

Her Husband—Jackson Randall Womack

Navy Seal—Rhys Garret

Specialist—Sydney "Spider" Rountree

Police Chief—Tommy John Parnell

Chief's Assistant—Carol Spoon

Connie's Best Friend—Dr. Kay Shirley

Officer William Weber

Officer Drew Tandy

Chief's Parnell's Sister—Beverly

Beverly's Daughter—Reese

Senator Winn Coleman

Senator's Wife—Patty Coleman

Coleman Children—Melissa & Elizabeth

Head of Security—Tony Hines
Nanny—Phyllis Grimes

Bodyguard—Eddie Miller

Coleman Family Attorney—Matthew Cohn

FBI Agent—Larry Talbert

Columbia Chief of Police—Roy Mannes

N. Myrtle Beach Chief of Police—Hank Johnson

Folks at Flynn's—Marty, Jane, Amanda, Larry, and Barry

Sex and Drug Trafficker—Cecil Locklear

Cecil's Cousins—Todd & Raymond Snyder

Cecil's Right-Hand Man—Skeeter

The Garrison Brothers

Cecil's Main Henchman—Cricket

Cecil's Other Henchman—Screwy Louie

Kidnapper—Curtis Todd Morning

Captain Theodore James Jolly

U.S. Park Ranger—David Ward

Tricks the Cat

Nebulous Deception

"If our American way of life fails the child, it fails us all."

Pearl S. Buck

Prologue

THE SUN WAS SETTING AS THE TWO YOUNG LOVERS KISSED.

THEY SIT ON THE SAND IN THE COOL of the ocean breeze as the sun sinks below the horizon of Folly Beach. The newfound lovers are in the throes of passion as he kisses his way to a young girl's heart. He then stops abruptly and looks deep into her eyes.

"Reese—that's right isn't it? Reese, do you want to go? Oh, never mind."

She looks confused as she looks up at him in the dusk of night. "Yes, my name is Reese and what is it you started to say?" She has forgotten his name already.

He sits up on his knees. "Would you like to go to one of my friend's house? It's just down the street over near the Pour House," which was a bar well-known for great live music off Maybank Highway. "They're having a little party. It's always a cool scene. Look, I know you don't know me but it's supposed to be a real good time, it always is." She waits a second before she answers. "Come on what do you say?"

She knows the right answer because she is staying with Susie, a daughter of her mother's best friend. But all the friends at Susie's house are not hers, and if her mother knew she ran off from Susie's and knew she is out on the beach kissing a total stranger she would dead already. But she cannot help but say the wrong answer. After all, she is 16 and he is real cute.

"Sure, it sounds like fun." And that's all it takes as they both stand up, brush the sand off their cutoff jean shorts, stop for a second to kiss each other one last time before the sun sets, and then run off the beach holding hands all the way to his car. They drive away.

There is no party off Maybank Highway.

SHE IS GONE!

Pillow Fight

Chapter 1

CONNIE WOMACK AWOKE AS IF that night had never ended and wished it had never happened as she noticed the fresh bruises all over her arms and hands. The long restless night had taken its toll, as she finally lost the fight with the lumpy set of pillows and very uncomfortable comforter. So she tossed all three on the floor at the foot of the bed in disgust and began to wiggle back and forward to get a so-called running start. She threw herself upward and outward, causing her to sit up in the bed long enough to turn and place her feet on the hardwood floor.

"Getting old is a bitch," Connie said out loud as she stopped just long enough to rub the soreness out of her back and to let her eyes focus on the clock that said 4:45 am. She then cleared her throat with a small cough as she started rubbing the sleep out from the corners of her eyes. She stopped and stared at her bruises once more and thought back to the last evening.

"Who the heck were those guys?" she said out loud as she thought they had balls to come in my house; they must have been looking for something.

Connie thought to herself, how they surprised her by grabbing her arms and hands and wrestling her out of the wheelchair, throwing her to the floor as they shouted, "You better stop looking into matters that don't involve you lady, it's none of your damn business."

"Stay the hell out, you hear me?" said the man who wore a red baseball cap and had a big black scar on his face.

She laughed out loud thinking how fast those boys ran back to their white pickup truck when she pulled out her .357 Magnum and thumb-cocked the hammer back as she pointed the barrel directly at their heads, making them first help her get back in the wheelchair before they ran off to the truck. She sat on the porch watching them drive off and wondering why she hadn't call the police.

Nevertheless she made sure they were gone

before she went into her home, and that all happened last night, she thought.

"Man, what a night. I wish I had just stayed up all night. Hey, I think you did," she said to herself. Still in a dream state, Connie sat there not moving, more like frozen in time for a few more minutes as she stared off into space till she focused, looking once again at the predawn time on her alarm clock glowing in the dark. "Matters that don't involve me? Really?" she asked out loud.

Suddenly, without warning, something hit hard up against her back. Connie didn't blink as she reached back and grabbed her cat Tricks pushing up against her. "I know, it's time to eat again," she said to the purring 20-pound black male cat that ruled the house. As she sat rubbing on Tricks her eyes started scanning the room till they found their target and there it was, lying on its side in the corner, her wheelchair.

You had to get mad at that thing too last night, didn't you, she thought, wondering how she was going to retrieve her chariot. After all, without it she was no good, at least when it came to getting around. But she was not through thinking of yesterday, as she lay back in the bed staring at the ceiling with the questions running like wildfire through her brain.

Who were those men that tried to rough her

up? What did they want from her? When might they come back? But the big question on Connie's mind was where were the kidnapped girls? What a case, she thought to herself. Connie kept trying to place the pieces in her mind but something wasn't adding up.

Bang! The loud noise came from the kitchen and Tricks the cat struck again by jumping off the bed hitting Connie right in the small of her back in his retreat. "Damn you cat! You scared the shit out of me!" But something was wrong; she could feel it as she sat up in the bed. Again more noise but this time the sound was of pots and pans crashing to the floor in the kitchen. Someone was definitely in the house. Without hesitation Connie pulled her Smith and Wesson out from under her pillow, opened the revolver chamber and checked on all six Remington's .357 cartridges. Once the bullets were inspected she closed the chamber and pointed it towards the bedroom door.

In a weak and fragile voice she cried out, "Is anybody there? Help me, I'm an invalid, I can't get up, please help me." She then removed the safety and eased the hammer back to welcome her new unwelcomed house guest with her best two friends, Smith and Wesson.

"Invalid my ass," said a man's voice. "Don't shoot, it's me Connie," as the door opened enough to where Connie could see the coast was clear. She quickly eased the hammer back in place and took a big sigh of relief as she recognized the intruder.

"Oh man, Willie, I could have shot your butt," Connie called out to her friend and part-time lover.

Willie pushed the door open enough to where Connie could see his face in the doorway. "Heck, you're the one that gave me your key."

"Yea, but most people call first. That's crazy just coming in here like that," she said as she laid the gun down on the bed. "What the heck are you doing here away?" she questioned him once again as she reached over for her night shirt to cover her nude body.

"What am I doing? You're the one that invited me over, dumb ass. Remember you called me yesterday afternoon, talking about not sleeping well and maybe having breakfast together. So here I am and I was looking for something to cook with. Sorry but I'm hungry. You know I do work night shift these days at the old precinct. I got off a little early this morning, so I came over to make you some pancakes if that's alright with you," he said, still standing in the doorway as he kept looking into the bedroom enjoying the view of seeing her in her birthday suit.

"All right peeping Tom, you got your eyes full."

She finished pulling the T-shirt over her head and was now covered up. "Why don't you come in and help an old lady, I mean a damsel in distress. It seems my wheels got away from me last night."

With that Willie was in the room like a flash. He really loved Connie and would do anything for her. Grabbing the wheelchair with one hand, he uprighted it quickly and slowly rolled it over to her bedside. "Here you go, Miss," he said like an English lord, tipping his hat at her. Connie responded with a makeshift curtsy, pulling outward on her shirt and nodding her head.

"Thank you, Sir," she said as they both laughed. Hearing the laughter, Tricks decided to join them once again on the bed, satisfied that all was well and no danger was at hand.

Willie quickly noticed the scratches and bruises on Connie's arms as he was helping her into the wheelchair. "Wait a minute, what is this," he asked as he inspected more closely. "Connie what is going on here, are you alright?"

"Sure thing, I'm fine Willie. Now help me turn this thing around," she said to stop his investigation, as she pulled on the wheels of the chair and they proceeded out of the bedroom into the kitchen with Tricks in tow.

Willie turned the wheelchair around so Connie

could see his face. “It’s that missing kids’ case, right?” Connie didn’t say a word; she sat there looking down at her nails as if she was doing a self-inspection of her manicure as Willie’s lecture continued.

“Connie, you know that’s an ongoing investigation. It’s not warm; it’s not cool, and damn sure it’s not cold. It’s active and about as active as any case I have ever seen. I’m talking from the FBI, the SBI, the Governor’s task force, all the way down to the local police and sheriff’s office. And by the way, you young lady, are not any of those folks, much less a policewoman. You have no authority in that case. You could be arrested.”

Connie stopped the inspection and looked up. “Oh Willie, nobody is going to arrest me. Plus I’m not pursuing any ongoing case dealing with kidnapping. I’m too old for that game these days. I’m just an old woman living out the rest of her life in this old house with her old cat,” she said as she rubbed the top of Tricks’ head.

“You sit up here working on old cold cases, that’s one thing. Getting involved with an ongoing police investigation is another thing all together and you know it.”

“Hey, pull your panties out of the crack. I know what I can and can’t do, William. The truth is you boys seem to be working a little slower than a few folks in town would like. And a couple of these fine people have asked for my help. Wait a minute, my help, that's all. They just want to see if I could help speed things up, turn over a few rocks, nothing more than that." Connie moved over to the coffee pot and hit the button that started the pot to brew.

"And by the way if they were your kids, you would ask for my help, too. Bull, you know you would." She then rolled over to the big bay window in the front of the house, pulled open a drawer to her mother's old secretary and grabbed an old pack of Marlboro Lights.

Again trying to talk her out of meddling in the kidnapping case, Willie walked over to the back of her chair and put his hand on her shoulder. "Connie, you are a retired insurance investigator, not a cop. You don't even have a concealed-carry permit for that hand cannon you keep with you all the time. And now I come over here and your place looks like it was ransacked, your wheelchair turned over on its side, and you have been roughed up by some damn body. And to this policeman it looks like you have already turned over a few rocks. Now what say you my pretty?"

"Well Willie, I didn't know you cared that much sweetheart. I do appreciate your concern, but dealing with kidnappers is not like working up a quote for State Farm. You know I have the skills."

She rolled the chair over to him, reached out and grabbed his hand. "Look baby, I'm trying to help some folks find their daughters and I'm going to try with or without your help, or Captain Tommy John Parnell and the entire Charleston Police Department. Now how do you like your coffee big man?"

"Black," said Willie, knowing full well that Connie was not about to give in to his tactics. She was not going to tell him and that's that. And she was right. She did have the skills. A tomboy from birth, she was a great athlete in most sports in both high school and college. At Duke she lettered in softball and field hockey and graduated second in her class.

She then joined the Army before the end of the Vietnam War. She was not allowed to fight in combat so she volunteered for the military police, where she served 20 years as an MP before she retired with the rank of major. She also was 22 years retired as an insurance investigator for Lloyds of London, traveling all over the world reclaiming stolen property. She knew about everything there was to know about people, law enforcement and the criminal mind. She was one tough lady and a lady in every sense of the word, but hard as nails and one good-looking woman, then and now. The years had added a few more pounds and her crow's feet and laugh lines a little more pronounced, but Connie Womack was still very striking to look at and someone most folks didn't want to mess with. She was also a little on the crazy side after someone blew up her house in Washington, D.C., killing her husband of 30 years and putting her in a wheelchair for life.

"How's the coffee Willie, need more?"

"No, I'm good for now. How about those pancakes? How many you want?"

"Pancakes, my butt is so big now it will barely fit in this wheelchair. Are you kidding me, no thank you, I'm good," she said as she moved the chair around the room and back and forth as though she was getting exercise.

"Hey, I know a way to lose weight," Willie said with a smile on his face, as he looked in the direction of the bedroom.

"Now that's the best idea you have had this morning." Connie turned the chair and raced into the bedroom. Willie was right behind her and Tricks shot in before the door closed.

Service Call

Chapter 2

THE MARQUEE SIGN OF THE SEA NYMPH MOTEL flickered VACANCY in bright pink neon light as the two lovers inside room 14 were working on their nonstop third round of sex. They had to get in all the romance they could in a short period of time because of their situation in life. One was the wife of a state senator and the other was her bodyguard. From the looks of things there was not one inch of her body he did not guard, ravish, massage, pamper or lust over. These two were on a mission and the mission had been a huge success as the two collapsed into a sticky heap of sweat and melted Ben and Jerry's ice cream, which had stained both the bed and the carpet. She laughed and giggled a little as he licked the inside of her thigh after rubbing his finger in the almost empty carton of butter pecan. She was covered in the stuff. The two looked like a Calvin Klein ad as they kissed and licked each other like a tootsie roll pop.

Their union was one of pure unadulterated sex and nothing more. Sure, they enjoyed each other's company but the raw sex is what the rendezvous had always been about. Intellectually they hardly knew each other, how do you do was never spoken or what's your favorite anything, much less your favorite show, color, food, places to go, anything. The one time Tony talked ill of her children, saying that they were odd and conniving, she didn't have sex with him for over two months. So sex was it with these two and they both were pretty good at it.

"Stop it! I can't stand any more, you will be the death of me," she said as she tried to catch her breath and leaned over and kissed him for the last time on his forehead. He sat up on the side of the bed, pulled out a cigarette and lit it.

"Your death, hell I'm the one having an affair with my boss's wife. I don't think you have much to worry about since he is screwing everything in town. Heck, I should know. I'm the one watching out for him. Ha, that's a joke." He was feeling sorry for himself, that was all. He rolled back over in bed and put his hand on her leg and slowly stroked it.

"Now wait a minute Tony," she said as she crawled back on top of him and they both shared the same cigarette. "The bottom line is that you have been faithful to Winn. The problem is that he has not been very faithful to anybody his whole life, including me. It's all about him, and it always will be. He's a born politician. Everything about him is phony, even his name. It's not Winn Coleman, it's Cornelius Pettigrew."

"No you're kidding me, Cornelius? That's great, Corny Peabody."

"No, not Peabody, Pettigrew silly."

"I know, I'm just messing with you," and he rolled over again putting the cigarette in the ash tray and starting act four. But before they could even finish the foreplay Tony's phone started to ring, and ring and ring.

"Are you going to get it or not?" she said as she stopped kissing on him and sat up on the side of the bed.

"OK, OK, Yeah Eddie what is it? This better be good! Winn, what about Winn, where is he now? What, OK I hear you, OK thanks. Baby we got to go. Your old man just announced on Twitter he is going to run for governor of South Carolina."

"Great news, I'm glad he didn't bother to tell

me first."

"Yeah, but out of all the motels in Charleston Eddie said Winn is bringing a girl to this motel so we have to go, and go now!" He grabbed her hand and helped her off the bed.

"What the hell," she said as they both started searching for their apparel. "I've got to take a shower and get this damn sticky ice cream mess off of me."

"Well you better hurry up, and do it fast. Damn girl, use the sink, we got to go!" As they both worked their way into the bathroom Patty pulled back the shower curtain, turned on the water and pulled Tony inside the bathtub.

"You're the one that made us a big sticky mess; I need a big strong bodyguard like you big boy to help clean this off. That sorry ass husband of mine will have to wait his turn." Both she and Tony both laughed as they made sure that act number four was not just a quickie but a complete success. They managed to escape from the motel room in mere minutes as they made it to their car and seemed to have fled the scene of the crime undetected and both squeaky clean.

Once in the car Tony cautiously checked to see if the coast was clear as he looked both ways before edging the black SUV cautiously down the back alley and out of the motel's parking lot in just the nick of time. Within moments Eddie drove up in the front driveway of the Sea Nymph. He didn't stop at the main entrance but drove the car further back into the adjacent parking lot trying to be a little more discreet. His instructions were to always park in the back, regardless of the fact that you are driving a black stretch limousine with blacked out bulletproof glass with the senator and his flavor of the month in the back seat. The senator said he would be less likely detected by the press if they parked in the back lot.

Not the smartest man in the world, next time use a Volkswagen, not a land yacht that covers three parking places, thought Eddie as he then left the car and walked into the motel's office to make the usual arrangements so as to not disturb the newfound lovebirds in the back seat.

"Man this shit is getting old," he said to himself, "but at least one of us is getting some," as he pulled out some cash and handed it to the attendant to pay for the senator's hour of lust.

We Need A Winn

Chapter 3

THE CHARLESTON PLACE HOTEL WAS FULL of excitement. The ballroom area was abuzz with the news conference that was about to take place. The ballroom was now serving as the makeshift local Republican headquarters and was full of potential voters, onlookers and reporters. The room was decked out in red, white and blue banners, balloons and American flags lining the walls along with campaign signs throughout the large crowd of about five hundred. You could bet there wasn't a fire marshal in the bunch, as the room was well over its legal capacity. The crowd poured into the adjacent hallways and they were spilling out into King Street in the heart of the city. The anticipation of this event was at full volume along with the patriotic music blaring out over the loud speakers. The cheers from the crowd reached a fever pitch as they awaited their candidate. Campaign signs dotted throughout the room were being waved about and bounced up and down, saying "WE NEED A WINN."

Suddenly shouts and claps erupted as a side door from the outside hallway finally opened. After being at least an hour late, Winn Coleman, the pride of South Carolina, finally arrived. He walked into the room, headed toward the podium, waving and shaking hands to a standing ovation. Once he got on stage he fought back the desire to blink and squint, even though his eyes burned and he was having trouble adjusting to the bright television lights. He thought to himself that he was a professional at this, no one was going to see him sweat regardless of how hot or nervous he truly was. The two-term state congressman and one-term state senator was now running for governor of South Carolina. So what if that heat radiating off the lights burned like a hundred sunlamps on his sprayed-on tanned face. That wouldn't cause him to blink one bit, and he didn't as he started his speech.

"Thank you, thank you, and thank you ladies and gentlemen. Thank you very much, thank you all. It is a great honor and privilege to be speaking to you today in this beautiful hotel, in this wonderful town of Charleston, in our great Palmetto state that we all love so much. There's one thing about you wonderful and diverse people... no matter if you are a Gamecock or a Tiger fan, whether you are from, be it the upstate in the Greenville, Spartanburg area or the midlands of Columbia and Florence, or from here, our beloved coastal low country, we all have one thing in common and that is we all care about our great state of South Carolina."

He stopped as the roar of cheers and shouts rose in volume as more signs were waved in the crowd. "And that's why I, Winn Coleman, your state senator, have come to be with you here today, to you the people of this fair state." He stopped again and pointed out to the crowd. "I will need a lot of your thoughts and prayers if I'm going to do this right. That's why with you and God's help today I am here to announce that I'm running to be your next governor of the great state of South Carolina. South Carolina," he shouted for the second time. That's when the crowd went nuts and jumped to their feet as the cheers went out throughout the crowded room and down the hallways of the hotel.

All the while his daughters sat in the first row of reserved seats like manikins with their smiles painted on, like the perfect children that they were, in public. Their mother was backstage waiting to be announced to enter the stage on his command. After a tedious 20 minutes of campaign promises and lies, he then motioned to her to be ready to come out and to walk over to her political husband.

"Come on out here sweetheart," he said to her as they met on stage, planting a fake kiss right on her lips as well. And the crowd went crazy with cheers once again. "Everyone this is my wife of over 15 years, Patty Lynn. Say hello, Patty."

"Hey, everybody, hello," she shouted in her best artificial southern drawl, being from New Jersey, as she embraced him again and stole the microphone. "I wanted to thank you all for the love and support you have shown to my husband and myself over the years and especially in these last few weeks leading up to today. Winn, I know thanks you, and I too would like to thank you, all from the bottom of my heart, thank you, thank you again. We need your vote if we are to beat those old mean democrats in November, so we can make South Carolina the great state she once was, a great state again," she said as she kissed him for the second time and blew a kiss to the crowd, moving to her place on stage beside, but slightly behind him.

The noise level went up even more as both

Winn and Patty held hands and held them high over their heads in a victory sign of sorts. The folks in the crowd loved it, and if truth be known, they always loved her more. And who wouldn't? She was real, not calculating and cold like her husband Winn. But she knew her role and she did her part well. So well that hardly anyone knew their marriage was a stage act all together.

The years of campaigning and traveling apart had turned them into something they were not when they lived together in a small apartment in Five Points, when they both were going to college at the University of South Carolina in Columbia back in the early 90s. But those days of being in love, going to the Vista for a few drinks with their college buddies and having laughs eating chicken wings at Leo's "the home of the wing" were over. The love flame was about out for these two, now strictly a campaign machine. They were much like a modern-day Franklin and Eleanor or a local version of Bill and Hillary. No Ronny and Nancy here, not with these two, they were all business.

Even the children were cold and more calculating. Patty made sure they were always dressed and groomed perfectly. These two were seen on local TV more than reruns of *I Love Lucy*. No way would Winn and Patty let them act up and ruin their political career. They couldn't afford the two girls getting out of line in anyway, much less pick their noises, or hit each other, or shout out loud, and heaven forbid them to look sad or say a bad word in public view or within earshot of a reporter. No, they were perfect little Stepford kids, in front of everyone, including their parents, Winn and Patty.

Precious children, one would think the first couple of times you met them. Elizabeth, 16, was the oldest by one year but Melissa was the brains of the outfit. Both girls were very deliberate in their actions and one would not dare do a thing without the consent of the other. It was as if they were twins, but without a doubt they knew each other inside and out, more like soul mates. They were more than sisters and best friends; they were inseparable and depended on each other religiously.

When they were younger Winn would call them Winking and Blinking to see them get mad. But most of the time if angered they would walk off and plan a surprise attack to get even. And boy, were they good at that. Their best attribute was to get back at someone but to make it look like someone else did it. That was their specialty and not getting caught at it was their second-best attribute. To be able to play such a game of charades was genius but with such devilish personalities it was truly a rare feat indeed and quite scary. Winn and Patty Coleman had their hands full with these two and didn't even know it. But soon they would.

"Great speech Winn, good job," said a few fans and donors who paid big bucks to be there. Working the crowd, Winn and Patty worked their way off the stage and headed to talk to the press at the makeshift spin room which was set up around the backside of the stage itself. Patty saw Phyllis Grimes standing among the crowd of people when Winn and Patty walked down the stairs.

"Phyllis, where are the girls? We need them with us for pictures and we are getting ready to meet with the press. Where are they?" said Patty, as Winn too, was curious not seeing their children with their nanny or bodyguard.

"I'm sorry ma'am. I thought they were with you two. They both got up and said they were going to the bathroom and were going backstage to be with you guys." Saying it out loud, Phyllis realized she might have made a terrible mistake.

"Are you crazy? You let them go to the bathroom by themselves in this crowd," Patty shouted.

"Dear please, hold your voice down. People are watching," Winn whispered, as some of the press was picking up on their conversation with the nanny.

“OK, I will make announcement on the microphone and we will find them in two seconds,” said Patty.

“You will not, you will not do any such thing. It will make a scene. I will tell Tony, and he will handle it. Dear, they are young women, not children. They walked off, they met a couple of boys, and they are probably standing outside right now for all we know and that’s what teenagers do. And you know we’ll find them shopping down the hallway in here or in the Straw Market some place. You’ll see.” Winn motioned over to Tony Hines, his head of security and soon to be his campaign manager.

“Yes sir, I heard the conversation. We can handle it. My people and I will find them.”

“See Honey, now let Tony do his job and you and I will go talk to the press. Now let’s go,” Winn demanded, and once again she did as he commanded.

Tony started calling in his security team and within seconds he was off like a hound dog on a new scent.

Police Need Help

Chapter 4

"IF YOU LIE TO ME ONE MORE TIME I swear I'm going to kick in this TV set so help me," said Tommy John Parnell, being so disgusted from what he saw and heard he grabbed the clicker and quickly turned off Fox News showing the Coleman campaign live on Special Report with Bret Baier. "That's all we need is another coldhearted lying son of a bitch for governor," he shouted as he finished drinking the last drop of cold coffee while dribbles ran down his shirt and tie. He then sat back down at his desk and was in the process of cleaning off the brown stain as the door opened.

"Chief, is everything alright in here? What was all that shouting about?" said Carol Spoon, his secretary.

"Yes, mama I'm fine. It's all this political crap, it drives me crazy, Carol."

"Yes sir I understand, political crap," she said, not understanding what in the world he was talking about. "Yes sir, crap. Oh by the way sir you have a visitor. A lady, a Miss Womack, and by the way she's in a wheelchair sir."

"Well, let her in, Carol, and the wheelchair too," he said sarcastically.

"I'm sorry I didn't mean anything by that chief. It came out wrong. I'm so sorry."

"It's OK, Carol. Please send her in," he said as he straightened up both the papers on his desk and his tie. "Miss Womack, right this way, would you please come in."

"Chief Parnell good morning to you," Connie said, as she wheeled into the large office and parked so she could look out the larger picture widow watching the passersby on the sidewalk and street. "Look at all those people out there. You sure have a big responsibility don't you, chief?"

"Yeah, I guess so," as he too looked out the window.

"I wonder if anyone stops and thinks about it

like that, you know, your job and all the responsibilities that come with it. Keeping the peace, solving crime, keeping the meter maid lady happy in more ways than one, you know what I mean, I believe her name is Judy?"

"I'm glad you're here, Connie, and I know you must be still mad at me. This is not easy for me either," Parnell said, knowing the last time they met was not very cordial. In fact it ended up in a fight of words with Connie and the chief leaving mad and upset.

"Look Connie I'll cut to the chase. The deal is I need your help. Someone, or I think it's a small group of people, are kidnapping innocent children and asking for ransom money. You know the story, if the money does not arrive in time; the kid is sold to the highest bidder, never to be heard of again."

"You say what, chief, you need my help? I believe I was the one that came to you the first time," she said as she quickly turned the wheel around to see his face.

"I know, Connie. You did tell me months ago we might have a problem, but at the time, Connie, we did not have the resources that we do now. Plus people are scared now."

"Oh I see. Someone or a bunch of someones called your boss the mayor and said that you better fix this thing before it gets out of hand. Was it something like that, Tommy John? Is that how it went down?"

"Look you win. You are on the case as a special agent, OK? Whatever you need you come to me, and if I can I'll make sure you will get it. Here, here's a badge," as he pulled a badge out of his desk drawer and laid it on his desk. "I need you on this job, alright, is that nice enough?" He stopped talking and stared at the floor. He was done apologizing. He truly needed help but he was not about to beg for it.

Connie looked and saw pain on Tommy John's face; she then rolled closer to him and grabbed his hand. "This is personal," she said. " Who do you know that was kidnapped, who is it, Tommy?"

"My sister called two nights ago. She's a single mother doing all she can. It was her child, her only child, Reese," he said in a low voice. "We don't have much money Connie, and we are not rich people. I don't know what to do at this point. My men, the FBI, SBI, everyone, we have looked everywhere and I'm out of leads. I need someone with your background. I need your help, Connie."

Connie sat up straight in her chair and started calling out demands. "Give me all the information on your sister's kid, school records, pictures, names and numbers of friends, and all the information you have on the other children that are missing in a two-hundred-mile radius. We have already lost precious time in that first 48 hours."

Tommy John was writing down her request so he wouldn't forget it as he looked up from her last comment.

"I'm going to need someone from your office to help me; Officer William Weber will be fine, he's a friend of mine. I will need several computers with a strong mainframe, the good ones with lots of memory, plus access to passwords and security clearance for codes to police computers and data."

The chief looked up from writing. "I can do that."

"I also need a cell phone with an unlimited plan, and a tablet, all preferably Apple. Don't be cheap, Tommy. I don't need an office, but if you have one that's open that's fine too. Now let me see, oh yea I do need access to the Federal Bureau of Missing Person's data base, and a van, wheelchair accessible so I can get around a little better, getting in and out of a car is a pain. Oh, did you know I use a wheelchair? Your secretary didn't?"

"Damn, Connie, anything else?" he said, looking up as he was writing down her demands.

"Yes, get me a concealed-carry permit. I keep

my gun with me all the time," she said as she patted her hip where her Smith and Wesson was hidden. She turned the chair toward the door and looked over to Tommy John before leaving. "We'll get your niece back, Tommy, and the rest of those children, so help me."

Tommy sat thinking as the door closed in Connie's departure. He looked at the picture of Reese sitting on his desk and picked it up and looked again at it real hard, as if she, in the picture, was going to tell him where she was. His eyes swelled a little with tears in the corner as he looked at her beautiful big green eyes and that head full of red flame, curly hair. She called it strawberry blonde. She hated being call a redhead. He attempted to hold back his emotions.

He moved the mouse over the pad and clicked the cursor as his computer came back to life to the page he was on earlier in the day reading, the National Center for Missing and Exploited Children. The phone number was there as well, 1-800-The-Lost. The website stated that over one in five children that are reported runaways are in fact sex trafficking victims. Tommy John quickly wrote down the number 1-800-843-5678, and grabbed his phone out of his pocket to call his sister Beverly and to tell her the good news about Connie being on the case. He then reached over and pressed the intercom button on his desk.

“Carol, come in here, I have some things I need for you to get,” he said on the intercom.

“Sure thing, chief, I’ll be right there!”

He kept reading about kids in Cambodia for sale for sex trafficking reported by Dateline. Tens of thousands of children each year are sold and bought in night clubs in Bangkok and in the windows of Amsterdam, among the most-well known destinations. It had become a multibillion dollar industry, sex tourism. He leaned back into his chair thinking the worst and shouted, “Carol did you hear me!”

Concrete Coffin

Chapter 5

THE DARK IS EVERYWHERE AND NOTHING BUT BLACK, pitch black. There is no light at all. She awakes naked, scared and cold. She pushes herself backwards till the hard concrete wall comes up to meet her as she feels the cold rough concrete cut into her bare skin. She sits shaking from the cold as she wraps her arms around herself trying to get warmer. She can feel the cold sinking into her bones. She hears the sound of a metal chain moving across the concrete as she tugs and pulls against the chain attached to her leg and feels the metal bracelet on her ankle. The pain hits her as the metal band cuts into her flesh when she moves, so she tries to remain as still as she can.

Her minds races on. What must have happened to her? There is just dark, not one ray of light, it is as if she had no eyes. She can see nothing, not even her hand as she waves it in front of her swollen and tender face that hurts when she touches it. But no matter how hard she tries, she has no idea of anything, nothing at all. How did this happen? Where is she? How did she get to wherever this is? All she knows now is the pain from the cold concrete on her naked skin, and the smell of mold and damp as she starts to cry again but quickly stops when she thinks she hears something or somebody.

She tries to stand but hits her head on the short ceiling as she tries to straighten up but falls back down on the concrete. Running her hands along the rough textured walls she feels their height which seems to be about three feet. Too short to stand up in but tall and long enough to get on all fours and to stretch, and to get off that cold and hard concrete for a second or two and that helps. Again her ears strain to hear anything, as she makes herself as quiet as possible by holding her breath. But there's nothing to hear as she sits back down on the cold floor and waits.

"Is there anyone there?" she says in a soft

voice. Again she cries a little more, this time more like a whimper, and then with a blast she shouts, “Help me!” The rebound of the echo is deafening as she covers her ears and cowers in a fetal position. She knows now she is in a very small space. And in pitch black darkness it becomes very claustrophobic. As she tries to gain strength and understand her predicament she senses that she is not alone. She reaches out and her outstretched hand accidentally touches something. She jumps back a little but after a couple of minutes her curiosity gets the best of her and she reaches out to touch the something once again. Her hand trembles as she slowly extends her arm, her hand, and her fingers.

And again she explores the unknown as she then feels the soft smooth surface of an object that is cool to the touch. She has no idea until she feels the free edge and hardness of the fingernails and realizes that it is someone’s hand she is touching and only a hand, no arm, no body. She screams in horror and pulls her own hand back quickly. She cries again as she sits and does the only thing she can do, as she waits in the black dark hoping to be released from this hellish concrete coffin.

Team Womack

Chapter 6

STARING AT THE BOTTLE CONNIE poured herself a second glass of Pinot Noir, a birthday gift from her husband Jack that she had saved for years. Why today?

Maybe because she finally gave up on the Isabella Gardner Museum theft of over 13 works of art valued at $500 million. The Gardner Museum caper was and still is, the largest-value crime of theft of private property in U.S. history, with a $5 million reward for information leading to recovery of the loot. It was around five a.m. on the morning of March 18, 1990, when the guards at the Isabella Stewart Gardner Museum in Boston allowed two men who were posing as cops to enter the museum.

Once the men were inside they quickly tied up the guards and made away with the stolen works of art. One was a self-portrait of Rembrandt, dated 1634, plus there were several more Rembrandt, Degas and other rare artifacts. Once the real police arrived all that was left were empty picture frames and pedestals. The case had haunted Connie as she had spent over 20 years on this one. Neither she nor anyone else has ever cracked it or had found even a good lead.

But as for opening the bottle of wine from Jack now, she did not really know the reason. It seemed like a good time and that was good enough for Connie. Spur of the moment was the way her husband would want it. She kept reflecting back on her day at the police station, and was pleased that she got everything she had asked for, but the overall weight of the situation had her worried. She sat in her wheelchair in the living room rubbing Tricks perched on her lap. As she replaced the cork back in the tall-neck vessel she started to think of her mission, her real mission.

Sure she wanted to save those kids but was she doing it just to get back in the game? She thought maybe so. After all it had been a long time since she felt like doing much of anything after losing her husband. Jack was the apple of her eye. He was her everything and what a man he was. "I miss the hell out of you Jack," she sighed, as she raised her glass of wine in the air to toast and to salute him. How would he handle this situation, she thought? No one would know better than Jack. He knew exactly what to do, and how to do it right, in just about any situation, and this job was going to take more than an average guy.

Jackson Randall Womack was no average guy by any stretch. He was tall, with Tom Cruise good looks but with jet black hair. He stood six-five and weighed about 250 pounds and was all muscle and one hundred percent all man. He played middle linebacker back in his football days at the Naval Academy in Annapolis, Maryland, and graduated in the top one percent in his class. He was a part of an elite Navy Seal team and did four tours in Vietnam, his last tour was in Iraq. Afterwards he started his own private security business for folks that needed protection. Even small countries asked for his company's help, and in just a few years, he managed and operated a small army, comprised mostly of his old navy and army buddies that were tops in their fields of expertise. Jack traveled all over the world as bodyguard and mercenary, with an army large enough to stop a small war in any third-world country.

Connie and Jack met at an Army-Navy football game after-party. He could not resist her Renée Russo looks and they fell in love at first sight. Before they knew it, they were a couple living in

DC. She was still in the military working at the White House under the Ford administration and he worked wherever he was needed throughout the world. He would be gone for weeks at a time but the reunion with those two was nothing less than a workout. They tried so hard to have children but after two miscarriages they stopped trying, but boy did they practice. They truly loved each other and nothing got in their way of lovemaking.

After Connie retired from the military she was looking for something to do. Jack had a friend, Bob Wesson; he was also a customer of Jack's who had made some enemies along the way in the insurance business. Insurance companies were always looking for good investigators.

Once Connie left the Army Jack thought she would be pretty good at something like insurance investigation. Investigating was right down her alley. She loved solving crimes. It didn't matter if the crime was stolen jewelry or precious art works. Crime solving is what she was trained for and after twenty years with the military police she was considered by the army as one of the best at it. The company didn't care about her skills at solving crime. They just wanted to recoup the money from the stolen properties.

After a few short years and several solved cold cases, Connie landed a job she could not turn down.

It was with the largest of all insurance companies, Lloyd's of London. They were interested in knowing how she did it. In a few years she was considered one of the best in the world at recovering stolen property. Not long after that she too was sent all over the world as a trainer, teaching other investigators her method. With Jack's help, she had found her niche, and had also found that she had a knack at solving crime. Jack was amazed at her ability, quite the Agatha Christie's Miss Marple and Nancy Drew all rolled into one.

Connie's method was quite simple. Find the person or persons who were buying the stuff. The old tried and true, following the money method, but Connie studied bank accounts and their paying method with off shore banks and their travel routes, finding the right shipping lines; everyone had their own routes getting to the right buyers. And that works in the drug trade and the kidnapping industry as well. It's hard enough trying to find the stolen Rembrandt or Hope diamond or even a kidnapped person, but the trail to the buyer will lead you to the prize every time.

But it had been a long time since Connie was in the field and as the years went by the use of computers was more prevalent and her methods of finding these trails were getting harder to do. It was a whole new ballgame in this new tech world with smart phones, Facebook pages, Twitter, and basically the whole Internet thing in every corner of the globe. She knew she had to get someone to help her in this department, and quickly, but who? Jack would have known who to call, but that would no longer be an option. She thought long and hard as she sipped on her wine and stared up at the ceiling, deep in a train of thought till her eye caught sight of a cobweb way up in the corner of the room and out of her reach to destroy.

Just like that the name popped in her head, Sydney Rountree, that's it, Sydney, known affectionately as Spider. He was the best in computers and communication, the best IT. man period. Spider had worked for Jack on several operations in Libya the Sudan, and a couple times in Chad. "Yeah, that's my guy alright." She stopped and thought again out loud, "I wonder if he still works with Rhys? He sure would come in handy. Now all I got to do is find them." With a smile on her lips, she finished off the bottle of Pinot Noir with that last swallow. She was so tired, not to mention drunk, as she placed the empty glass of wine on the table, grabbed Tricks, and wheeled both herself and the cat into the bedroom. It had been a long but very productive day.

Last Straw Market

Chapter 7

TONY LAMAR HINES WALKED ALONG THE STRAW MARKET in downtown Charleston for hours looking for clues. The girls were nowhere to be found. The Market was in the center of historical Charleston, which began across the street from the Charleston Place Hotel and went down to the restaurant district on East Bay Street. The Straw Market was an open-air market where you could buy anything from handmade straw baskets to T-shirts and souvenirs. At night the vendors had to leave and take everything with them. In the morning they were back setting up shop again and selling their wares. Tourists loved the place, the location and the history. The fact that back in the day they sold slaves there was very intriguing to a lot of folks. In fact, it was one of the largest slave markets in the South. That's the history of Charleston. Once a slave market, now the Straw Market, an odd place indeed, full of bars, shops and restaurants and a great place to get lost in.

That's what Tony was thinking being a local kid himself. Tony knew this town like the back of his hand. He graduated from the Citadel and did two tours in Afghanistan, and he was good at his job. But never in his wildest dreams would he think he would end up being a nursemaid to these two punk kids. He never liked those two. Something about them was odd, not your typical teenagers by any means. He had his hands full with these two but a job is a job, and working for the senator overall was a good one. At least working for Mrs. Coleman was a good gig, but he never thought he would fall in love with her.

"Eddie, if you're over on King Street check out Jacobs Alley. It's between Archdale and King Street. You can't miss it," Tony said in his phone.

"Will do, boss, I'm on it," said Eddie as he hung up the phone. Tony had the rest of his men search from the Arthur Ravenel Jr. Bridge and south on Highway 17 north of the hotel to Queen Street and down to the Battery Park, back to the Straw Market and all points in between. Tony and his team were feeling frustrated and tired of coming up empty and now it was time to tell his boss Winn and his wife Patty the bad news. Tony stopped for a second and looked through the open-air window at the folks having a great time at Henry's, a local watering hole in the Straw Market. He wished to himself that he was there instead of being out in the heat on this wild goose chase looking for the two sisters. He stopped his daydreaming and pulled his cell phone out of his pocket, but before he had the chance to call anyone, his phone started ringing. Caller ID said unknown.

Who could that be, he said to himself, but answered anyway.

"Hello, Tony Hines here," said Tony to no answer but he heard crying on the other phone, and again he tried, "hello, who is this?" The noise of the street was loud, making it hard to hear. "Hello, I can't hear you."

"Mister Hines it's me, Melissa," the crying voice answered. "They have Elizabeth, help me! Help me! I don't know where I am. Help me please. They got Elizabeth. I got away." The phone went dead.

"Hey! Hold on, hello, hello! Melissa is that you? Damn," he said as the line went silent. Are you kidding me? he thought to himself. He hit redial on the phone but no luck, the number was blocked. There was nothing but the sound of a busy signal going off like an alarm as he hung up the phone. He quickly texted to his men to meet him at Henry's in the Straw Market.

"That makes no sense," Tony said out loud as he reviewed the conversation he just had with Melissa. "She calls me, not her parents, from an unknown phone number, does not say where she is and then the call is cut short. It does not make sense," he said again, shaking his head. He then began texting to Winn as he stood on the corner of North Market and Rafters Alley. The street was packed with people for the opening weekend of the Spoleto Festival, a huge annual performing arts event held in Charleston for the past 17 years.

Tony moved in and out of the crowds of thousands as he danced around the masses in the street the whole time he was texting on the phone. He never looked up; he was concentrating too hard on his business at hand. He never saw the white Ford truck or the people around him who were jumping out of the path but Tony didn't move and it was too late. The truck's horn never sounded and the truck never skidded to a stop as the two collided at the intersection in the Straw Market where Tony stood. The sound of the cries and screams was the last thing Tony heard.

More screams and cries rang out through the crowd of pedestrians and onlookers. "Watch out, oh my God!" shouted someone from the crowd.

"Oh my God, move, get out of the way!" cried another.

As the crowd reacted to the mayhem of what had occurred, Tony's head hit and broke onto the pavement after his body was thrown yards into the middle of North Market Street. People circled his body as the life quickly ran out of Tony Hines. His outreached hand was still holding on to his phone as the life in his eyes went dark for good. He took his last breath and was gone. The circle of people stood in shocked silence.

Patty and Winn were in their hotel room when Winn's cell phone dinged with a text. It was Tony with the news. Winn read the text from Tony explaining the call he just received from Melissa and answered back by writing *OK, please call back ASAP*.

"Who was that?" Patty asked after hearing the dinging of Winn's phone.

"That was Tony, dear. He said they have not heard anything but they are still looking."

"That's it; I'm not waiting one minute more Winn Coleman. We must call the police."

"Come on Patty, let the pros do their work. We don't have to involve the authorities and the press.

Heck you know the drill. It will be in all the papers, TV, Internet, everywhere."

"Pros? Who the hell do you think the police are? I just don't understand Winn, our little girls are out there all alone. We can't wait any longer, people go missing all the time, and this is not going to hurt your campaign. Oh' the hell with your career," she snapped as she grabbed her phone from her purse.

"I said Tony is on the case. The girls will be alright, dear."

"Do I look like a damn deer to you asshole? I'm calling the police now, Winn, that's it." Patty had had enough and was not stopping till she found her little girls and the hell with her so-called husband and his political career.

Winn slumped down on the piano stool in the beautiful suite in the Charleston Place Hotel and finished off his last swallow of Pappy Van Winkle's Family Reserve, at a price tag of $3,000 a bottle of Kentucky bourbon, given to him by a secret campaign supporter.

"Yes, 9-1-1, please give me the Charleston Police Department. This is an emergency," Patty said in a strong voice as she looked over at Winn in disgust.

The hotel was only a few blocks away from where Tony Hines' broken body lay in the middle of the street. Patty and Winn were completely oblivious to the tragedy as they heard the sirens of both the ambulance and EMT fire trucks from their penthouse suite. It was just more noise in the big city to them.

By the time the police and ambulance got to Tony the crowd of people was so large it covered the entire width of the street. It was like a shark sighting. Everyone had to get in the act and see what was going on. It took a long time to get to the body, not to mention the crime scene was completely contaminated.

"Back up people. Let us do our job, please move back," said Officer Wayne Johnson. "We will need to get your names, addresses and phone numbers."

"Please we need your cooperation. Please move back," shouted Officer Bill Morrow as he pushed his way to Tony. Upon hearing the call for names, numbers and addresses most of the crowd broke away pretty quickly. Their curiosity lost out to the fact they would rather remain anonymous, so they wouldn't be involved. Officer Morrow looked down at Tony and started to take a few photos with his cell phone. Tony's cell phone was not in his hand, nor was it at the crime scene.

Officer Johnson grabbed a couple that were

still in shock and started asking what they saw. "I saw a truck come out of that alley and hit the man as he was texting on his phone," said a young man who looked about 20 years old.

"I saw nothing, but heard something and then I saw a man flying in the air; they must have been moving pretty fast, I don't think they put on the brakes," said a young lady.

"I saw little white Ford truck with one, maybe two men inside," offered a college student in an East Carolina University T-shirt.

"I think that's the truck that hit him," said a little girl holding her mother's hand.

"I didn't see a thing," said one guy as he turned away and walked off.

Wayne looked over at Bill. "Are you hearing this about a truck? I don't see any truck."

"Me either. I'd say this is a hit-and-run." He reached up and grabbed the microphone on his shoulder.

"Central dispatch we have a 480 in the Straw Market needing assistance."

"10-4, officer assistance is in route."

"Roger that dispatch over and out," replied officer Bill as he noticed several people running up to Tony. Eddie Miller, Tony's number one man, was the first to reach the scene, pushing back people and ducking under the police tape till he saw Tony. He could not believe it as he stood there with his hand over his mouth in horror. They had just talked on the phone two minutes ago and now this.

"Hold it fellow. This is police business. You can't come in here."

"That's my boss Tony Hines. We work for Senator Coleman," said Eddie Miller as he showed the policemen his credentials. By that time the rest of the team was there as well. They could not believe what they were seeing, and thinking it can't be Tony, but it was.

Not Two Suite

Chapter 8

CHIEF PARNELL STOOD IN THE LOBBY OF the hotel waiting for Connie to arrive at the Charleston Place. He had already received the information from his officers on the hit-and-run of Mr. Hines and had read over the statements of his men. So he knew everything about the two missing girls plus the fact that the senator and his wife were pretty slow in coming forward about that situation all together. And he was pretty pissed about the whole thing by the time Connie and Willie pulled up to the valet parking in front of the hotel.

"Hey chief, how's things," said Connie as Willie helped with her wheelchair. "So how to you want to play it?" she asked.

"Play it? I'll tell you how I will play it. I'm going to kick the shit out of those two upstairs till I get the answers I'm looking for, that's how I'm going to play it," said a mad and pissed off chief of police.

"Well, that sounds good to me, chief, since one of the two upstairs is a sitting state senator who announced today that he is running to be the next governor of this state, and by the way, they, too, must be hurting. Their children are missing. So how about we turn it down a notch or ten and we go ask them a few questions. We might learn something. What do you say, chief?"

"Well they have already talked to the SBI and the FBI. I don't know what we are going find out, but OK Connie let's go see the loving couple. I'll be nice," said Chief Parnell as he held the doors to the elevator open so Connie could wheel inside. As she rolled in she looked up at him. "I promise," he said as the doors shut.

Winn and Patty were back to their senator and Mrs. Coleman faces as the three entered the room of the beautiful presidential suite at the top of the hotel. They all said their hellos and were offered drinks to which they all said no. Connie broke the ice. "Mrs. and Senator Coleman, when was the last time you saw your children?" Connie pulled out her tablet to take notes.

They both looked at each other and Winn said, "Today at the rally, here in this hotel." Connie did not look up before she asked another question.

"Mrs. and Senator Coleman, when was the last time you talked to your daughters?"

"We said today at the rally," said Winn as he seemed to be getting a little mad with the questions.

Connie didn't miss a beat and asked another. "Senator Coleman, when was the last time you let your wife talk?"

"How dare you lady, I'm a state senator."

"Willie, could you please take the state senator into the other room so that the chief and I can have a few words with Mrs. Coleman. I'm sure the senator understands."

"Chief, I thought you were in charge of this case," said Winn as he walked back into the other room with Willie.

Connie and the chief pulled their chairs up closer to Patty, and Connie put her hand on her leg. "Mrs. Coleman, we are going to find your daughters, don't you worry. We just need to understand this situation. I heard the 9-1-1 call and it's clear you and your husband were not on the same page with calling the police. Now listen to me," Connie said as she leaned in a little closer. "Do you think your husband is involved in any way?"

"No, no way, not Winn, of course not. You can't be serious." Patty sat up a little straighter in the chair. "By the way, we were having a campaign rally today. He wants to be the next governor. Does that sound like someone who kidnaps his own children?"

"I understand Mrs. Coleman. I did not mean to get you upset. I have to ask the question that's all. Now a couple more if you don't mind. What kind of relationship did you have with Mr. Hines?"

"Tony, what about Tony? Why are you asking me about him? You don't think he is involved in this, do you? By the way why is he not here? Tony is in charge of my husband's security."

"Mrs. Coleman your husband has not told you about Tony Hines?"

"No, he has not told me anything about Tony, what?" Her body began to tense up and her hands had a slight tremble.

"Mrs. Coleman, Tony Hines was in an accident today," said Chief Parnell. Patty put her hand over her mouth. "He was involved in a hit-and-run just down the street here in the Straw Market."

"Is he OK? Will he be alright?" she said with

fear in her voice.

"I am sorry to say Mrs. Coleman, Mr. Tony Hines was killed," Tommy John said as he placed his hand on her shoulder.

"Oh my God," she gasped, as the tears started to flow. "I can't believe it, not Tony, and Winn knew all along?"

"We don't know for sure."

"So why are you telling me this? Is Winn being investigated because Tony and I were . . ." She stopped talking and looked over at Connie. She paused for a couple of seconds and regained her composure. "I'm not saying another word till my attorney is present."

The chief looked over at Patty. "Mrs. Coleman nobody thinks you did anything wrong, but we do have questions about your husband, so we are going to take the senator downtown for some questions about withholding information, that's all. If you would like to go with us to make it look a little better for your husband's campaign you and your attorney are more than welcome. But the first thing and the only thing I'm studying on are to get your daughters back home safe. I wanted you to know that."

Connie watched Patty's reaction to the chief's

statement and could see that she wanted to help Winn even if it meant losing her children. There was a very strong bond between those two and Connie could not put her finger on what the connection was.

"Why can't you ask your questions right here? He is not going anywhere, plus that kind of scandal would be the death of his campaign, even if indeed he is innocent. And chief I believe you are an elected officer as well, are you not, and a Democrat to boot? I believe this whole thing would look a little fishy in the voting public's eye, don't you agree?"

Connie looked over to the chief, not seeing that one coming and motioned to talk to him alone. The chief got up and walked over to Connie and wheeled her chair away from Patty so they could talk without her hearing them. "Let's go, chief, let's leave those two here. I think we can get more out of them if they stay together. Something is not right."

"I agree, Connie. That sounds good to me." He turned to Patty. "Well Mrs. Coleman you make a compelling argument and we both agree to your terms but on one stipulation. Our men will be here around the clock guarding you and your husband outside this door."

"So now we are all on house arrest, is that it?"

“No, I think of it as more like guarding you two for your safety. Again, your daughters are missing and if they are kidnapped somebody, at some time, will be asking for money. And to me kidnapping a state senator is as good as money, even better, do you understand?”

“Yes sir, I’m sorry. It has been one heck of a day so far, again I’m so sorry,” she said as she started crying again. The chief motioned to his officer at the bedroom to let Winn out of the room, and then turned back to Connie and Mrs. Coleman.

“Connie let’s go and let these two talk about today’s events.” Winn stood beside Patty and tried to comfort her. “Here’s the deal, we will be back tomorrow, but my officers will be here all night making sure you two are safe. If you need anything let them know. If you need to call me feel free. Just remember we are in this thing together. Your girls’ lives are at stake. We have notified the Amber Alert, the SBI and the FBI. Hopefully somebody will see something and call. By the way I had your phones tapped and we are hooked up on your sever for your emails as well. You never know how they will contact you. Now if you don’t have any questions we will see you in the morning.”

Winn looked at the chief. “Chief, I thank you for not taking me in, and I ask for you to do everything in your power to find our little girls, and

I'm sorry for losing my head earlier." He shook the chief's and Connie's hands, and thanked them again for their help as they left the apartment.

Riding down in the elevator they both were quiet for the first few floors and then Connie spoke. "That man is something," she said.

"He's as plastic as a Christmas tree ornament," Chief Parnell said with a smile on his face. Connie looked up from her chair and cracked a smile as well.

"You know something, chief, I was wrong. I think I'm going to like working with you a lot."

"I'll call you in the morning, Womack. Get a good night's sleep." He looked over at Willie and walked off.

Myrtle Beach Days

Chapter 9

THE BOARDWALK WAS FULL OF TOURISTS who were vacationing from all over the United States. They were enjoying all the hot sun and fun Myrtle Beach, South Carolina, had to offer as Todd Snyder stepped out of the summer heat and into the cool air-conditioned air of the arcade. In his hands were two footlong hot dogs along with two orders of cheese fries and two Pepsis. The refreshing cool air was full of sounds of people playing and the rings, bongs and dings of the pinball machines that filled the huge concrete slab room. More games lined the walls, adding the thud and clunky noise of the skeet balls. All of these money-making machines gave the players the expectations of winning anything from cheap stuffed teddy bears to an array of toys or tickets that could be exchanged into the prize of their choice. There was no doubt the place was raking in the money as the dollars poured in by the thousands.

All the while Todd's brother, Raymond, sat watching this spectacle take place, wondering where the hell his brother was. After all, he was gone for over an hour, and it seemed a whole lot longer than that to him. He couldn't take his eyes off all the young girls parading in their bikinis as they pulled and pushed and twisted their hips as if they were dancing or even making love to those machines. Raymond's daydreaming led him to lustful thoughts, as he started moving his hands in his pockets a little more as he sat with his eyes closed, rubbing himself faster and faster.

"Hey," Todd shouted, "wakeup, dummy. What the hell are you doing, Raymond? People are watching you," said Todd, as Raymond opened his eyes to reality.

"Where the hell have you been, lightning?" Raymond said as he pulled his hand out of his pocket and reached out and grabbed a hotdog.

"Where do you think someone gets hotdogs dumb ass. The line circled all the way around the block, Raymond. I got back here as soon as I could, and you are welcome brother."

"You know we're on a time schedule brother. Now give me one of those Pepsis."

"Ease up. We got till tomorrow morning, plus we got plenty of time. Those girls ain't going anywhere, that's for damn sure. Plus this time we are the ones calling the shots, big brother, not Cecil. Hell, if this thing goes as planned we might be able to buy you one of these here arcades."

"What would I do with a game room, knucklehead?" asked Raymond. "I ain't got no quarters." He picked up a pair of sunglasses someone had dropped on the floor, placed them on his head and smiled at a young lady sitting across from them at the next table. She smiled back. Quickly Raymond turned back to his brother. "Yeah look at me. I bet she thinks I'm a doctor."

"A doctor? Really? Well Doogie Houser, why don't you take this dollar and go play that pinball machine over there. Maybe this time you could win one of those teddy bears, while I call Cecil and let him know everything is on go.

"Sure Todd, but if you go outside again let me know. I hate being by myself, you know that."

"Sure thing big brother, I will," said Todd as he sat, chewing on his hotdog. He watched Raymond run off like a 13-year-old boy, not a 42-year-old man. He couldn't help but think that after the folks died he was all Raymond had, and he was not about to put his brother back in that so-called hospital for special needs people.

Besides they were doing good now with this job their cousin Cecil set them up with. The money was pouring in and all they had to do was make sure a few runaway girls didn't run off again. Plus all they were doing was holding the girls for a few days, maybe a week or so, and then giving them to Cecil when he called so he could find nice homes for the girls and they all would get a reward for it.

Cecil was their first cousin on their mother's side and was a lot older than both Todd and Ray, but to Todd, Cecil seemed to be a pretty good old boy, and had been the best of buddies growing up. It was a surprise when Cecil called with these jobs since they had not heard a word from him in years. Sure he had a few scrapes with the law and spent a few years in the big house, but overall Cecil was real likable and friendly to Todd and Raymond. Not knowing much about his drug dealing, those two always looked up to Cecil as a big brother of sorts. He was the one with the brains, Todd thought, as he typed a number in his cell phone and waited for an answer.

"Hey Skeeter man, let me speak to Cecil. What do you mean he's not there? This is his phone number. Where is he? Well we're here, and all is going according to plan." Todd listened and spoke again. "No, I did not leave him at home. Raymond is with me and he is not a half-wit. He'll be fine; you just leave him to me. Are we still on for the morning or not? Have Cecil call me back." He listened again. "That was not our plans. He wants us to come there tomorrow night alone, why? That doesn't make sense. He wants us to drive all the way out in those woods. That's over an hour and a half drive and at night. Why? I don't care, have Cecil call me anyway!" Todd turned off his cell phone. "I hate that guy," he said as he placed the phone in his pants pocket.

He noticed Raymond playing at the pinball baseball machine. He got up and moved closer to watch him play and noticed he had 28 runs. Just two more and he was about to win. And sure enough before Todd reached his brother the game went off with all kinds of whistles and bells. Raymond had just won a teddy bear. You would have thought he won a million dollars by the look on Raymond's face as he turned and saw his brother standing behind him. He jumped into his arms and gave him a big hug.

"Winner, winner chicken dinner," Raymond kept saying as the two walked out of the arcade to the white Ford pickup truck with a broken left headlamp. It was parked off Joe White Avenue, on Ocean Boulevard near the Sky Wheel in a handicap parking space, as everyone around them was enjoying the hot summer night at the beach. All the while Todd was thinking about getting back and getting the girls ready because, tomorrow was going to be a big day.

Drive-By Willie

Chapter 10

CONNIE AND WILLIE SPREAD THE INFORMATION out on the kitchen table so they could compile everything to the computer tablet. This way they could both see and examine any evidence they may have. Connie typed as they both read and called out evidence that they had written down in their notebooks and on pieces of paper when the situation occurred.

"Two, no three girls missing in the last 48 hours," said Willie.

"Check that, plus one in the upstate near Greenville and two more near Georgetown last week just an hour up the road from here," said

Connie. "All in their late teens and all from financially well-off families. Now where did they take them and how, what is the mode of travel? The question is, who is paying for this? Who is the master mind? And what about the white Ford pickup? Who was driving it and why the hit-and-run?"

"Do you think it's a part of this case Connie?"

"Without a question," she answered. "That was no accident, no way. And to your question on where, I bet somewhere with a lot of people, a tourist town somewhere like here maybe?"

"You would not want to go far. Someone might see you. Or maybe you wouldn't know you were looking at kidnap victims. They're girls, no big deal, it's not like they would be wearing chains around their necks and handcuffed to each other," said Willie as he changed the subject. "Or maybe it's like your best friend not telling you what happened a couple of nights ago when this so-called friend tried to shoot me," Willie said as he looked right at Connie.

"Now hold on partner. We are talking about a different case here. Let's stay on the subject."

"Let's don't," said Willie as he started to drill Connie for more information. "Someone was giving you a shakedown Connie. Now who was it? When

I got there the house had been ransacked, you had bruises on your legs and arms, and your Smith and Wesson was out and ready to go. Now something is up."

"They drove off in a white Ford truck. That's pretty much all I know."

"What? You saw those people who killed Tony Hines at the Straw Market?"

"No, not exactly, I went to the police station that day and talked to Chief Parnell. A nice couple wanted to hire me on that first kidnapping case and Chief Parnell didn't want me to have anything to do with that case. I got pissed and left. You know me; I was just asking a few questions. Well you know how great that turned out, so when I got home someone had been in my house. As I came around the kitchen door, right here," as she pointed to a place on the floor, "someone hit me and knocked me out of the chair and started roughing me up. I only saw one of them. The other wore a hoodie and a mask. I never saw his face."

"There was more than one? There were two guys," Willie said as he listened to the story.

"Two, yes I believe so, I really don't know how many for sure, all I know is I got the crap kicked out of me and my house torn to shreds. Well heck Willie you know, you saw the place the next morning."

"The next morning? You mean it was that night?"

"Yeah, you just missed them by about an hour or so. That's why I'm convinced now that no one kidnapped those two senator's girls. It does not make sense," said Connie as she looked up from the computer and faced Willie. "First of all, who would have the balls, and second, who would have the ability to pull that off? I mean really, at a rally in front of hundreds of folks."

"No way, this was planned Connie. They had the balls to invade you house and whip your ass. Plus that's the kind of thing that does happen. Kids go missing in broad daylight all the time."

"Not like this. I agree it was planned alright, but not by a kidnapper. This was an inside job," she said as Tricks jumped on the table and lay beside the tablet and started licking himself.

"So you are telling me the senator took his own daughters? For what? For money or to ruin his own campaign or maybe he was getting even with his wife's lover? So a hit-and-run? Are you telling me he killed his own head of security to make it look like a kidnapping?"

"No, I'm saying it doesn't look like a kidnapping

and I'm not accusing the senator. I'm looking at the evidence and the senator's fingerprints are not on this. But someone's are, that's all I'm saying Willie, but you are bringing up some great points."

"Thanks, what points, which ones?"

"Who would gain from kidnapping those girls?"

"I know, a kidnapper silly," said Willie as he laughed.

Then out of nowhere three gunshots rang out, then again three maybe four more, as the glass windows shattered along with a table lamp as the light was shot out. Connie threw herself out of the chair and hit the floor as two more bullets hit the kitchen wall. The sound of car tires screeching on the wet street could be heard outside Connie's house.

Connie slowly pulled herself up toward the wheelchair and leaned over with her gun in her hand but it was too late. Whoever it was had gone. You could hear the glass break as she moved on the floor to check on Willie as she called out. "Willie, are you OK? Willie they're gone, are you alright?" All the while she was feeling her way through the dark room full of broken glass. "Willie, answer me."

Her eyes tried to adjust to the dimly lit room. The only light in the kitchen was that of the tablet computer spinning like a top as it hung in air halfway between the table top and floor. It appeared to be floating in air and being tethered in place by only a power cord. Connie watched as the spinning computer slowed down its revolutions till it quit moving all together. She reached out and grabbed it with her cut hand. She used the computer like a search lamp till she saw Willie still sitting in his chair with a bullet hole in his forehead, his blood trickling down his handsome face with his eyes still wide open. He never knew what hit him. Connie froze as she stared into his wild expression, as if he was saying, watch out.

"Damn it Willie," she said under her breath as she dropped the tablet and pulled her cell phone out of her pocket and called 9-1-1. She started to cry as she looked at his lifeless body. "Oh, Willie, I'm so sorry." She reached out and touched his hair, and then she closed his eyes. She really loved Willie. He could never replace Jack in her eyes, no one could. But Willie was an old shoe that fit her just fine and now he was gone as well.

Team Bravo

Chapter 11

THE RAIN POURED DOWN AS THE WIND POUNDED the windows of Chief Parnell's office while both Connie and the chief sat thinking of Willie without saying a word. They could not believe the events last night had happened and he was gone. They both thought the world of Willie as his body lay downstairs in the morgue, one as a good cop and the other as a good friend and part-time lover.

"He was a great kid, I'm going to miss the hell out of him," said Chief Parnell, as he poured himself a drink and offered one to Connie. She shook her head to the bottle he kept in the bottom drawer of his desk. "I can't believe that boy is gone.

Do you have any idea, Connie, who could have done this? It's obvious they tried to stop you and they surely don't want us to find out anything about this kidnapping case."

"Or is it? Maybe we stumbled into something that's bigger than this case and we don't know, at this point, what it's all about. There's something that doesn't seem right with this case and I can't put my finger on it, but someone is trying to stop us from finding out, in the first place. Who knows?" she said as she threw her hands up in the air. "But what I do know is some of their evidence is embedded in the walls of my house. And if I do anything I will catch the sons of bitches that murdered our friend, and you can take that to the bank."

"Hold on little lady, you ain't got to get all riled up," said a small thin man with a pencil thin mustache standing in the doorway to the chief's office.

"Spider, is that you?" said Connie as she quickly turned the wheelchair in the direction of his voice. She then promptly moved closer where they both could hug. "I'm so glad you are here. Your timing could not be better." As they broke apart she turned and introduced Spider to the chief, wiping the tears for Willie out of her eyes. "Chief Tommy John Parnell, this is Spider. I mean Sydney

Rountree, aka Spider, the best computer and communications man there is in my book," said Connie as she hugged him again.

Spider was about five foot nothing and weighed just over 100 pounds, if that, and sported a large black widow spider tattoo on his neck, and long brown hair tied in a ponytail. He looked like an old hippie with small round glasses like the ones John Lennon wore, but he looked more like an angry protester in search for his next rally at the National Mall.

Chief Parnell stood up and extended his hand for a shake. "My pleasure, it's nice to meet you, Mr. Rountree. We were sitting here saying our goodbyes to a dear friend of ours and one of my best officers. He died last night at Connie's house, shot in the head . . . never knew what hit him."

Spider turned back sharply to look at Connie. "Damn girl, are you OK, and did you get hurt?" He stopped and thought for a second. "What the hell Connie! Do you always have to live in an Alamo?" alluding to Jack, Connie's husband, being killed at home as well.

Connie reached out and touched his hand. "No Sydney, I'm fine and thank you very much, but Willie Weber was a very close friend of mine who I loved. He was a senseless victim of a drive-by shooting."

Spider was not about to believe that. "Yeah, sure, a drive-by, right, I bet you 10 bucks."

The chief saw Connie's face turn to a frown as he stood back up and looked over at Spider. "How 'bout we go down the hall and take a look at all that new computer stuff I ordered for you and Connie. I can't make heads or tails of that stuff and we really need to get ready for business."

Spider stood up as well and patted Connie on her shoulder as if to say he was sorry, and she touched his hand to say it's OK. "Where can I set up? I got my computer and hardware with me."

The chief put his arm around Spider as he walked around in front of his desk. "You don't have to worry about that son. I have you set up with your own office right down the hall here," said Chief Parnell using his finger to point down the hallway. "We got everything Connie asked for and then some. I think you will be impressed with the quality, hope so anyway. Right this way young man."

As the two started their way down the hall to see the computer room that Chief Tommy John had assembled for Connie's operation Spider stopped and turned back toward Connie. "By the way girlfriend, Rhys is outside in the car. He was on the cell phone when I came in. I'm sure he'll be here in a minute."

Connie quickly looked up at the news. "Rhys is here as well?" She could not believe both Sydney and Rhys Garrett, Jack's right-hand men back in the day, came to help her and were both here. Thinking about Rhys, she had not seen or heard from him since the funeral and that had been at least eight years ago, she thought as she counted up the years, thinking how quickly they had gone by. "Great. can't wait to see him. You two go on down the hall. I'll be right there. Give me a minute to powder my nose."

"Sure thing," both men said as they left and headed toward the computer room for the second time.

Rhys Garrett, Connie thought as the two men left. She had all kinds of thoughts going through her mind. Rhys was the best recon man in Navy Seal Team Six. Jack hired him when they were in Afghanistan together back in '02. Jack never knew that Connie and Rhys dated a few times before she met Jack. And why tell him, those dates didn't mean much and besides, those two men became very best of friends. Connie and Jack would go out with Rhys and his flavor of the month whenever the two boys were back in the states at the same time. Jack and Rhys were very much alike, bigger than life, fun to be with; always stayed in great shape and both were great at their jobs as mercenaries, and really easy on the eyes. Her thoughts drifted into daydreams of her days loving the two men in her wonderful life before everything ended in Jack's death.

"Hey, Connie girl wakeup," said a tall man standing in the doorway of the chief's office with his arms outstretched covering the doorway and a cigar in his mouth.

Connie quickly opened her eyes and there he stood. "Hello Rhys," said Connie with a smile on her face and a tear in her eye. "Come over here and give me a hug you big ape." Connie moved her wheelchair over closer and the two embraced for a long time and kissed each other on the cheek. Rhys stood back up and looked Connie straight in the eye.

"Lady you look great, but then again you always do."

Connie realized she was not the girl she used to be, being now in a wheelchair. "Yeah, it's like being a hood ornament attached to a Buick," she said, with a little laugh as she hit down on the wheelchair's armrest with her hand. She then looked back up and said, "It's great to see you too Rhys, but why are you here? This case is domestic. We aren't going to bomb a village or start a national uprising. I'm trying to find a few kids, that is all, two of which are a state senator's children, but wow, the two of you here to help me. I feel honored."

"Well it's not exactly what you're thinking. You see Connie, my sister Kay lives here in Charleston, well north of here up Highway17 over in Mt. Pleasant." Rhys found a chair to sit in so they could talk eye to eye.

"Yeah I know Kay. We talk a lot. She's a great girl and a super psychologist. I wish I had her brain. But she didn't tell me you were in town." Connie then turned her head away from Rhys. "Oh, I see." She leaned back in her wheelchair, feeling a little down, as if she was a second thought and she wanted to see how he would react. "So you really didn't come here to help me at all."

"No, now wait Connie, you know I'm here for you too!" He moved his chair closer to her.

"Sounds like it." She played along, acting as if she was begging for more sympathy.

He moved his chair even closer. "But I have to leave in a few days."

"Why did you even bother coming over here Rhys? We don't need you and it's not like you called and checked on me every day since Jack passed."

"Now look here Connie," he said as he grabbed the wheelchair. "Spider told me about your situation and I had to come. You know I can see my sister anytime. I'm here to help you in any way. You know that, but truly I don't know how much time or help I would be to you."

Connie looked up at him eye to eye. "You haven't written, called, emailed, or tweeted me since Jack's passing. He loved you like a brother and I always . . . "

"Connie, I know, I should have called. But I'm here now and when Spider told me he was coming down here, well I had to see you. I think of you. I mean, I think of Jack and you all the time. I miss him so much. What a guy he was. Plus in my profession, well, we are not very good at funerals. OK?"

"I know Jack wasn't either, I understand Rhys, and I miss you and all the guys in Jack's outfit." She had him right in the palm of her hand as she pushed back on her wheelchair. "Let's go down the hall and check on Spider before he talks the chief to death about the working of a computer or something technical."

"Yeah sure," he said as he stood up and moved his chair out of Connie's way so they could head to the chief's office as he grabbed the wheelchair handles.

Connie started making small talk so she would

not get too emotional. “How do you like it down here?”

“It sure is hot.” He stopped and looked out the windows, watching the rain. “It reminds me of Thailand or Cambodia, humid as all get-out, and floods every time it rains, pretty much like today.”

“Glad you like it. Jack always said you’d bitch over ice cream.” They both laughed. “I see you haven’t changed in that regard. Come on Mr. Happy, let’s go see all the new toys that Chief Parnell rounded up and save him before he gets electrocuted.”

“Yeah you got that right girl. Ain’t no telling what Spider has gotten into.” The two left the office with Rhys behind, pushing the wheelchair for Connie and heading down the hall.

The Room And Roommates

Chapter 12

THE DAYS PASSED WITHOUT COUNT AS SHE LAY in her concrete prison. Her mind moved in and out of a drunken subconscious state. Daily her body was subjected to injections of all kinds of narcotics to keep her in a controllable condition, but mostly she stayed passed out. But today she heard loud squeaking noises coming from the metal hinges of the door to her cell as it was opening. Not knowing if it was real or a dream she lay still, as if she had a choice. Her body could not move.

"Grab her legs, stupid, before she falls. Cecil

will kill us if anything happens to her."

"I am Todd. Don't you worry brother, I've got her." Just then her head hit the metal door.

"Damn you, I said watch out, man you're stupid."

"Oh shut up."

They wrestled with her body like it was a 100-pound bag of Jell-O and finally brought it to rest as they put her on a table. She opened her eyes only to experience instant pain from the light and quickly closed them as tightly as possible. Those were the only muscles she had control of. The rest of her body was useless after laying on that cold wet concrete for days with no food, no water, and near death.

The two men once again picked her up to move her to the other side of the room away from her concrete prison. She could barely hear them talk but her mind could not comprehend what they were saying or doing. They then wrapped her naked body up in a blanket and placed her on a small bed, more like an army cot, on the floor. They repeated this same operation twice as they retrieved the other two girls from the same hellhole. The small room looked like an operating room you would see on the TV show *MASH*. IV drips were placed in all three girls' arms and a leash was attached to replace the chain to the girls' ankles. Before leaving the room the two men stopped to inspect their handy work and then turned off the lights and shut the big metal door that concealed the torture chamber from the rest of the house.

Slowly the hours ticked off before any of the girls made a sound. The drugs finally started to wear off. She pulled on her leg and felt the leash pull back against her. She brushed her hair out of her eyes, and in the dark she could see that the blacked-out windows had been freshly painted. A small paint can with a paint brush was sitting on the windowsill. There was enough light still bleeding into the room for her to scan over her surroundings of the small twenty by twenty area made of cinder block with a large metal door, something you would see on a meat locker. Cameras were set up beside the two small transom windows that were blacked out, and two more on the other side of the room. As she looked, she could see that the room was surrounded by cameras. All were up high and out of reach.

The walls were damp and she could see water on the floor. We must be in a basement, she thought. But the one thing that was really strange was the toilet and sink were oddly placed back to back in the center of the room, not much privacy. But after being stuck in a concrete tomb for days, who cares? she thought. She then looked over at the other two girls. "I do not know them," she said, as they both started to move around a little under their blankets. Was this really happening? she thought, as she looked them over again, thinking how really young they seemed, mere children compared to her ripe old age of 17.

Again she tried moving her legs but no luck, only one of her arms would move a little and she could turn her head some but her neck was still sore at this point. If she could only get some water to quench her thirst. She kept licking her lips as she stared at the sink like it was a wishing well, hoping that cold water would come rushing out for her to drink. Her mouth was so dry that just trying to say hello to one of the girls was close to impossible but she kept trying and slowly, "hello," came out in a very quiet and soft but hoarse-sounding voice.

"It's OK, I can hear you," said another in the same voice. It was hard for her to talk as well and the room was quiet again.

"What is your name? Mine is Reese," she said and waited for the response. A few minutes went by.

"I don't know, I can't remember." The other girl started crying as she scooted back under the covers, hiding her head as if to escape from her embarrassment.

Reese wanted to comfort her with words like "Sweetie, don't worry it will come back. Your head is still a little messed up. Your memory will come back, you'll see, don't worry little one." But all she could muster was, "it's OK."

The girl pulled the covers down from her face as if she was saying, thank you Reese, then closed her eyes. This time she knew she was not alone in this bizarre menagerie as she closed her eyes to sleep once more. Reese, too, closed her eyes to rest, thinking she had to get out of this hell, but how? For right now, she would rest and dream of a solution as she remembered the name Todd, one of the brothers. She drifted off to sleep once more.

Cash Call

Chapter 13

THE EMPTY BOTTLE OF COMPLIMENTARY CHAMPAGNE was still floating in the bucket of water that once was ice, and the red, white and blue campaign helium balloons were void of almost all life, flying at a low or no altitude which caused them to dance and bounce as they dotted the floor of the presidential suite. Winn and Patty sat in uncomfortable chairs across the room from each other. The silence was deafening as the two wondered who would be the first to speak. Each stared accusingly at each other; finally she won, as he spoke.

"Did you love him?"

“Did you kill him?” Patty said as she returned the volley. She sat ramrod straight in her chair glaring at Winn, ready for his twist. She was well aware of the way he twisted most conversation in his favor like the great politician he was. But this time he didn’t. He just turned away from her glaring stare and waited.

“Well did you or did you not? He was your friend. How could you, why Tony Winn, why?”

Winn then answered. “First of all I did not have anything to do with Tony’s death. I did not kill him and I can’t believe you would even think something like that about me. Hell Patty, everyone knew you two were having a romantic fling and I understand. We have not been the best of couples in the last few years. But to accuse me of murder, you know me better than that.”

“I don’t think I know you at all anymore,” Patty said as she stood up and walked over to the bar to make herself a drink. “Want one?” she asked. He slowly turned his head away again as if to say no to her. “Tony and I did love to be with each other and yes we enjoyed each other’s company, but you and everyone else were wrong. There never was a love affair, no romantic interlude between us.” She was lying and Winn knew it. He just let her ramble on with her talk.

“Tony was too much a gentleman for that, plus

he thought the world of you, Winn. Sure I dreamed of the day he would grab me in those big arms of his and pull me close in his embrace. I can't lie. He was in my dreams a lot of nights. But the bottom line it never happened, because the man you hired to watch over me did just that and nothing more. Unlike you Winn, Tony was true blue, straight up a great guy. I can't believe he is gone." She slammed her glass on the bar. "And if you didn't kill him, then who? Who the hell Winn, who would run him down like that and kill him like a dog in the middle of the street in downtown Charleston in broad daylight? Who?" She threw the glass up against the wall.

"Calm down Patty," Winn said as he heard a knock on the door. He jumped up from the couch and walked over to the door, calming himself down as well. "Come in."

"Is everything alright in here?" said the policeman that was outside the suite. After hearing all the noise inside he wondered what was going on.

"We are fine, officer. Everything is OK," said Winn as the officer noticed Patty sitting in her chair crying. "We are fine, just a typical husband-wife thing, nothing more." Winn then walked over and put his arm around Patty and gave her a big hug. "We are fine," he said again.

The officer was still looking for confirmation.

"Ms. Coleman, are you OK?"

"Yes, officer, I'm fine, sorry to bother you."

"No bother, Ms. Coleman. It's my job and if you are sure I'll leave but I know you two must be going through a lot. Look, if you two need anything just ask. I can get a counselor if you need one, anything, OK?"

"No sir, we are fine, really," as they both bobbed their heads in agreement, and with that the police officer turned and walked back outside to stand his post as he left the suite.

"Take your damn hands off me," Patty said as she fought and got out of Winn's arms, showing that the charade of their marriage was over between them.

Winn walked over to the bar and poured a tall glass of Ketle One Vodka. "Don't mind if I do," he said and took a big drink. Suddenly the phone on the big table in the middle of the living room started ringing. Winn and Patty looked at each other, and they decided that Winn would answer.

"Winn Coleman here," said Winn as Patty stood by wondering who it was on the phone. "Hello this is Senator Coleman," he replied for the second time. "Hello, is there anyone there?"

"Don't hang up if you want to see you little girls

again," said a mechanical sounding voice on the other end. It sounded like a robot. It was obviously meant to disguise someone's identity and to Winn it was working pretty well.

"Who is this? Where are my children?" Winn shouted into the receiver.

"You need to shut up and listen or I will hang up and you don't want that, trust me." Winn motioned to Patty to come close to the phone so she too could hear. She had her hands over her mouth and tears in her eyes.

"I understand you are in control. What do you want us to do?"

"Let's get a couple of things straight. First there will be no police involved. Do you understand me?"

"Yes," he quickly answered.

"And second, we want $100 million from your campaign fund wired to our offshore bank account so it cannot be traced."

"I can't do that. It's against the law, and besides, I can't get my hands on campaign money. I'm the politician. The only person that has that ability is—" he stopped talking.

And Patty spoke up "That's me now. The

campaign manager and treasurer would have been Tony. He was in charge of the campaign fund," she said, as she shook her head.

"That's right Ms. Coleman. You are! And as soon as the money is wired your daughters will be returned. We will call you back in 24 hours and you better have the bank account information so we will be able to make this transaction work."

"Twenty-four hours? I can't get that kind of money in only 24 hours! We will need more time."

"I hope not, for your daughters' sake, because that's all the time your kids have."

"Wait, I want to talk to the girls. Please wait." The phone went dead. Winn looked at Patty with shock on his face. He could not believe it. As he fell back onto the couch, Winn wondered what in the world to do.

Then Patty spoke up. "We've got to call Chief Parnell now."

"Are you crazy, what part of 'no police' do you not understand, Patty? You call the police and they will kill the girls."

"We can't do this on our own, Winn, it's too much and no, we can't lose the girls but we have to do something. How about that Connie lady who was here with Chief Parnell, Ms. Womack? She's not the police."

"No, but she is working as a liaison with the police. That's as good as being one, don't you think?"

"Who gives a shit, liaison or not, damn Winn it's our children. We can't let this happen to them. We have to call Ms. Womack and call her now!" Patty grabbed Connie's business card off the bar and pulled out her cell phone. "You need to be with me on this one Winn, you have no choice." She punched in the number on her iPhone. "Ms. Womack, Patty Coleman here. You need to come over please. We have been contacted by the kidnappers. Thank you. We will see you then."

"What did she say?" Winn asked.

"She's coming and if you screw this up, Winn, so help me I'll kill you."

Winn backed down as he got up and made himself another drink.

Relative Reality

Chapter 14

THE WIND BLEW AROUND THE LITTLE WEATHER-BEATEN HOUSE that sat several miles down an old logging road deep in the woods in the little community of Sampit. The location was about 45 miles from Charleston, a little over halfway between Monks Corner and Georgetown, South Carolina, off Highway 17 Alternate.

"Damn, Todd, we are so far in the woods you'd have to go toward town to go coon hunting! We're so far out in the country I bet its 20 minutes by telephone," Raymond laughed.

"Shut up Ray, Cecil said to come out here so here we are. I can't help that plans have been changed. Now come on and get in the house," Todd said as he held the screen door open for his brother.

"Man it sure is spooky out here in the dark and all," said Raymond as he passed Todd on the steps and stepped inside the door, where two men were arguing. One was Cecil, Todd noticed. Both Todd and Raymond stopped before going inside the house and watched the two men argue from the porch.

"I said if you ever disobey my order again I'll kill you dead you son of a bitch! Do you understand me?" said Cecil as he slapped the man down to the ground with one swing. "Who told you to go to her house and try to scare her off anyway? And if she's anything like her old man, you two are lucky she didn't shoot your dumb ass. Now get the hell out of here till I call for you."

"Yes sir I understand, yes sir," the poor man with a black powder burn on his face said as he grabbed his red baseball cap off the porch and left the house holding the side of his face and passing Todd and Raymond as he walked out the screen door. The rest of the men stayed seated at the kitchen table inside and didn't dare move from Cecil's card game. Cecil turned and saw his cousins standing close by with their mouths open in shock.

"Where the fuck have you two been? You're late as hell. Get in here," Cecil barked as he held the screen door open

Todd started right off trying to make an excuse for getting lost about 10 times and even Raymond knew to keep quiet. "Well you see, Cecil, we left Myrtle about three hours ago and well you see . . ."

"Shut up, Todd. It's a two-hour drive at most. Now you two hammerheads go sit down in that other room while I get these boys straight on another matter. Are we all together OK?"

"Yes sir, Cecil," said Todd as he and Raymond made themselves at home sitting in the living room down the hall. The room was full of stuffed animals, a taxidermist's paradise. Raymond sat down in a big old chair full of dust and looked around the room as all those animal eyes stared back at him, making him feel a little uneasy to say the least.

Suddenly out of nowhere they heard a loud bang and then another that sounded like gunshots. They both jumped up out of their seats and ran to the kitchen where the noise seemed to be coming from. The first thing they saw was a dead body lying on the floor. Smoke was still coming from Cecil's gun when they arrived at the scene; their mouths gaped wide open as they stood looking at the guy with the powder-burned face lying on the floor.

"What the hell!" Todd yelled.

"This ain't got nothing to do with you boy!" Cecil shouted over the body covered in blood. "That son of a bitch came back with a gun and tried to shoot me in the back," Cecil said, while he kicked the body with his bone-white alligator boot to make sure he was truly dead. He was the same fellow that Todd and Raymond saw Cecil arguing with when they arrived. His red ball cap was still on his head. Cecil looked over at the other two men who were still playing cards but were still alive at the kitchen table. "You two take this piece of shit outside. I want you take him down the road a ways and lay him down beside the swamp so the gators can get him, plus that makes less work for us, and we don't have to worry about burying him."

"Hell he'll be gone in a couple of hours if not sooner," one of the other men said.

"I bet you a hundred dollars," said the other.

"You're on, a hundred bucks."

Cecil looked over at the two fellows. "Just be quick about it and get him out of here. Come on Ray, you and Todd don't worry about that shit. Nobody liked him anyway. He was an asshole." He could feel the brothers shaking as he put his arms around them both. "Come on boys, let's go back here and talk, so they can clean this mess up, OK?" They all three walked down the dark hallway back toward the zoo of the dead. As they passed one of the bedrooms Cecil grabbed the doorknob and opened the door to a dark room. He pushed the brothers inside enough so they could see a young girl handcuffed to the bed. She was nude and had an IV in her arm. It appeared that she had no idea where she was.

"She will be ready for delivery tomorrow but before then if you boys want some of that," said Cecil with a laugh while Todd and Raymond took in the scene. "I didn't think so," he said as he pushed them back so he could close the door and they started back down the hall to the zoo and sat down. Cecil looked at both of them to make sure they knew he was all business.

"I'm sorry about that stuff back in the kitchen boys, but that boy had it coming. He disobeyed my order. We can't have that, now can we, plus he was out to get me and well that's that. Here is what I need you two to do. I need you two to get all three girls and bring them here tomorrow night and be sure you blindfold them. Todd, here's some money for gas, food and a few other things if you need it.

Here are the keys to that big gray van," Cecil said as he handed Todd the keys plus $200 in cash.

"Leave the white Ford truck here; I'll have the boys paint it something real nice, maybe powder blue, and fix that dent in the front. Now listen to me, you need to be here no later than midnight to stay on schedule with the buyers. They hate to wait for anything. If you are here a little early they will be able to get out of here and make it out to the interstate highway by one or one thirty. Now look here boys, you need to drug them up a little. I don't care how much; just make sure you two don't kill them. Or I'm afraid the gators will be chewing on your two asses as well, you understand me?"

Todd had a little smile on his face, knowing Cecil had to be fooling around like he always did when they were growing up together. "But Cecil, we are your cousins, we are family, you know you can trust us," Todd said with a half smile, not sure if Cecil was kidding or not.

Cecil jumped straight up out of his chair, knocking it over. Towering over Todd and Ray, Cecil looked down at the two with a stern look on his face. "Does it look like I'm messing around to you?" Both men were shaking their heads as the smiles were erased from their faces. Cecil quickly moved over to the couch and sat down. "I don't give a shit who the hell you two are," he shouted and he pulled out his .45 Glock and laid it in his lap.

"If truth be told, my family ain't ever liked your side of the family that much anyway. Your mama treated my mama like shit her whole life and that's the truth. Besides I'll kill you both if you screw this thing up. You two understand me? I'll kill you

Todd, and you too Raymond, is that clear enough to you boys?" he said pointing his finger at his gun. "Now I showed you how much medicine to give those girls to put them asleep. They better be alive when you get here. Now that you know how to get here, it better be no later than twelve o'clock midnight tomorrow night or you two sons of bitches are gator bait. Do I make myself clear?"

"Yes sir," they said at the same time, still shaking.

In an instant, Cecil's personality changed back again. "Now look boys, I don't want to do anything rash and you know I won't if we stick to the rules and plans." Walking around to the back of the couch Cecil patted them on the back. "All I ask is that you pay attention and do your job and do everything like I taught you and it will be fine. And yeah, there will be plenty of money to go around for all," Cecil said with a smile on his face. "Plenty of money. You two will be rich, so get ready to make some money boys and I'll see you two back here tomorrow night, right!"

"Right, yes sir," they both shouted.

"OK then, you two go out that back door and I'll see you tomorrow. I've got to help those boys in the kitchen clean up a bit. You understand don't you?" Cecil walked the two brothers to the back door. "You two watch yourselves and be careful," he said as he patted them again on their backs for good luck. They walked out the door and headed to their new ride, a gray Chevy van, leaving the white truck in the dark beside of Cecil's SLC Mercedes-Benz.

Raymond looked over at Todd. "Mama said it was bad luck to go out a different door than the one you came in on."

"Shut the hell up, Raymond, just shut up and get in the van, holy shit," Todd shouted.

"But that's not our ride. We came in the truck over there, the white one," he pointed. "Why are we not getting in the white truck Todd? I sure liked the white truck."

Todd could not believe what they had seen and heard; the Cecil he once knew was gone and had now truly turned into a monster. He shot that man down like a dog right in the kitchen, and then jumped all up in his and Raymond's shit for no reason. That dude is stone-cold crazy.

What was he going to do, Todd thought, trying to reason and make sense of the whole thing with his brother? Todd knew Raymond was scared. He was too simpleminded to show it, but Todd knew he was, and he also knew he loved his brother. But now Todd was afraid of Cecil and for the safety of his brother and himself.

"I said get in the van for the last time damn it. Raymond, get in the van!"

"OK, but I liked the white truck better."

It was an hour before the two spoke to each other as they drove north back to the North Myrtle Beach area. Todd pondered, maybe drugs had warped Cecil's brain, and there's no telling what they did to him when he was in the Army. Whatever, neither of them had ever seen that side of Cecil and they hoped they never would again.

Todd started trying to think of a way out of this whole deal all the way back to Myrtle. He wondered what the hell they had gotten themselves into. One thing for sure, they would find out indeed if they could not come up with a different plan. Cecil would surely kill them if he knew what they were thinking. Hell he might kill them both just because they saw him kill that other fellow, who knows. But there was one thing for sure; they had to think of something fast.

Todd reached up and turned on the radio and tried to relax as he listened to the music. Even Raymond enjoyed the sounds of WEZV, the easy listening radio station as the van entered the city limits of North Myrtle Beach. As they passed the tourist landmark of Barefoot Landing and Oscar's hamburger joint, hunger was finally replacing fear.

Eye In The Sky

Chapter 15

"**CHIEF YOU MIGHT WANT TO SEE THIS**," said Officer Drew Tandy as he handed Chief Parnell a photo of a white Ford pickup truck leaving the crime scene in the Straw Market at the exact time when Tony Hines was hit in the streets of Charleston.

"Where did you get this?" he asked.

"Got it from the video camera on top of Henry's bar. It's right beside the alley where the accident occurred."

"I know where the hell Henry's is! Tags, I need to see license tags. Can we make them out? I want to nail those sons of bitches."

"No tags. This was taken from the front of the truck. We can tell that there are two people in the vehicle and the driver is wearing a red ball cap but that's about it, sorry chief. But that's not the only camera in town and now that we have the right time, we'll get them."

"Good work, Tandy. Let me know when you get something else. And take that info down the hall to Mr. Rountree and see if Spider can do something with that. That's his world so I hope he can help. Connie said he's the best so let's see."

"Yes sir, you got it."

"Speaking of Connie, where is she? She was supposed to be here hours ago."

Carol Spoon, the chief's secretary, looked up as she overheard the conversation. "Chief, she told me to tell you that she was going over to see the Colemans after they called her. I think the kidnappers contacted them and they asked for her."

"What? The kidnappers contacted the Colemans and I didn't know about it and they called her? What the hell is going on around here? I'm the chief of police and I appear to be the last one to know anything around here, damn it. I know, we need to take down the police station sign and put up a sign that reads 'Connie's Place'. Yeah that would work and I'll just go home."

"Yes sir, I mean no sir, I'm sorry sir," Carol said as she went back into her office and shut the door so she could not hear anything else in the hallway.

"Hey chief, check out what Spider's doing. Come in here."

He turned and went towards the voices. "OK, what's up fellows?" Parnell said as he looked over the shoulder of Officer Tandy and started to watch the computer screen on Spider's desk. The Chief watched closely. "What have you got there Rountree, home movies?"

"No sir Chief, just watch. I'll start back at the beginning." Spider pressed enter on the keyboard and the video started back. The computer monitor showed several screens of roads and highways. In the top screen it showed a white Ford pickup sitting in the alley beside of Henry's bar. Then from a stopped position the truck appeared to take off and run right into Tony Hines. The truck hit him so hard it threw him into the middle of the street. After the hit-and-run it then proceeded down through the Straw Market and took a hard left on East Bay Street at a high rate of speed and almost hit someone else coming out of the Noisy Oyster restaurant. The picture then shifted over to a different screen picked up by a camera this time on the on-ramp of Highway 17 north going over the Ravenel Bridge headed towards Mt. Pleasant. The truck then seemed to slow down and go the speed limit till it turned off the bridge down the off-ramp in the area called Patriots Point where several old Navy ships like the USS *Yorktown* are located across the harbor from downtown. At that point the truck disappeared under the canopy of trees.

"Where the hell did they go?" Parnell shouted. Spider quickly worked away on the computer for a couple of minutes and then stopped, looking up at the chief.

"OK, chief, here is where we are, over here in this area," as Spider pointed his finger at the screen. "That truck is going to come out somewhere. It might take a while so be patient. I'll call you when I get something else on the IP cameras."

"What is an IP camera? Is that the same as traffic cameras?" said the chief.

"IP stands for Internet Protocol. Yeah, but no, the old traffic cameras were closed circuit. You know, CCTV, right, Closed Circuit Television. Well this is the newest thing. IPs are cameras that communicate through the computer network and in this case it's the TKH high-tech fiber optic equipment set up by the state of South Carolina. They have one of the best surveillance systems in the country, believe that or not, from traffic cameras to variable message signs, VMS. And the best part is the data can be sent and received via a computer network, and brother we got a good one here. So you hang on. I'll have this thing working to find that old truck in a jiffy."

Spider was on it like a dog on a bone, so the chief was not about to interrupt his train of thought. He slowly eased back out of the room like he was on the bomb squad and let this boy do his thing. Connie was right, he was good at it. The chief walked up the hall to his office and his thoughts turned to Connie. She was over at the hotel talking to the Colemans, getting the information he needed in this case.

That's when his phone rang and he answered, hoping it was her. "Chief Parnell speaking."

"Tommy John it's me. Do you have any word on Reese? It's been over four days. Please tell me you have something. We are all going crazy here; tell me you got some new information on my little girl, tell me something, please."

"Now Bev, hold on, we are working as hard as we can, and yes I think we have a lead on a hit-and-run vehicle that may point us in the right direction but these things take time. I also hired a specialist that deals in kidnapping cases and she is on top of it as well. Plus the FBI, the SBI, everyone is working hard on it. You just have to believe me Sis."

"Damn it Tommy, it's my only child. She is all I got."

"Beverly I'm going to send Ms. Womack to your house so she can get a better picture of the situation. But before she gets there you need to write down anything you think will help find Reese. Who, what, when, where, people she knows, places she has been, her likes and dislikes. Can you do that for me? That will help more than you know."

"OK Tommy, I'll start a list, but I told you and the FBI about the night she left Brenda's house for some boy she met at the beach. I don't know anything else to tell. I feel like you have me doing nothing but busy work and maybe it will help, who knows. I'll talk to you later, love you."

"Love you too. Please hang in there. Something will break. I just know it," and they both hung up their phones.

"Got 'em, chief, come in here quick." The chief heard shouting from down the hall in Spider's office. He quickly got up from his chair and headed in that direction.

"There they go," Spider said as he pointed to the monitor. They saw the white Ford truck traveling up Highway I-26 several miles north of the North Charleston area headed toward Summerville. He shifted over to another screen and this time they could see that the license tag had been removed. It was not on the truck. How could a trooper not see that? The truck exited the highway on the Summerville offramp headed to Highway 17 Alternate and that's where the surveillance ended as the truck drove up the offramp.

"Damn it, get it back! He's getting away again," shouted the chief as the picture went blank. "We don't know which way on 17 they went, right to Summerville or left towards Monks Corner and Sampit. Spider this is great but stay on it. We have to apprehend these guys."

"I'm on it, chief, don't you worry," as Spider twisted his chair back around and focused like a laser beam on his computers.

Flynn's Tavern

Chapter 16

TODD PARKED THE BIG GREY VAN UP BESIDE THE CURB outside of Flynn's Irish Tavern, a local's favorite located on Main Street in North Myrtle Beach. Several local customers were sitting on the front porch enjoying a friendly conversation and adult beverages with their buddies. Todd and Raymond sat in the van, still numb from the long drive from Cecil's house. Hardly two words were spoken on the whole trip back. Todd was not yet ready to face the captive girls in the basement of the farm house which was only a few miles up the road from North Myrtle in the community of Wampee. He was sick of the whole situation. It made his head hurt for all the thinking—what to do with Cecil, the girls, everything? Plus he was tired of driving and was pretty hungry and ready to get out of the van.

"Look Raymond, I'm hungry. I'm sure you are as well. Now look, we are not going to sit on the porch, not with all those people. Don't talk to anyone OK? Now let's go inside and get something to eat. I heard the food is really good. Plus I know you have to be tired as well so let's unwind for a few minutes and relax with a nice meal, what do you say?"

Raymond didn't know how to say it but he, too, was tired of the ride and had not eaten all day as well. "Sure, I've been hungry the whole trip. Let's eat," Raymond said and jumped out of the van and headed in the front door of Flynn's.

The place looked like a true Irish sports bar, with New York Yankee's baseball and professional boxing memorabilia covering the walls, along with signs for every type of Irish beer and whiskey imaginable. There was also an array of Gaelic artifacts, causing the restaurant's appearance to resemble a real Irish pub like you would find in Galway or Dublin, Ireland. It was a real neat place.

As Todd and Raymond entered, the owner's

daughter walked through the swinging door that separated the kitchen from the bar. "You boys thirsty or hungry?" said the attractive young bartender with long blond hair pulled back in a ponytail.

"Both," Raymond shouted.

"What will it be boys?" she asked again as she kept wiping down the bar. Behind her were literally a hundred bottles of liquor plus about every type of Irish whiskey you could think of or ever heard of.

The two brothers slowly walked up to the bar as if they had never been in one like this before. They sat down on two barstools and looked up at the pretty young lady. "We are hungry and thirsty," said Todd as Raymond shook his head in agreement.

"Well, alrighty then. My name's Amanda. What's yours?" The two looked puzzled as to what to say as they looked at each other. Todd then spoke. "Can we see a couple of menus please? And it's Tim," as Todd pointed to himself, "and that's Bob," as he nodded over toward Raymond.

"Well of course you can. Here you two go, Tim and Bob," she said as she quickly handed them two menus. As the door opened, another customer came in and sat down at the bar beside of Raymond.

"Hey Larry, what will it be today? Let me guess," as she paused like she had to think, knowing full well what he got every single day. "I know, how about a shot of Powers and a Miller Lite?"

"You guessed right Amanda, I'll take a shot and a beer please," said the little fellow with a beard. The man was obviously a regular. Larry then turned to greet the brothers. "Hey Hognuts, you boys come around here often?" the little man asked trying to be funny and start a little small talk.

Raymond was oblivious to Larry's conversation as he seemed to be deep in his own world, looking around the room at all the pictures of famous ball players and boxers that dotted the walls, not to mention all the liquor bottles.

"I'm sorry sir. He doesn't talk much. We're from out of town," said Todd, trying to apologize for his brother's rudeness.

"No shit. You must be Yankees," Larry said as he grabbed his two drinks and headed out the door to be with his friends on the porch. He stopped before going outside to his permanent seat with his other drinking buddies. "Hey boys, have you ever had your ass kicked by a leprechaun before?" He then laughed as he turned towards his drinking buddies.

"Don't worry about him. He's just playing. He's harmless, but he is funny," Amanda said as she tried to do the apology thing herself, this time for Larry. Both she and Todd laughed.

"Hey, look Amanda, can we just get a couple of beers, Miller Lites, and two Ruben sandwiches would be fine. We'll take the sandwiches to go if that's OK."

"Fries? You got it Tim," as she drafted off two cold beers from the taps that were in front of them. "Here's your beer and I'll go put your order in right now," she said as she went through the swinging kitchen door to place their order to go.

Todd leaned over and in a whisper he tried to get Raymond's attention. "Raymond, look here, Raymond I'm talking to you," Todd said.

Raymond then slowly turned toward Todd. "You said my name was Bob. Which one is it, Bob or Raymond? Make up your mind Tim," and Raymond started to laugh.

"Quit dicking around. We're getting out of here soon as you drink your beer. This wasn't a good idea at all; I should have stopped at McDonalds or something."

Then another regular customer sat down at the bar, this time on Todd's side. "Hey boys how's tricks," said Berry Brown, a retired gentleman from upstate New York. He didn't have to even motion to Amanda and as quick as a wink Berry's beverage sat before him. "You've got to love this place," Berry said to Todd. "And the service ain't too bad either," he added as he looked over at Amanda. "Where are you boys from?" He took a swallow of his drink and then looked back over at Todd.

Todd was scared to answer and he hesitated with his reply and then his lie came out. "We are from New York state."

"No kidding, that's where I'm from. Where exactly?"

Todd was stuck and was scared to answer. A few seconds went by before he replied, "upstate."

"Really? That's where I was raised, over near Malone up not too far from the Canadian border. You know that area I bet."

Todd could not believe that he told the one wrong lie, and this guy came from the one place he lied about. But faith intervened and saved Todd at that moment when out of the blue there was a loud horrible sound of tires screeching and a boom as two cars crashed out front. Everyone in the place turned to see what happened outside of the restaurant. Then like a flash the door blew open as Little Larry the Leprechaun came flying inside to bring the bad news.

"Hey boys," as he looked over at Todd and Raymond. "I think Charlie Thompson just found his parking spot. The bad news is I believe your gray van was sitting in it."

Everyone abandoned their food and drink to run out to see two damaged vehicles; Todd and Raymond remained seated, not believing what happened. "Damn Todd what do we do?"

"Shut up, I'm thinking. Don't you say a word."

The front door opened again and this time a man walked up to the two brothers. "Hey that's your van outside sir?" the man asked.

Todd was slow to answer and finally he pushed out a "Yes."

"Looks like old Charlie hit your van pretty good out there, but I don't think there is much damage. Look guys, my name is Marty. I own this place and Charlie Thompson is a dear friend of mine but I'm afraid he's had a little too much celebration today already. And I don't want to see him get into any trouble. How about I pay for your damages. I'll give you a few hundred now. And if you think it should be more, go get a couple more estimates and I'll pay you the difference later, what do you say?"

Todd could not believe his luck. He could not say yes fast enough. "OK I need to look at the van first but that sounds fine with me, let me check." The three walked outside and inspected the car and van. "Sure we're good with that. Come on Tim, let's go. Thank you, Marty. I hope your friend Charlie didn't get hurt." They looked over at the crowd nursing Charlie back to health. The crowd of folks was sitting out on the front porch of the bar attending to their friend, as someone was handing Charlie another Power's whiskey shot to get his head right.

"I think he'll be fine, and here's $800. You think that should do it?"

"Yes sir, but shoot, that old van isn't worth much more than that anyway. That's awful nice of you Marty. I sure appreciate it, thanks again." With that the two strangers got in the van. All the folks on the porch, including Larry, started waving good bye as the brothers drove off. The rest of the customers started to walk back inside, as Marty's wife Jane came out to the street with two to-go boxes.

"Marty, did they just drive off?" Jane asked. "Well here is the food they ordered and by the way, they didn't pay for a thing, including the beer!"

Todd felt relieved from that situation and worried about the next as they drove up Main

Street headed to the Wampee community about five miles north up Highway 90 from North Myrtle Beach where the girls were being kept.

Raymond turned to look at Todd. “I sure am hungry Tim!”

“Oh shut up Raymond!” Todd shouted as they drove down the road. “Just shut up!”

The Winn Blows

Chapter 17

CONNIE AND RHYS ARRIVED AT THE HOTEL shortly after seven o'clock that evening, about two hours after the Colemans had called, asking to see her as soon as possible dealing with the disappearance of their two daughters. This would be the first case of this kind that Rhys had ever dealt with. He was used to blowing up towns and villages but he was not much with the emotional side of putting lives back together.

"Hello, Ms. Connie, good evening," said the police officer that was on duty at the hotel as they got off the elevator to the presidential suite. Rhys was drumming his fingers on the handles of the wheelchair as he waited on Connie's niceties.

Connie looked up from her wheelchair with a smile. "Officer this is Mr. Garret. He's with me tonight and you might be seeing a lot of him in the future."

"Hello sir," the officer said to Rhys as he opened the door to the Coleman suite, and Rhys nodded his head as they went by, pushing the chair into the larger foyer of the apartment.

"Hello again Connie," said Patty with a drink in her hand as she offered one to each of them.

"No thank you, Patty, we are good. Thank you anyway," Connie said, answering for them both. "Patty, this is Rhys Garret, a dear friend of mine," Connie said as he shook Patty's hand hello.

"Hello Ma'am, don't mind if I do. I would love a vodka tonic with a lime twist if possible?" Rhys asked.

"Sure of course," Patty replied as she eyed Rhys' perfectly shaped body with a long gazing look before she then turned, feeling her face blush. She quickly peered over to Winn standing behind the bar. "Dear we need another VT please! You two come on in and please, have a seat." She looked at Connie as to say she was sorry for undressing Rhys with her eyes. Connie didn't say a thing, as if to say it's alright, as they worked their way into the room.

Patty introduced Rhys to Winn as Winn handed Rhys a drink. They all found seats in the living room area of the suite, as if they were from the chamber of commerce on a social call. Patty and Winn sat in their chairs across the room from each other. Connie had the convenience of placing herself anywhere in the room she liked, so she parked herself between and facing them both. Rhys stayed standing at the bar, to overlook the conversation like an official referee ready to blow his whistle and get the game started.

"OK folks let's cut right to it. What's going on, what's the big news?" Connie asked as she stared at both Patty and Winn.

"They called us, Connie!" Patty was the first to speak.

"Who was it, do you know, did you two recognize their voice? Did anything stand out to either of you in the conversation?"

Patty replied, "No they sounded like a machine; they must have put something on the phone that made them sound like Darth Vader."

"And they said no cops, so what does my wife do but call the cops, great!" snarled Winn as he rose from the couch to make himself another drink. Rhys held his hand out to stop Winn from getting hold of the bottle of vodka.

“Hold on cowboy, let Connie do her thing before you get all liquored up, alright?” said Rhys as he grabbed the bottle, daring Winn to take it away from him, knowing Winn would lose.

“Hey look Patty. This guy has muscles like Tony. Maybe he could become your next boy toy as well.”

“Shut up Winn and sit down so Connie can find our baby girls.”

“Yeah, our sweet little harmless babies, right! I shouldn’t have ever adopted those kids in the first place. They have been trouble from the get-go. Babies, hell they are teenagers and something is wrong with those two and you know it as good as I do!” he shouted to Patty.

“Shut up, just shut up!” Patty started to cry and she put both her hands to her face. Connie moved over to console her as she placed her hand on Patty’s shoulder. Connie then looked up at Winn.

“Senator Coleman you need to leave this room, I’ll talk to you later.”

“I’m not going anywhere. You can’t make me,” he shouted, looking over at Rhys as Rhys crossed his arm and flexed his muscles a little. Without a word Winn turned to leave, stumbling a little as he tried to walk. It was not close to a straight line but he made his way to the bedroom and closed the door behind him.

"Yep he's a state senator alright. Wow lady, how much have you two had to drink today?" Rhys said, as Winn barely made it to the room without falling down.

"You're right Rhys, he's drunk, me this is only my second drink of the day. I'm fine to answer any questions. And yes, they called and said not to call the cops, but I had to do something so I called you. You're not a cop are you?"

"That's OK, Patty, we are here to help. Rhys and I are old friends from way back and my friend Willie that you met yesterday, well let's just say he couldn't make it. Now first, whose cell phone did they call?"

"No it was that one," as she pointed to the house phone, "right there on the table."

"They called here to the hotel's phone? Well they knew you're here that's for sure. What do they want? How much money did they ask for, Patty?"

"Well, here's the thing. They asked for us to wire $100 million to an account offshore but the money must come from Winn's campaign fund. Since Tony was killed that makes me Winn's campaign manager and treasurer. I'm the only one that can get that money. They had to be the ones that killed Tony. How would they have known that?"

"Inside job, that's what you got here Connie," Rhys shouted out loud as he walked over closer to the two women.

Connie looked up over at Rhys like she could kill him. "Thank you, Rhys. What else was said Patty, like where and when do they want the money?" Connie asked her.

Patty leaned toward Connie. "Tomorrow afternoon at five o'clock, they gave us only 24 hours, or they are going to do something horrible to the girls. We have till five, or else."

"Or else? Hell they are bluffing," said Rhys.

"Or we will never see the girls again," Patty said as she started crying again.

"OK, Patty, here is what I need to get from you. I need cell phone numbers, all of them, every family member's phone, email addresses, plus passwords and the name of the company that is the service provider. And we need to go to your house in Columbia tonight if possible and go through your children's rooms and get their computers. We must find something that will give us a clue. Are you up for that?"

Patty stopped crying and looked up at Connie. "Anything that will get our girls back, and by the way don't pay attention to Winn acting like an ass too much. We had a fight over the girls just before you two got here. He'll be alright. Right now he is a little mad and drunk, that's all."

"Rhys, you get the senator and I'll get Patty ready and call Spider. We are going to be taking a road trip to Columbia."

Without hesitation Rhys whipped out his cell phone and called Spider. "Brother, you need to get our recon and intel gear together. We are going on a road trip ASAP. We should be there in a half an hour or so. You good with that?"

"No problem big man, but there is one thing, bro. Your so-called sister called and she is pissed that you have not returned any of her messages she has left on your phone. F.Y.I., she said she loves and misses your big strong body. That's some sister," he laughed.

"Just get the shit ready to go, I'll deal with that mess later. I'll see you in twenty."

"Roger that Casanova, catch you in a few."

Rhys checked his phone and sure enough he counted about 20 messages from the number Spider was talking about. He smiled and walked over to the bedroom door where the senator had been placed in time out. "Hey Winn, we are ready to go sir," he called out but no answer. "Senator Coleman sir, where are you sir? We are going to take you back to Columbia, sir." Again no answer. Rhys surveyed the room and then checked every room in the suite.

Patty and Connie looked up and Connie asked, "What are you doing Rhys?"

Glancing behind the bar Rhys straightened and looked at Connie. "The son of a bitch is gone."

"Gone!" both ladies shouted at the same time. While Connie digested the new turn of events, Rhys went outside to tell the officer to call for backup and have this section of Charleston blocked off, if possible.

"Connie, you better call Chief Parnell and 9-1-1," shouted Rhys as he found the policeman lying on the floor beside the elevator. He quickly checked for a pulse, and was happy to find one; he then loosened the officer's tie and pulled him over and sat him up against the wall to rest, as the man started to come to.

Both Patty and Connie couldn't believe Winn would do this. Connie called Chief Parnell for help on her cell phone. In disbelief, Patty went back into the suite and checked every room to her satisfaction, and finally admitted to herself he was truly gone. "Damn you Winn Coleman!"

Out on the city street Senator Winn Coleman stood in his stocking feet while holding the door handle as he nervously scanned two city blocks, looking back and forth and up and down the intersection before getting in the passenger side of a black SUV. With a big smile on his face he slid in the vehicle which was parked in front of Hyman's Seafood restaurant, down a couple of blocks from his hotel.

"Sir if you're ready, we need to go," said Eddie Miller, who sat nervously behind the steering wheel of the getaway car, and now the new head of security.

Winn, too, was nervous. He looked again down the street to see if he was being followed, then back to Eddie. "Did you get everything?" Eddie nodded yes like a good servant and the two drove off undetected into the night headed for Columbia.

Free Bird

Chapter 18

REESE STARTS TO COME TO AS SHE HEARS THE BEEPING SOUND of the intravenous machine. She notices that the pouch is empty of fluid, and the other two girls' IVs soon would be as well. She also notices that she is not as groggy as she was before and now definitely more aware. Again she has awakened before the other two have, and once again her eyes start casing the joint and inspecting the room for every small detail, from surveillance cameras that appear to be off with no red light on, to the locks on the door, to the color of pink paint on the walls. Her ears try to hear something but there is no sound but her own breathing and her heart pounding. Her legs and arms seem to have no restrictions as she has no trouble moving them now. To her delight the medicine has surely worn off.

She can now sit up on the edge of the bed and reach out and grab the small table with a scalpel, some cotton balls and a syringe. Knowing she cannot cut off the metal leash attached to her leg, and not knowing when her assailants are coming back she grabs the scalpel and places it inside her pillow case. She then returns the table to its original spot in the room and that's when she notices the opening in one of the transom windows on the other side of the room. Her mind is on fire trying to think of ways to get to and out of that window. It must be at least six feet off the floor so how can she possibly do it? Her mind races as she thinks of escape, but first she has to awaken the others. She reaches out and grabs her IV stand and uses it to grab the other stands and pulls them closer to her. Once she has them lassoed she then pulls all of them over close enough to her to remove the needles from their arms. Now she has to wait and hopes they awaken before those men get back. Hurry up, she thinks, and it is a race against time.

The window, how do we get up there? she thinks as she kicks the footrest of the small bed and it moves. It moved, she thinks, as she kicks it again and bam, down goes one side of the bed. She has broken it. Without hesitation she slips the leash right off the bed. She is speechless as she starts to cry and laugh at the same time. Soon she regains her faculties and quickly sets out to leave the hellhole. The others are still out cold, and there is no way she can wake them up as she tries by shaking their bodies and slapping their faces.

Still not knowing if anyone is home she tries to be as quiet as possible, but precious time is ticking away. She thinks to herself that nobody is here in the house. It's too quiet. She can't hear anything or anyone. The hell with it, and once she makes that decision she realizes she is on her own. All she thinks about is getting out immediately and she herself is her only hope. What will I need? she thinks, as she then realizes she is standing there in the nude. Well that's obvious she thinks, grabbing the bed sheet and cutting a hole in the middle of it and, like Rambo, starts making a poncho.

She then slips it over her head and cuts off a piece of plastic tubing making a belt, tying it around her waist. She moves the broken bed over to the side of the room with the opened window.

Leaning the bed against the wall and using it like a ladder she makes her way up to the window and begins to push but it won't move. It must be painted shut. She climbs back down and grabs the scalpel. She wedges her toes into the bed frame to climb back up. This time she runs the blade around the edges between the windows and the window casings, cutting away the paint. This time she pushes with all her might and it opens but suddenly the bed starts to move as her weight shifts. At the same time the window opens and the bed slips off the wall and hits the floor. One of the girls starts to move a little as the noise of the collision must have awakened her but she is still out cold. It was then that she sees headlights from a gray vehicle reflecting off the transom windows.

"Oh shit, they're back, damn it!" she says out loud and now she has to move and move even faster. Quickly she grabs the bed and places it against the wall but this time she wedges the IV stands against the post in the center of the room to the foot of the bed to keep it from slipping. She stops to hear the men at the vehicle beside the house; she listens to their conversation outside.

"Damn it, Raymond, we'll get something to eat inside the house. Now get out of the damn van and quit acting like a baby," Todd says as he slams the car door.

"But Wendy's is just up the road, Todd."

"Damn, what did I ever do to deserve this; I said get out of the van Raymond, damn it." As Todd goes inside the house, Reese can hear his footsteps upstairs in the house. The screen door shuts and she can hear the hardwood floors creak as he is directly overhead.

Her heart is now beating like crazy as she can hear him coming down the steps just outside the door to her room. Quickly she gets herself together, inspects the bed one more time, grabs the blanket off the bed, and climbs to the top of her bed ladder again. As she opens the window slowly so as not to make any noise she can hear the keys in the door lock and she starts to pull herself through the window. At the same time the door to the room opens and Todd walks inside and notices the bed is not where it should have been. His eyes see Reese as her legs kick the air, trying to escape as she hangs in the window above his head.

"No, oh hell no, damn it!" shouts Todd as he runs over to stop her from escaping through the transom window. Reese's body is half in and half out of the window, trying to free herself. Todd then starts shouting to his brother. "Raymond help, she's getting away, Raymond she is in the window!" Todd tries to grab her feet but she kicks his hands away.

She then kicks and wiggles her way out the window. She's out! Once outside she looks for some sign of direction. She sees the man in the van with his door open. She then gets down on her hands and knees and slowly sneaks around the front of the vehicle and stops.

Raymond hears Todd shouting but he can't

make it out. "What Todd, what's going on?" he shouts back to his brother. Reese looks over and quickly sneaks over to a nearby tree to hide behind. She looks up at the stars in the night sky but she has no idea about the constellation she sees. She thinks it is the North Star but she has no idea and no understanding of what direction to take but she knows she has to move and move now. Suddenly she feels a hand on her shoulder. She jumps from the touch. It's Raymond, the other guy.

"Now hold on little girl. You're not supposed to leave. We have to take you to see Cecil!"

Reese turns and faces her assailant and in that moment, without thinking, she sticks the scalpel right into Raymond's neck. Todd could hear the scream as he runs out of the house, headed toward the sound. As Raymond falls she turns and sees Todd standing in the back doorway. He sees her as well, as he starts his pursuit after her and she starts running away in the dark from both brothers.

"Raymond get her," Todd shouts, as Raymond makes it to his feet under his brother's instruction and starts his chase. Todd quickly catches up with him, but not knowing the severity of Raymond's injury, Todd runs right by Raymond in his pursuit of catching her. Raymond stops, feeling the pain in his neck. He then removes the scalpel from his neck, opening the wound even more as the blood starts to pour out from his jugular vein, and it can't be stopped. He places his hand on his neck and tries to run to catch up. The blood drains as he runs, but after less than hundred feet or so he feels faint and his run slows to a walk. He becomes a little light-headed and he feels dizzier and dizzier as he stops moving all together. He then starts to lose consciousness, dropping to his knees for a few seconds. Then, like a big oak tree, he falls face first to the ground in a pool of blood. Todd, being caught up in the moment, has no idea he just lost his brother. He continues to run but has no idea in which direction to go.

She can hear the sounds of a highway now as the night sky is lit up with the glow of town and headlights from the interstate. Her feet hurt with every step of rock or stick she steps on but she cannot stop, no way.

Todd now realizes he doesn't have a chance in hell in catching her. Soon Todd is exhausted and stops his chase. He looks around for a second but she is nowhere to be found. He knows it is truly over. He then turns his attention to the whereabouts of Raymond as he retraces his steps to find his brother.

"Raymond! Raymond, where are you?" he shouts. After a few minutes in the distance he sees something that is lying on the ground. He picks up his pace as he starts to run, faster and faster as he runs back to find his brother. When he gets there he is terrified to see his dead brother in a pool of blood lying on the cold ground and he starts to shout. "I will kill you girl, I will kill you!" He falls to his knees and starts to cry over his lost sibling. "Raymond I'm so sorry, I'm so sorry," he cries. He reaches out and holds his brother in his arms, not believing this is happening as he cries in pain.

Reese is crying as well, but for joy, as she makes it to the highway. She waves her arms for someone to stop but they don't. Car after car and truck after truck, no one seems to care. She stops and strips off the sheet. "What the hell," she says to herself as she stands nude in the median so everyone on both sides can see her in full birthday suit apparel. Within seconds cars and trucks come to a screeching halt. She falls to her knees as she realizes she is saved. She sees the red and blue light of a South Carolina Highway Patrol car. Exhausted and beaten up and worn out, she lies there knowing her prayers are answered. She starts to cry as she prays again.

She's Alive

Chapter 19

THE LITTLE EARLY BIRD DINER OFF THE SAVANNAH Highway near Wappoo Road was packed with hungry customers and Chief Tommy John Parnell. He was sitting in his favorite spot in a booth in the back of the restaurant eating a late-night supper when his cell phone rang, creating more attention as it played Dixie. He stopped cutting into his country style steak dinner, including mashed potatoes and green beans, a fresh roll and sweet tea for a bargain of $5.99. He placed his knife and fork to the side of the today's special and answered the phone. It was a number that he was not familiar with, and on his dinner hour too, but for some reason he answered it anyway. He cleared his throat with a sip of tea and sat up in the booth as if someone was watching him answer.

"Chief Parnell here," he replied, but he heard nothing, so he repeated himself. "Hello, Chief Parnell speaking, hello?"

Trying to get her words out she finally spoke. "Uncle Tommy, it's me, Reesy, I escaped! I'm OK, I'm in the hospital, and the police saved me!" In shock he dropped his glass of tea on the floor. He wiped his mouth with his napkin as tears formed in the corners of his eyes. Was it really her? He could not believe his niece, who was kidnapped just days ago, was calling on his phone.

"Reesy, oh my God, dear are you sure you are OK?" He placed his finger in his other ear so he could hear her better over the loud din of the diner. "Oh God this is great! Where are you sweetheart? I will come and get you right now."

"I'm in Myrtle Beach, no they say, North Myrtle Beach. I don't know where but please come get me, please. Here, they want to talk to you," as she handed the phone to the police chief.

"Hey Tommy John, this is Chief Johnson here. Hey Buddy, just wanted you to know she is fine and we have her at the Grand Stand Hospital right now."

"That's great, but how is she really, Hank? Can you talk?"

"Yeah I can talk; I'm stepping outside of her room right now. Look Tommy I'll tell it to you straight. She's been through hell and back. Tommy, it looks like they pumped her full of all kinds of drugs. The doctors are in the process of detoxification right now, and the good news is she looks pretty good. There are no broken bones, a few cuts, but there is evidence of rape. I am so sorry, Tommy, but I'm afraid it appears she was tortured and raped multiple times. Doctors don't know the severity of her condition at this point, but I thought you might want to know so you could be the one who breaks the news to her mother; it might be easier coming from you."

"Sure, thanks Hank, but what about the investigation?"

"My men are searching over and under every inch of those woods. It's about five miles from town so the sheriff's office is involved as well. As for Reese, she wants to go home in the morning but she is a sick girl right now and she needs to rest. She has a strong will Tommy. Your family should be proud of this young lady. She's been through a lot, and don't you worry, I will have around the clock security on her. She will be fine till you get here."

"I don't know what to say, Hank. Thank you and your men so much. I'll call my sister right now and I'll be there first thing in the morning. Thanks again chief. I'll see you guys in a few hours," as he cut off his phone.

He grabbed his walkie-talkie off his shoulder and called the dispatch. "Dispatch, Chief Parnell here, please connect me to Officer Tandy, Drew Tandy, over."

"Sure, Roger that, chief, over."

In a few seconds the chief's radio squawked. "Tandy here, chief, what's going on? Do you want me to go Columbia to help Connie, over?"

"Connie? What is her situation, over?" he asked.

"You better call her sir; I'm not at liberty to say over the open air waves, over."

"Roger that, but I need your help in the morning. I need you to go with me to North Myrtle Beach, over."

"10-4, sir. Is everything OK, over?"

"Everything is great. They found my niece. She's alive and well, over!"

"That's fantastic I'll see you in the am, over."

"Thanks Drew. I'll see you in the morning at the office, seven o'clock, over and out."

The chief could not get off the mike fast enough so that he could call Connie. He paid for his food and apologized once again to Betty, the waitress, tipping her big for breaking the glass and quickly went out the back door of the restaurant and called Connie while standing in the parking lot. He waited for Connie to pick up. "Connie what is going on?" he said as she answered.

"You will not believe it, Tommy; the senator just knocked out your policeman and took off. He escaped and we can't find him."

"What? The hell you say! He escaped, hell we were protecting him!" he shouted.

"We believe he is headed back home to Columbia. Rhys is with me and we're picking up Spider on the way out of town. We are almost at Spider's now."

"I knew the son of a bitch was up to something, damn him. Well you won't believe this. I have great news. I just talked to my sister's girl Reese. They found her and she is OK. I'm going to pick her up tomorrow morning in North Myrtle Beach. But back to the senator, I'll call Chief Mannes in Columbia and have him help you in any way you need, OK?"

"Sounds great, and that's fantastic about Reese, Tommy. Thank God, she is OK," she said as she disconnected.

Tommy looked up his sister Beverly's number on speed dial and pressed the name that said Sis. He explained to her all about Reese and that he was going up in the morning and she could ride with him if she wanted to or take her own car, anyway was fine to him.

"Oh my God Tommy, I can't believe it! Thank you, thank you brother! I love you so much. Is she OK? Do you know if she is or not?"

"Yes, she's fine. They are still doing all kinds of tests but so far she's checked out just fine."

"Oh thank you God" Beverly said. She then talked about cooking Reese's favorite foods and cleaning the house and having her bedroom just right, never mentioning why Reese left in the first place. Tommy had no way of knowing that Reese and his sister had parted on bad terms. And maybe, Beverly thought, it might be best if Tommy went up there alone and she stayed at home and had everything ready for Reese's homecoming. She knew he wouldn't understand why she was not going and she wasn't about to tell her brother, right then and there, that Reese hated her because of that no-good boyfriend. She wasn't about to tell him anything about her boyfriend's abusing Reese. Tommy hated Wayne Bowman with a blue passion anyway. If Tommy John knew that Bowman had even touched Reese, much less slapped her away in his drunken stupor and maybe worse, Beverly knew he would truly kill Wayne. Beverly even questioned herself on why she was still with a piece of trash like Wayne and figured maybe now was the time she left him for good. She did not have an answer, but at the end of the conversation the brother and sister agreed that Beverly would be there waiting for her little girl to come home and to give Reese all her love, as the two hung up their phones.

But there was still police work that needed to be done, as Chief Tommy, still sitting in his police cruiser, next called Chief Mannes in Columbia. "Roy, Tommy John here. Looks like we a have a situation going to be happening in your fair city tonight. My folks are on the way," as he explained the particulars to the chief and filled him in on the kidnapped girls and the whole ordeal.

"You got it, Tommy John. We'll have that house staked out and ready for your guys to show up. Anything else you boys need from us up here in the state capital?"

"No sir, you have done enough and we sure appreciate it, and will rotate it back to you in the future. Have a good night sir and thanks again Roy." With a smile on his face Tommy John put the key into the ignition of his police car and drove out of the parking lot, headed back to the station to get a few things for tomorrow's trip.

What a night! She is safe, he thought as he drove off.

Todd's Cleanup

Chapter 20

TODD SAT ON THE GROUND LOOKING AT HIS BROTHER. Raymond lay at his feet, dead and covered in blood. She killed him, he thought, as he stood up and grabbed Raymond's arms and started his journey back to the farm house by pulling him back down the path. Every few feet he stopped to rest but he never stopped cussing her for Raymond's demise. An hour went by and he finally reached the house. He stopped and rearranged Raymond again to get a better hold of his arms before he pulled him through the back screen door and into the kitchen where he laid him down beside the kitchen table. Todd stared at Raymond's lifeless body once again, all the while thinking what he should do first. Still upset about Raymond, he blamed himself for what had happened.

I was supposed to watch after him after mama and daddy died, he thought. That was my job till she killed him. He never hurt a soul and she killed him. That thought kept running through his mind till he remembered Cecil. Oh God, Cecil. He needed to call him, but calling Cecil was not what he wanted to do at all. He would have to at some point but not now, he thought.

He quickly stood up and went to the sink, pouring water over his hands and washing the sweat and blood off his face to cool himself down a little before he went back downstairs to check on the girls. He knew that the police would be in this area soon.

Once again he thought of her. "Because of her I'm not at all ready, but she will get hers, she will alright," he shouted out loud as he walked through the entire home, turning off all the lights, giving it the appearance of looking empty and abandoned. He then unlocked the door to the downstairs and shut it behind him. He turned on the lights to the stairway and went down to the larger metal door and unlocked it. As he walked into the room he noticed that the two girls were still asleep. He checked the leashes on their ankles making sure they were secured and then started to move the broken bed off the wall to its proper place.

All of a sudden he jumped. The sound of both IV machines began to beep as they ran out of anesthetic; he quickly reached over, fumbling with the knobs, trying to turn off the loud beeping noise of the machines. After several tries he finally hit the right buttons and the noise ceased. Sweat popped out on his forehead and his hands started to shake as he opened the door to the small refrigerator in the corner of the room. He noticed there were only two remaining bags of anesthetic. Carefully he removed the two bags with the name Atracurium-Acris 25 mg printed on them. Todd cradled them like a baby as he carried them over to replace the empty ones hanging on the two stands.

"Help me," he heard, and suddenly he jumped as a hand reached up and grabbed Todd's leg. In the process, Todd dropped both bags of anesthetic. He scrambled to catch them but was too late. One of the bags had indeed broken and was pouring out fluid all over the concrete floor.

"Damn you," he shouted as he kicked the bed. What to do now? That was all the meds he had, but he had to do something fast. It would be only minutes now before the other one awoke. Todd quickly replaced the bag in the one IV machine.

"Since the other girl is awake I'll have to tie the one up, that's right," he thought out loud. "Now wait a minute. I have some GHB in the refrigerator." He turned around and retrieved the liquid ecstasy, the number one date rape drug on the market. That would slow her down. At least she would be easy to work with and feel no pain, he thought. Just as he was reading the label on the bottle he jumped again as his phone rang in his pocket and he dropped the bottle on the floor. It, too, broke.

Are you freaking kidding me, he thought, as he looked down at the broken bottle on the floor. He could not believe his luck tonight as the phone kept ringing. It was Cecil. He just knew it and was scared to look but he did and sure enough it was Cecil. He lowered the sound of the ringer and did not answer. What in the world do I do, he thought. Trying to think of a solution, he felt like his brain was on fire. All he could think of was to get the hell out of there before all hell from the police fell on him.

"Are you going to kill us?" said one of the girls. It was the one with red hair. She looked up at Todd with tears in her eyes. He did not know what to say, as he looked into the eyes of a little girl. He never saw them as girls; they were only things, or money to him.

He looked down at the young girl, trying to

think of something as a smile came to his face. “No dear I’m here to save you. My name is Todd; I’m here to get you two out of this hellhole.”

“Oh thank you. Please help us, my name is Melissa. That’s my sister. Is she going to be alright?”

“She’s fine. I need to give her some more medicine and with your help we are going to get the heck out of here, OK?”

A small smile crossed her lips. “That sounds good to me,” she said, not knowing who Todd really was. She sat up in the bed rubbing her eyes and trying to wake up from days of medication.

Todd was feeling pretty good at that point, thinking she had no idea who he was, as he removed the leash from her ankle. “Now you sit here for a few minutes. I don’t need you passing out on me, OK?” he said as he did the same to her sister’s leash. Leaving the room for a minute, Todd returned with a couple of shirts so he could get them out of the house, since it would be hard to transport someone who is naked. “Here put this on. It’s too big of course, but it’s something to cover you up anyway.” She pulled it over her head and slowly got up and went over to dress her sister.

“Now the moment of truth with Cecil,” Todd said aloud, wanting to get it over with. He stepped away from the girls and pulled out his phone. His hand was shaking as he called and waited for an answer on the other end.

"Todd, tell me what the hell is going on," shouted Cecil as he answered.

"Cecil, I can explain."

"Damn it, Todd, it's all over the police scanner that a girl was found up in North Myrtle Beach and she says she had been kidnapped. Now tell me she is not one of ours, please tell me that."

"She killed Raymond, Cecil."

"What, she is ours? Damn it, what the hell are you and your brother doing up there?" shouted Cecil.

Todd's voice remained calm as he spoke to his cousin. "Raymond is dead Cecil. She killed him. I'm getting the others ready for travel to your house right now. I can't stay here. The cops will be here in minutes. Now tell me what should I do Cecil?"

It took Cecil a second to understand the situation. "OK Todd that's good. Stay calm and do what I say! Take anything you think you need to get here and burn that old house down to the ground with Raymond in it, you understand me? You need to haul ass right now. I can't believe you're still there. You need to hurry up. Now listen to me; everything will be fine, don't speed whatever you do. Drive slowly and take the old country roads for the most part. It will take longer but take your time and be sure not to leave anything that can lead the police back to me. Again stay calm and be cool, I'll see you in a few hours. Be safe."

"Yes sir, I'm on my way. I'll be there in a couple of hours. Thanks Cecil."

"That dumb son of a bitch," Cecil yelled as he threw his phone across the room, kicking over the ottoman as he lowered himself into a nearby chair. His blood was boiling; he could not wait to see his cousin now! She got away, holly shit; all hell is going to come down on us now! "Skeeter, where are you?"

Quickly one of Cecil's men ran down the hall from the kitchen to see what Cecil needed. "Yes sir, you need something?"

Cecil finished his glass of bourbon and looked at his man. "Skeeter, I want you and Freddie to go down to the cabin and clean it up and make sure the generator is full of gas and everything is in working order. Also stock it with some drinks, bottled water maybe, some cokes and a couple of bottles of that date rape stuff, GHB. We are going to have some guests staying the night. Call me if you need something."

"You mean now, tonight sir?" Skeeter looked at his watch.

Cecil jumped out of the chair and placed his hands around Skeeter's neck, staring straight into his eyes. "Yes damn it, right now you sorry piece of shit, yes tonight," he shouted. He then stopped and let go. He turned around and in a calm voice he again looked at Skeeter who was now shaking and scared. "I'm sorry Buddy, just go clean the place up and call me when you are finished. By the way you have about two hours so don't hurry. Everything will be OK." Cecil walked over and poured himself another glass of bourbon, looking back at Skeeter again. "Don't worry Skeeter, this shit will be over soon. Now you boys get to work, and call me."

Back at the farm house Todd was getting ready to leave. He grabbed a small bag, the one Raymond's clothes were in, and started putting the bottles of GHB inside it and gathering anything else he could think of for the trip to Sampit. After that he put blankets and towels down on the floor board of the van to form a makeshift bed. He then got Melissa to help him carry her sister, as they struggled getting her up the stairs. They stopped and rested a minute in the kitchen, and luckily she never saw Raymond or his blood that was all over the floor. Making their way out the door they slowly made it to the van and placed the girl on the blankets in the back of the van.

"Here you go, you need to take this. It will help your headache." Without thinking Melissa took the pill. "Wait right here. I'll be back in a second." Todd left the van and went behind the house to an old out building for a few minutes. By the time he got back to the van Todd had emptied a five gallon can of gasoline, pouring it all over the property, both inside starting with the basement and all through the living quarters, and outside working his way to the van.

By the time he was finished Melissa was sitting in the front seat and well on her way to dreamland. As she looked at the house in flames, she said in a soft voice, "The fire is so pretty." That would be her last words for a while. Todd got into the van and looked back for the last time, thinking of his brother Raymond. He drove away from the inferno, turning the van out of the driveway and taking the back roads to avoid the police and several roadblocks. Todd drove down several dirt roads, like the old path that ran beside the Waccamaw River. He then turned onto the Old Wampee Road, turning left onto a blacktop road, which ran parallel with the Little Pee Dee River heading south. Melissa and her sister remained quiet and still. Todd finally started feeling pretty good about the trip as they made it to Highway 17 just north of Murrells Inlet, with only an hour or so to go before they would arrive at Cecil's.

The firemen spent hours fighting the blaze at the old farm house outside Wampee. There was no hope in saving it. All they could do was contain the fire to the house and not let the woods catch on fire. By the next morning the old house was reduced to an empty shell, burned completely out and gutted, with very little remaining. It was hours before both the fire and police chiefs could walk through the burned-out foundation and basement where the IV stands and the rest of the medical equipment were found, blackened and burned with charcoal stains. Both men inspected the outline of bed frames and restraints, knowing now they were standing at ground zero. They opened one of the doors to the concrete prisons. They were very small, not much larger than a large drawer, only three-by-three-foot spaces, more like a square coffin, which held the girls in prison for days.

"Who could do something like this?" one of them said. The fire chief saw something inside and on further investigation he reached inside the space and pulled out a manikin's fake hand.

They both looked puzzled at finding an artificial hand. "What the heck?" the chief of police asked. He placed it in an evidence plastic bag and continued the search. They had the assurance that no one would be tortured there again.

Antebellum Alibi

Chapter 21

WINN WASTED NO TIME RUNNING UP THE STAIRS TO HIS OFFICE in the big old antebellum home where he and Patty raised their girls. Eddie sat outside in the SUV as instructed by his boss, not understanding why they were in Columbia since Winn did not reveal his intentions. The house was more like a shrine to Winn than a home to raise a family. The walls and shelves were full of his accolades and awards along with photos of himself with the rich and famous, from South Carolina legendary Senator Strom Thurmond, to Speaker of the House Newt Gingrich, to James Brown, "the Godfather of Soul," to Steve Spurrier, a head football coach. But once in his office Winn went straight to unlock the wall safe and, once opened, he quickly rifled through it in search of something he obviously wanted badly but could not find. As he frantically searched, the lights in the room suddenly came on.

"Looking for this, senator?" said a lady's voice that Winn knew. He waited for his eyes to adjust to the lights, standing quietly a moment before speaking.

"Well good evening, Phyllis," said Winn as he looked at the girls' nanny holding a thumb drive in her hand.

"Looks like I beat you to it, Winn. By the way, thanks for sending me back here to check if the girls came home. I would not have found this memory stick if you had not told me to come home."

"Now Phyllis, I think we could work out some kind of agreement, don't you?" He paused for a moment. "Now let me see, the girls are missing and you are here, so I'm guessing you have some evidence that could incriminate me, is that right?"

"You are not getting out of this one Winn, you sorry snake of a man. We got you this time," as she shook her fist in the air holding the thumb drive. "I can't believe that I loved you at one time. But for years you treated me like a slave, your very own concubine making me do horrible things for your sick sexual appetite. I don't know how you can live with yourself; my God, those children, Winn, how could you? How could you have your own children kidnapped?"

"Kidnapped, now hold on Phyllis. Don't get so worked up. You know I still love you. Everything is alright. Just give me the thumb drive and I will act as if this night never happened. Remember you, too, are on that memory stick, and no one needs to know that. Trust me; I did not have anything to do with Elizabeth or Melissa, sweetheart. Hell I was hoping they were here with you, not still missing. You have to believe me!"

"Winn, you haven't called me one time to check to see if they were here. You know as well as I do, you don't care, you don't give a rat's ass about those girls. You hated them as much as they hated you. I'm sure of that. You know Winn, when you have sex with your own daughters, well that sometimes causes them to hate you." He had nothing to say as he sat down on his big leather chair behind his large mahogany desk and took in every word she was saying. He placed his hand under his chair, and as she was still talking he pulled out a small handgun he had hidden there, placing it in his lap where she could not see it.

Out on the street, a man walking his dog eased up to the SUV and looked in at Eddie behind the steering wheel. "Sir, do you have a light?" Eddie dug in his pocket and pulled out a lighter. When he looked up he was staring at a gun. “Sir, put your hands on the wheel, Columbia Police Department. Hold it right there,” said the walker as he flashed his police badge in view. Eddie froze as he looked up at the light in the office window. Within seconds police cars and Connie’s van showed up and surrounded the house.

“Phyllis, please hand over the thumb drive,” Winn calmly asked as he revealed his surprise resting in his lap. Winn stood and walked around the desk. He touched her face gently. “You know it doesn’t have to be this way. You know you still love me and I love you. Please give me the memory stick,” he said, walking closer to her. She could not resist. He still had a spell over her and she handed it over without a fight. He placed it in his pocket and then looked deeply into her eyes, their lips coming together. They were still kissing as the police made their way up the stairs and into Winn’s office.

“Sir, please stand against the wall. Ms., you too please,” said the policeman as they entered the room.

“Gun!” shouted one of the policemen, as everyone else pointed theirs at Winn.

“No, you don’t understand! OK, I can explain!” shouted Winn. “She’s my girls’ nanny. I thought she had broken in the house, but she did not. Everything is fine officers."

"Officers, everything alright in here?" asked Chief Roy Mannes of the Columbia Police Department as he walked into the room. "Winn, are you and this young lady OK?" He had known Winn for years, long before he was a state senator. They had gone to school together.

"Roy, it's good to see you," said Winn after seeing his old friend show up. "Roy, everything is fine. I thought someone broke into the house, but it was only Phyllis. You've met Phyllis Grimes before; she is our children's nanny. Patty had asked for her to come home to check on the girls. That was a surprise to me. I didn't know she had asked her to come so it's a complete misunderstanding, that's all."

"Have a seat Winn. I'll take that gun if you don't mind. Yes, I remember Ms. Grimes, yes I do." The chief motioned to his men. "Could you please excuse us officers and take Ms. Grimes downstairs? I'm sure when Connie gets here she will have few questions for her. I need to talk to my friend here, alone. Thank you."

Once everyone left the office, Winn started to talk. "Man, it's great to see you Roy. You got here just in time." Winn looked so relieved.

"Shut the fuck up you dumb son of a bitch.

Have you lost your mind coming back here? Now where are they?" The police chief walked straight up to Winn's face. Winn acted like he had no idea what the chief was talking about. "You know what the hell I'm talking about. You're not the only person on those files with those kids!" he said as he moved even closer to Winn. "Now where did you put those disks or tapes, or whatever they are on?"

"Man I don't know what you are talking about. I don't have any tapes, Roy, I promise, I don't," Winn pleaded.

"You know what they'll do. They can't afford for names to get out. If they think you are lying to me they will surely kill you. Now look, I'm here to help you, Winn. You must know that?" He suddenly stopped talking when he heard someone coming up the steps.

"Well hey senator, knocked off any more policemen lately?" asked Rhys as he walked into the office, seeing the two of them talking. Winn looked surprised to see Rhys and knew Connie had to be close by.

"Hey, Muscles, where's Connie?" asked the senator as he started to straighten up his clothes and himself a little after being roughed up by Chief Mannes earlier.

"She's downstairs. I am sure she will have

several questions for you before they haul you off to jail or whatever they do to lying state senators in this fine state. If it's like everywhere else in this country, hell they'll make a statue of you for sure."

"Well, I don't know about jail sir. He is a state senator so I believe we can make accommodations, being that it's Winn Coleman and all," said the police chief.

"Damn, you boys sure are nice down here in the South and all," said Rhys as he grabbed Winn by the arm and pulled him out of the room. "Come on senator. Let's go see Connie. I'm sure we can work something out," as he headed Winn downstairs with the police chief in tow.

"Well Senator Coleman, did you enjoy your little trip to the state capital? I understand Ms. Grimes was here with you as we arrived. She doesn't seem to know very much about anything, or at least is not willing to elaborate. Maybe you could please help shine a little light on the situation," Connie said as she rolled her chair closer to him and pointed to a chair for him to have a seat.

"Thank you, Connie. Situation, what situation are you referring to?" Winn said as he boldly pulled the thumb drive out of his pocket and slapped it in his hand, pretending to dust off his pant leg. Winn placed the thumb drive between the arm and the seat cushion of the chair. Connie and the others in the room failed to notice the action.

"Ask him about the gun and whatever else he has in his pockets? I would like to look inside that safe as well, if you don't mind?" said Rhys.

"Winn, would you please place whatever you have in your pockets on the table in front of you please?"

"I have nothing to hide," Winn said as he pulled out his cell phone and about $20 in $5 bills, along with a few coins, and placed them on the small hexagon table.

"And your coat pockets please sir?"

"There is nothing in them." Winn stood up and pulled his pockets inside out to prove his innocence. "See, nothing." Rhys rubbed his head in thought, knowing the senator had to be in this house to retrieve something, but what?

"Well, you did assault the policeman when you knocked him out in front of the hotel suite tonight so we can hold you on that charge alone," said Connie as she wheeled her chair around Winn's chair.

Winn looked up at his buddy the chief, as if to ask for help. "Hold on there, little lady," the chief said. "I understand you are in charge of this case in

Charleston but the fact of the matter is that you are in my jurisdiction, not Tommy John Parnell's. So if you don't mind we will take custody of Senator Coleman, Ms. Womack."

"Well here's the thing, chief. This case is now a federal jurisdiction matter, stated under the Kidnapping-Federal Jurisdiction law under Title 18 USC section 1201. It provides special rules for offenses involving children where the victim is under the age of 18 years and the offender has obtained such age and is not a parent, grandparent, brother, sister, aunt, uncle, or person having legal custody. Which means it's a federal case, not local or state. I would like to re-introduce to you my colleague, Rhys Garret, former FBI agent, former Navy Seal and now special task group coordinator for the Federal Bureau of Investigation of missing children. This time it's a federal case so he is coming back with us but not until we check out this house. Here's our warrant for that and the computers and any other devices found on these premises, chief. Any questions on that?" Connie said with a slight smile. She noticed Winn's personality changing as he looked a little more serious minded.

The chief read over the papers, folded them back up, and handed them back to Connie as he looked over at Winn. "It looks like everything is in order, Winn. Looks like you're headed back to

Charleston when they are through here with the house and all. There's nothing I can do. Come on everybody, it's their ballgame now. We need to leave." And with that, after the handshakes and goodbyes, all the chief's personnel were gone.

"Spider you need to go through the house and get every computer and cell phone you can find and take the senator with you. I need to talk to Rhys alone," said Connie as she looked over at Rhys.

"Since when did I become an FBI agent and the leader of a special task of what?"

"Oh shut up, it worked didn't it? That country bumpkin chief didn't check to see who you were, let alone ask to see your credentials, and besides, you look like an FBI agent. I wouldn't worry about that guy."

"Don't know if you have checked lately but impersonating a federal officer is a felony offense, sweetheart."

"Now did you show them an FBI shield? No, you did not. Did you tell him that you were an agent? No, you did not, so come on Rhys and be a man. Grow a pair! I'm the one that lied, not you. It will be OK."

"Thanks, I feel better already."

"But I do need you to go help Spider gather up

all those computers before that crazy senator tries to run off again, please."

"I've got to hand it to you, Connie, you are some kind of tough lady, some kind of tough," Rhys said as he walked off down the large hallway to find the others.

Connie sat in her chair, thinking that they might have gotten a break in the case, not knowing that the information she was looking for was wedged in the seat cushion directly in front of her the whole time.

Medical Rescue

Chapter 22

THE HOSPITAL LIGHTS IN THE HALLWAYS WERE DIM as the two men hired by Cecil crept out from the stairway on the fifth floor in the wee hours at the Grand Strand Medical Center. Using the stairs to avoid security they moved with caution as they slowly inspected and looked in every room, but Reese was not to be found. They quickly stopped just short of what they thought was her room. Easing around the corner they noticed two policemen standing in front of a room door. They stopped and listened as they overheard their conversation.

"You want another cup? I'm going to get me one for myself. Staying awake up here is hard enough with coffee, much less without it," said one of the officers going downstairs to the cafeteria for some more coffee.

"Sure, why don't you tell Debbie to make us a thermos full, and a couple of doughnuts sounds good to me. We got all night."

"You got it," he said, adjusting his hat and heading toward the elevator. Quickly the two men backed up and stepped into an unoccupied room. One man motioned to the other, and as the policeman passed by their hideout he was struck in the back of the head with the butt handle of a gun and down he went. Quickly they pulled him into the abandoned room, using his own handcuffs on him and taped his mouth. That was too easy, and now the next one, they thought. They waited a few minutes thinking on how to trap their next victim, knowing they only had a short period of time before the next nurse would show up. Once they devised their scheme one of the men went back to the elevator as it came up. He stepped inside and called out for the other policeman who was out of view of the elevator and could not see who was talking. As the elevator doors opened again with a ding the one inside called out.

"Hey Buddy, I need a hand with all this food and coffee."

"Oh yeah, sure thing, be right there," the officer said without a clue as he left his post. As he rounded the corner another man fell in behind and followed him. Surprise registered in his brain when he saw someone else, not his partner, in the elevator. Before he could react the blow of the gun handle found its target and down went the second cop. Again the pair quickly handcuffed and taped the officer up in the same abandoned room and then made their way to room number 521.

One of the men slowly turned the door knob and crouched down slightly, peering into the room. He saw his prey, Reese, heavily sedated, asleep in bed. The two men cautiously and quietly entered the room. They inched closer to the bed, ready to do what they had been assigned to do. Without warning Tommy John Parnell stepped out of the bathroom doorway with his revolver drawn and shouted, "Hold it!" The first man turned to fire his weapon and Tommy took him out with one shot, as his body hit the bed and bounced as he hit the floor. The second one made it out the doorway but was met by four of the North Myrtle Beach's finest as they wrestled him down to the floor, removing his gun and any hope of escape. Tommy quickly checked on Reese, finding her unharmed, and could not believe she was still asleep. He then went outside in the hallway where his prisoner was standing with his head down as if he was ashamed of his deed. Tommy approached the man with questions.

"Who sent you here? What's your name?" Tommy reached out and quickly grabbed the man's shirt around the neck. "I said, who the fuck sent you to kill my girl you son of a bitch?" he shouted. A couple of policemen grabbed and pulled Tommy off the man and as they did, two shots rang out and down the prisoner went. The bullets came from the gun of the first man who had crawled out on the floor and before he died shot and silenced his partner. In a reflex motion two policemen returned fire on the assailant. Tommy looked at both assassins. They were riddled with holes as their blood poured out and down the hallway.

"No, damn it no," shouted Tommy John as both men lay dead on the floor. The hallway quickly lit up with lights and it seemed that everyone in the hospital was on the fifth floor wondering what just happened as Tommy John walked over and looked down at one of the dead men. "Well, that surely ended the questioning and answering segment of my interrogation," he said as he kicked the gun out of the hands of the first subject still lying halfway in Reese's room.

Tommy walked back in to see and check on Reese. He placed his hand on her hand and touched her hair. His mind wondered off, as he could not believe all of this was happening. It seemed like just yesterday when she was bouncing on his knee or playing in the sand box behind his sister's house. His sister and he did not see eye to eye on some things but he did love her and Reese. He knew the relationship between his sister and her husband Carl was not that good but he couldn't believe Carl would ever touch his own daughter. The way it all came out in court and with those pictures . . . it was horrible. Tommy thought it was a good thing Carl killed himself, saving Tommy from going to jail because he would have surely done it for Carl.

Reese and her mother were never close after that, one blaming the other for something neither one had anything to do with. Years of counseling, alcohol and drug abuse had taken a toll. It was no wonder Reese was constantly running away from home. But that was all in the past he thought, as he watched her now. What a beautiful young lady she had become, with her whole life ahead of her. He made a vow right then and there to be more of a father then an uncle to her and to help mend the relationship between her and her mother. With tears in his eyes Tommy John walked out of the room and closed the door.

"Tommy John, do you have any idea who these men are?" said Chief Johnson as Tommy again looked down at the bodies on the floor.

"No Hank, I surely do not, but I wish like hell I did. I'd like to get my hands on whoever is causing this nightmare, I'll tell you that," he said.

"I'm just glad you decided to come up early and not wait till morning. I am afraid something bad would have happened if you had not been here," he remarked as he walked over and placed his hand on Tommy's shoulder. "Man, this kidnapping for sex trade thing is crazy, Tommy. I don't know how it is in Charleston, but here, I can't tell you how many runaways we have every year, and it seems like thousands. I imagine you could double that figure for Myrtle Beach. I don't know where they all are coming from, but at least the result you had is a good one," and the two old friends shook hands.

"Thanks Hank, thanks for everything. We'll be leaving in a few hours after the doctor releases her. If you need me for paperwork or anything call me. OK?" and with that Tommy turned and went back in Reese's room to sleep a few minutes before dawn.

Catch And Release

Chapter 23

THE VAN SAT ON THE SIDE OF THE ROAD NOT FAR from Cecil's hangout with the engine still running. Todd sat quietly wondering what to do with the girls. If he took them to Cecil they surely would be shipped off to who knows where, and most likely be placed in a sex-slave lifestyle, a world of prostitution, or end up dying somewhere, or both. Not to mention his very own fate, with Cecil's mindset, there's no telling what Cecil had in store for him. How did he let this happen? He thought it was supposed to be a quick and easy way to make a buck like Cecil had said. All Todd and Raymond had to do was hold a few girls for a few days that Cecil had stashed away in an old farmhouse and bring them to one of his cabins when he called. Todd had no idea that hit-and-run, cold blooded murder, kidnapping, and torture were going to be involved. This was crazy and too much to take in, not to mention losing his brother in the process. Todd's head hurt from thinking so much, as he wondered what to do about Cecil and the whole situation.

Suddenly a voice caused Todd to jump a little in his seat. "Hey what are you doing man? Why are we sitting out here in the middle of nowhere?" Melissa asked. She had started to come to and think a little more clearly, questioning this whole thing of kidnapping and being drugged up and burning down the house and everything else she had experienced. "I thought you were a cop or something. We were being rescued, right? Well, where are the cops and why did you burn down that house? You did burn it down, I think you did anyway. What the hell is going on here?" she was shouting. Todd could not take it and reached over and knocked her out with one punch. Bam, she was out like a light, but the pain in his hand was real.

"Oh shit that hurt!" Todd grabbed his hand in pain. "Damn it, I think I broke it, oh shit, dumb ass," he said to himself as he felt the hand going numb. "That's great, now your hand is broken. Way to go, Todd." He kept scolding himself till he saw the headlights coming toward him. He covered his eyes from the bright head lamps of the Humvee approaching. The vehicle stopped just short of the van's bumper, throwing dust into the air.

"Get out of the van, Todd. Cecil sent me to come get you. Did you break down? If so I'm here to pick you up," said Cricket, one of Cecil's hired guns Todd saw in action at Cecil's cabin. He was one of the ones that helped take that dead guy down to the swamp to be eaten by the alligators.

"I remember you. No man, we're OK, we just got lost a little bit, that's all," Todd lied with a smile.

"Lost, your ass is four hours late. That ain't lost, brother that's hiding." He opened the van door and grabbed Todd by the arm, pulling him out from under the steering wheel till he hit the ground, as another man took Todd's place behind the steering wheel.

"Louie, you go ahead with the girls, I'll take care of this one. Tell Cecil I'll be there shortly," and with that, the man drove off with the girls in the van as dust filled the air once again. Todd knew his time was up if he didn't think fast, but how? This guy was a mountain of a man but not the smartest kid in class, he thought.

"You know Cecil came up with this plan. He was using you and your brother as patsies and you two dumb asses didn't even know it? Hell, you two desperados killed the head security guard that worked for a South Carolina state senator. Yep, killed him deader than hell by hit-and-run, two bad sons of a bitches ran flat over him in that white Ford pickup truck, yep you sure did. Well, that's what the cops think anyway and that's what really counts now doesn't it!"

"We didn't kill anybody and you know it. Now take me to Cecil. Where is he? I need to talk to him," Todd shouted as he got up from the ground.

"You ain't talking to anybody, not much longer anyway. Now get in the Hummer and shut the fuck up, clown; you and your brother were a joke. Cecil knew you would fuck something up but I got to hand it to you, we had no idea it would be this bad. Now get in the truck." The two got in the vehicle and they, too, drove off but not in the same direction as the van.

"Where are you taking me?" Todd asked as Cricket turned onto another dirt road but this one was a lot rougher and muddy.

"It's a shortcut. Don't you worry yourself. Enjoy the view. The swamp is beautiful this time of night ain't it," he said as he drove farther into the wetlands in the Francis Marion National Forest. "You know it's hard to pin a crime on a fella, being its federal land and all. That's what I like about this old swamp," he laughed.

Todd slowly pulled his cell phone out of his pocket when the guy was not looking and held it out the window. He kept his arm out of the window till he saw a landmark or something he could remember to help him find the way back if needed. Hopefully Cricket wouldn't notice.

"You know Cecil set this whole thing up so he could pin this whole kidnapping thing on you and your retarded brother to keep the cops off our ass, and so far it's working pretty good, don't you think?" He drove down to an intersection where he turned onto Highway 17, staying on it for about five miles before turning right on another dirt road. This time they were at a federal park. Todd didn't say a thing as they drove by the big brown sign that read, Francis Marion National Forest, Boat Ramp Ahead. Todd dropped his phone as close to the sign as possible in hopes it would be there on his return trip, if there was a return trip. Deeper and deeper into the swamp they went till Todd noticed the vehicle slowing down, and up ahead a clearing. It was a dirt parking lot area, which was the starting point for several hiking trails and for camping overnight in the forest. At the end of the parking lot down the road a ways was a small, beat-up camper with a light on inside. That's where the Hummer pulled up to and parked.

"Get out, slowly." That's when Todd saw the gun pointing at him. "Get inside," Cricket ordered, and again he pointed the gun. Todd slid out of the vehicle and slowly walked across the sandy ground into an old fishing camper of sorts where two guys were playing some card game, maybe two-hand poker. He wasn't sure.

"I guess this is our man?" one of the men at the

card table said, with a cigar hanging out of his mouth. He was a big fat guy with long greasy hair and was wearing an eye patch. They were a really good-looking bunch, if you like the redneck gangster type with cutoff-sleeve shirts, lots of tattoos and mullet haircuts, right out of the Dukes of Hazard.

"Have a seat, Lucky, we'll be with you in a few minutes," said the other thug. Todd sat down on the bar stool beside the back door.

Cricket never went in because there was not enough room so he stood outside, looking in the doorway. "OK, Buddy, I'll tell Cecil this matter is closed and we'll see you guys later. Nice knowing you dumb ass." And like that the Hummer driver was gone.

Todd wondered how much time he had and what he could do; he had to get away, as he looked all around the small camper for something he could use. The camper was so small there was hardly room for the card game, much less escaping. It would be difficult in such a small space, but what to do? Think damn it, think, he ordered himself, and that's when he saw the fire extinguisher right beside the small stove. That can work, he thought. Without hesitation Todd stood up and started his walk out the door.

"Sit down, Lucky. We ain't ready for you yet.

Where do you think you're going?" said Eye Patch, sitting at the table still playing cards with his brother as Todd slowly walked by him and the other man on his way out.

"I'm only going right here," Todd said as he turned with one quick move, grabbing the extinguisher off the wall and hitting old Eye Patch in the back of the head while spraying a stream of fire-squelching agent in the eyes of the other brother. He backed up till he made it out the camper door, and once out the door, Todd took off like a rabbit through the woods.

The two men blindly fought their way through the carbon dioxide filled camper and found the doorway as they exited the trailer. Outside they both fell to the ground on their knees, coughing and spitting, one holding his bleeding head and the other rubbing his painful eyes. They tried to force in as much fresh air as possible to relieve the burning to their eyes and face. The chemicals made it almost impossible to breathe or see so they were forced to stay put, cursing Todd the whole time.

"Don't you worry little brother, we'll get the son of bitch," said Eye Patch, as he wiped off more blood streaming down from the back of his head and coughing up more spit. The two helped each other up, using the truck hood to hold themselves upright. One man grabbed a beer out of the cooler from the back of the truck and used it to rinse out his eyes.

Meanwhile, Todd was still on the run, down through the swamp waters and crossing several dirt roads till he finally got back to an area he recognized. It was a boat ramp, but he could hardly go any further. He had to stop, so he tucked himself in a pine tree thicket, dropped to the ground and rested while he took time to look at the stars in the night sky. "OK, MacGyver, what's your next trick," he thought, as his heart was pounding and he tried to catch his breath and stop thinking of Cecil. I can't believe he wants me dead, my own cousin; damn this has gotten messed up, he thought. And then the thought of saving those girls ran through his mind, but first he had to save himself and get the hell out of there.

He slowly stood up and brushed the dirt off his pants. While doing so he looked over to his right and that's when he saw a large sign, spelling out the trails and where you were, like being in a mall at the food court. There was a 'You are Here' with a big red arrow pointing to Todd's location. What good luck! Hell, my name is Lucky, he thought, as he looked at the map again in search for roads, maybe even Highway 17, knowing that would be the best bet to get help and maybe find his phone. His finger traced the black lines of roads and trails on the map till he saw what looked to be a small lake or pond and right on the other side was the entrance to the park off Highway 17.

"That must be the other boat ramp where I dropped my phone. Well that's it then, that's my route I'll take," he said out loud to himself but then he heard the sounds of a truck headed his way. He quickly ran back into the thicket of pine trees where he waited to see who was coming down the dirt road. He held his breath and watched as he saw Eye Patch and his brother pass by in their old beat-up black Ford pickup truck. The good news was that they kept going but he watched till the brake lights were out of view before he got up. What now, he thought? He would have to stay off the roads if he didn't want to get caught.

The lake was his only answer to survival, which was the only thing that stood between him and that cell phone, and pretty much his only hope if he wanted to get out of this thing alive. OK, big boy, I guess I'm up for a moonlight swim, he thought, as he took another quick glance at the map for memory.

Standing up and brushing himself off again Todd set out in quest for his phone. He headed straight down the concrete boat ramp into the cool water, clothes and all, plus everything else that was alive in those swamp waters. He looked in all directions making sure he saw no alligators nearby and then waded through the old black swamp water. Surprisingly, he found that it wasn't any deeper than waist deep for the most part. Hearing fish jump startled him but he kept going. A few times he stopped dead in his tracks, thinking he saw a few water moccasins crossing his path, but he wasn't sure. The moonlight seemed to be playing tricks on his eyes but so far no gators had crossed his path that he knew of.

Todd was about half-way across when he saw his first gator lying on the bank of the marsh. I hope he is asleep, Todd thought, as the gator did not move a muscle. Todd danced with his arm outstretched and on his feet he tiptoed across the lake's bottom, bumping into cypress knees and stumps along the way. In the distance, he could see what he thought was Eye Patch and his brother in their truck as Todd could see headlights driving along the dirt road that encircled the lake. He had to make sure that those headlights were as far away on the other side of the lake as possible when he made his escape from his own Water World and hit dry land.

But that was still a long way away and with plenty of swim-dancing to go. He suddenly heard a big splash. Maybe the fish were jumping again, but then he heard it again. His heart stopped as he promptly noticed the moonlight reflecting off the water, making the wake very visible and it was coming full steam ahead and headed straight at him. Todd looked all around to find something to protect himself with, but there was nothing. A little group of cypress trees were about 50 feet off to his right. Then swim for those, he thought, as he hurriedly dove forward and started swimming as fast as he could. The hungry alligator was right behind him and gaining ground. Todd swam and kicked with all his might. Not much farther to go, he thought. He hit something down in the water with his hand, but he kept swimming because he was too scared to stop.

What Todd didn't realize was the water was not deep in that part of the lake and it was the bottom he was touching. Going full speed ahead he soon ran aground, hitting the muddy bottom and coming to a complete stop where he had to stand up. Once he stopped he quickly looked again to get his bearings. He saw the trees and started running for the grove, or at least doing the best he could in knee-deep water. The closer he got to the trees the water soon became mid-calf, then ankle deep as his pace picked up for the last 25 feet or so, and he finally made it to the grove of trees.

His heart was pounding in his chest as his wet shoes slipped on the bark of the tree. He kept slipping down a foot for every two feet he climbed, making it very hard to climb up, but after several tries he finally made it to the first few limbs. He sat still, terrified, with his heart in his throat as he watched his pursuer circle the base of his oasis. After a couple of minutes he was pretty sure that the gator could not climb the tree and it looked as if the pursuer lost interest. Todd's heart rate began to slow down a little and he let out a sigh of relief.

"Holy shit that was close!" Todd shouted, as his eyes never left the alligator's, just feet below him. "Wow, oh my God, that was too close!" Starting to calm down, Todd started looking at the tree he was in and looking for something he could use for defense. He eyed a small dead tree limb, one which he could break off with his bare hands. He reached over and did just that and started to clean off the twigs as he inspected his new weapon. He thought to himself, this will make a pretty good club, beating it against the larger tree limb, checking its strength. Damn I wish I had gotten one of these before I decided to take that little swim in the first place, he thought. But there was nothing he could do about it now, and the best thing was to start strategizing on how he was going to leave the safety of the tree and make it to dry land without being an alligator buffet. Suddenly he noticed the waters below him began to move. There was something else out there, but this time the gator was not the one causing the motion. In the dark Todd could not see well enough to make it out, but whatever it was, another alligator or large fish, it had the complete attention of the gator below as it slowly moved away from the grove of trees. The mystery creature swam away from Todd and out in the deeper water, stalking its prey.

Now, right now, was the time to jump down and move like the wind, he thought, as he quickly slid down the tree with club in hand. He was off to the races once again. This time it was mostly mud and tree stumps and thicket and the main body of water was behind him. His quest to escape the gator, plus those two brothers, was looking better all the time as he finally felt solid ground under his feet for the first time on this side of the lake. He was not stopping now!

Just Too Nice

Chapter 24

PATTY COLEMAN SAT BY THE PHONE BUT CLOSER to the bar as she made herself another drink of vodka over ice with a splash of tonic water and lime. It had been hours since she last talked to Connie and surely she did not want to talk to her lying snake of a husband Winn.

"Winn, how did he ever get that name, Winn being such a loser? I know you made it up," she said out loud as she stirred her drink, feeling a little lonely in that big old empty suite in downtown Charleston. And by this point she was feeling pretty sorry for herself, as the drinks kept coming. Her phone lit up and the ring tone started to play the song she had not heard in a long time, which was the Allman Brothers Band classic hit, "Melissa."

"Oh my God it's Melissa, it's her phone!" she shouted as she dived for the phone lying on the armrest of the sofa and quickly answered it without realizing the situation. She wanted to hear from her girls so badly.

"Yes, Melissa is that you? Is Elizabeth with you? Are you OK sweetie?" she cried out on the phone hoping to hear their voices but instead it was the cold machine voice again, as reality came crashing down on Patty. She was horrified as she stopped to catch her breath. She could not stop the tears from running down her face. This nightmare is not over, she thought. No matter how much liquor she drank, it could not mask reality. She brushed her hair back with her hand and threw her shoulders back as well, as she tried to regain her composure and stop the flood of tears.

"No, this ain't Melissa Ms. Coleman. It's me again with a friendly reminder that you have less than twelve hours to wire that money. After that I'm afraid there won't be a sweet Melissa, or Elizabeth either, do you get me lady? You and the asshole senator husband of yours better come up with that money or no more girls. Here's another Allman Brothers' classic for you to think about—'Whipping Post,'" and the phone suddenly went dead.

"But wait, how do I know they're alive? Hello,

damn it," she said as she dropped the phone back on the couch. "Shit!" She stood with her hands covering her face, but then she thought of something. She went back over and picked up the phone to check the phone number, and once again she saw where the phone number read unknown. How can that be? she thought. That was Melissa's ring tone. Something doesn't make sense. She quickly hit contacts on her phone and pulled up Connie Womack's number and called, pacing the floor, waiting on an answer from Connie.

"Hey, you have reached Connie Womack, I can't get to the phone right now but if you would please leave your name and number and a brief message, I'll get back to you as soon as possible. Thank you for calling." The call went straight to voicemail.

"Connie, this is Patty. Please call me back. I just had another call from the kidnappers. They were using that damn mechanical voice machine again. Call me back!" She lay the phone down on the bar and reached over and picked up her glass, looking at it like it was a crystal ball telling her the future. She watched the ice dance in the swirl of the liquor and after a couple of minutes she set the glass back down. She had had enough of this shit. She had had enough of everything.

She heard the doorbell and walked to the foyer.

A nice policeman opened the door. "You have a guest, Ms. Coleman," he said, as a young man, a college-aged kid, walked in the door.

"Can I help you?" Patty said to the young man, as she wondered who he was and what did he want with her.

"I have a note for you, Ms. Coleman. Some guy gave me a hundred bucks and told me to deliver this note, so here you go," he said as he handed her the letter.

"Is that all? Do you need a reply or anything?"

"No, I don't need anything."

The policeman looked at Patty. "Do you want me to hold him till the chief gets here or take him downtown for questioning?" The young man looked scared as he looked back and forth at her and the cop.

"No, he can go. He looks like a nice young man. He is free to go."

"Thank you, Ms. Coleman," said the young man. He turned and exited by the stairway, as he took the stairs down to the lobby.

Patty looked down and opened the blank envelope and pulled out the letter and a picture; the look on her face was one of surprise as she read the note. **Thank you for letting me go Ms. Coleman. You are a kind person. Unfortunately neither I, nor the people I work for are. If you do not get us the money soon your daughters will be dead or gone forever. So you better hurry the FUCK UP lady, we mean it! You have less than 12 hours now!**

Patty dropped the letter as she placed her hand over her mouth in shock and started crying as she ran back into the apartment. Officer Barber picked up the envelope and the picture that fell out onto the floor. The picture was of her two girls with their hands bound behind their backs and a breathable ball gag strapped across their mouths. He immediately started to the elevator, grabbing his handset at the same time.

"All units in the Charleston Place Hotel, secure the stairways and elevators. Don't let anyone out of the hotel till I get downstairs. I repeat, do not let anyone out of the hotel." He then closed the door to the suite, made sure it was locked, and set off after the young man who delivered the note.

The young man went hurriedly down the stairway as quick as he could run, jumping down six and seven steps at a time. He was flying. When he made it to the second floor landing he stopped and looked through the small window in the door to see if the coast was clear. His heart was pounding as he slowly opened the fire exit door and went inside the hotel. Being very cautious, he started walking down the hallway, looking back and forth till he was at the spot he was looking for, room 211. He knocked three times on the door and stopped, waited a second or two, and then knocked three more times. He was looking around the hallway as the room door opened and he quickly went inside. Officer Barber never saw him, as he too was on the second-floor hallway.

Patty lay on the bed crying her eyes out. After a few minutes she realized that Officer Barber was not with her. "Officer Barber? Officer Barber, do you hear me?" she called, but no answer. He was not there. She got up and went to the living room area to see where he was. She then went out into the foyer and again he was not to be found. She heard her phone ring in the other room and she quickly went to get it. As she picked up the phone she noticed it was Connie.

"Oh Connie, I'm so glad you called. Please hurry back here. I had a phone call like I said on my message, but he was here in person. He came to my room! Damn, he was here!"

"Hold on, Patty, slow down. Who was there?"

"A guy, he had a picture of the girls tied up and gagged. It was horrible. You have got to get back here. I'm scared to death!"

"A policeman is supposed to be with you at all times. Where is he?"

"You mean Officer Barber? I don't know. He ran off after the guy I guess. I don't know where the hell he is Connie. All I know is that the letter said I have less than twelve hours or the girls are dead or gone. Please hurry, Connie."

"OK let's take a deep breath and relax. You are fine. We are only minutes away. We are on I-26, a few miles out. We should be there within the hour. Hold on Patty. I will have another officer at your room in seconds, OK?"

Patty felt better. Hearing Connie's voice and knowing they were close by was really all she needed to hear after being in the hotel room by herself all day. She said her thanks and goodbyes to Connie and felt pretty good about making herself a drink. Why not? You deserve one, she thought, as she placed two ice cubes in her glass but before she could pour a drink the doorbell rang again. Man, they sure are fast; Connie must have lit a fire under someone's ass at that police station. Patty looked through the eye hole and sure enough a policeman was there and on duty. She opened the door. "You sure got here quick," she said to the policeman with his back turned from her. As he turned around she could not believe it. It was him, the young man that handed her the note earlier. He was there again.

“I told you, Ms. Coleman, you are way too nice,” as he grabbed her and placed a chloroform-soaked rag to her nose and mouth. She had no time to think, or to run as the rag stifled her efforts to be heard. Despite her desperate attempts to fight back her assailant quickly overpowered her as her strength was soon depleted. Now with the upper hand, he easily pulled her toward the fire exit and onto the stairway landing. The chloroform made her struggle seem useless and her body appeared lifeless, causing one of her shoes to fall off before the exit door had time to shut.

“Here grab her arm,” he ordered to another man who was waiting to meet him there on the landing. Between the two they easily carried their victim down the stairway, with Patty appearing to be nothing but drunk to any passerby. And just like that she too was gone.

Still Too Sick

Chapter 25

REESE TRIED TO REMEMBER WHAT HE looked like, knowing how important it was to catch those guys. The lady police officer sat beside her bed and kept flashing mug shots of every mean-looking felon and ex-con they had and still no luck. Reese turned her head away, as if it was hurting her to look. Her mind was whirling from the medication and the sheer shock of what she had just gone through.

"That stuff plays on your brain don't it," said uncle Tommy John as he stood in the doorway eating a doughnut. Reese smiled when she saw him. "Hospitals and police stations. There's always a doughnut somewhere hiding out, and I found mine." Tommy John walked around to the other side of the room to get a better look at his niece, still eating his find.

"Uncle Tommy I can't," Reese said. "I can't find him or the other guy either. They are not in here."

"Oh, there were two men, not just one that kidnapped you? See, you helped out already sweetheart. Now, work with officer Becky Sue. She'll help you find them." The chief's phone started to ring. He looked down as he pulled it out of his pocket and caller ID said it was Connie.

"Yes ma'am, how's things in Chucktown, Connie?"

"Tommy, you won't believe it. Patty Coleman is missing! She's gone! The door was left wide open; her phone, clothes and all her personal items are there. Nothing looks to be missing but her."

"What the fudge, she's gone! What about my officer? Is he alright? Barber, he's one of my best. What about the senator, where the hell is he?"

"Everyone is fine, but the senator is in your jail for right now. Barber is fine as well, but he is giving his statement to Rhys and one of your guys right now as we speak. How's your niece? Is she doing better?"

"She is real strong. She's doing fine," he said as he looked over and smiled at her and she smiled back, knowing they were talking about her. "Look here, I'll be there in two hours if not less, but the first thing you need to do is shut down that hotel. No one in or out."

"That's done, and your people are doing a great job with that. This going room to room might be a little sticky, but if she's here we'll find her. See you in a few," Connie said, as she cut off her phone.

Tommy turned and looked at his niece. "How are you feeling sweetheart? You think you feel good enough to travel?"

"Did you say travel? She's not going anywhere mister, no, not this little girl," said Nurse Howard, standing in the doorway with her hands on her hips. Standing beside her was Dr. Greene.

"She's right, Chief Parnell. I think it's best if she stays with us a few more days before she has to travel. The toxicology report is showing all kinds of bad things like arsenic, heavy dosages of cisatracurium besylate and troycurium, still in her system. That's my recommendation, chief, and you know I can't stop you from taking her, but she is real sick."

Tommy looked over at his niece. "What do you think I should do, Reesy, it's up to you sweetheart?"

"I'll be fine uncle Tommy. You go do your job,

but you better come back for me in a couple of days," she laughed. "Please tell mother I'm so sorry and that I love her so much. Will you tell her, uncle Tommy?"

Tommy John walked over and kissed her on the forehead. "I sure will sweetheart, I sure will," and kissed her again. Tommy looked at the nurse and doctor. "I truly thank you for all your help and care of this young lady." He then turned back to Reece. "I'll see you in two days, sweetheart," as he winked at Reese.

Tommy placed his cowboy hat on his head, tipped his hat, and left the room. He stopped outside and shook officer Becky Sue's hand. "Thank you for your help officer, but you better take good care of my niece in there."

She replied, "Yes sir, you can count on it."

"I am," said Tommy as he turned and left the hospital, hoping it was the right thing to do, but knowing in his gut it was not.

Once he got in his car and made it up to the highway he radioed ahead to the South Carolina Highway Patrol requesting an open road to Charleston, and it was granted. He brought his car up to speed and set his cruise control on 100 miles an hour and headed south on Highway 17.

Hundred-Dollar Straw

Chapter 26

CECIL STARED AT THE LINES OF COCAINE he had cut on the mirror as his face steadied itself for the shock and rush of the buzz he was about to receive. He tightly rolled up a $100 bill to perfection, as he would soon turn his respiratory system into a Hoover upright. He placed the makeshift straw into his right nostril and placed his thumb over the other nostril and began to inhale the mind-alternating narcotics with one long snort, as the straw quickly chased the white powder across the mirror till the line had totally disappeared up his nose. He pinched his nose closed with thumb and forefinger and held his breath. He stifled a couple of coughs as his body arched back and he rose up from the mirror with a mighty exhale. He then kicked back in the chair as his face and hands trembled, feeling completely alive and awake as the blood rushed to his face. He sat there a couple of minutes taking in the rush as it flooded all his senses. He had never felt more alive in his life, or not until the next time, he thought, as he placed the $100 straw on the mirror and handed it to the naked girl sitting beside him.

"It's your turn, sweetheart," Cecil said to the young girl sitting there completely in the nude. Her dirty blond hair covered most her face and breast as she held her head downward trying to use her long hair to cover her naked body as much as possible. Her hands were shaking from fear, if she did not accept it, or if she did. She didn't have a choice as Cecil pushed the mirror closer to her as a threat. She hastily caved in as she reached for the mirror. Her action was abruptly stopped by the handcuffs attached to her right arm. She didn't even flinch. She was used to the pain. She then regrouped and used her left hand to grab the tray, and without delay she inhaled the line of cocaine as instructed by her master.

Cecil watched her body as the young girl's cocaine rush caused her body to react as she kicked back and forth in the chair revealing everything her hair once covered. She then stopped and sat back with her mouth wide open as she exhaled, feeling the narcotic rush for the first time in her young life, as the drugs flowed throughout her body. Cecil could not be more turned on at this point. He was ready to take her to bed. Bed hell, right here's good, he thought, as he tore off his shirt and pushed her down to the floor with her hand still handcuffed and attached to the arm of the chair. He watched her squirm a little as he hurriedly tried to remove his pants but they made it only down to his ankles around his cowboy boots, as he fell on top of her. His weight crushed her till he could get up on all fours and, like an animal, he mounted his prey. All during this abuse she thought to scream, but she knew he would not stop. He never did and no one would come for help. They all worked for him, so she lay there knowing the outcome and knowing it would not be much longer. At least he wasn't beating her, not yet anyway.

Once he was through he pulled her up into the chair and threw a comforter over her naked body. He redressed himself with only his pants, as he pulled them up and walked down the hall to the kitchen to get a beer. The cocaine was working on his mind as he stood in the kitchen drinking cold Bud Light. After the coke and the sex he was still thinking and he was still pissed with his decision to let Cricket take Todd to the Garrison brothers and have them do away with him. Hell, he's family, Cecil thought. I should be the one to do him if anyone does, not a couple of dipshits that live in a damn fishing trailer, he thought, as he finished off his beer. He looked out the window when he saw the lights of the van pull up outside of the holding cabin. He was still mad he let one of his hired gunmen talk him into this so-called plan, as he headed out the kitchen door to greet the new arrivals. Screwy Louie backed the van up to the cabin's door where all the newcomers go, and Cecil went to meet him as Screwy cut off the engine and opened the door.

"Hey Boss, Cricket just called and we got a problem. That chicken-ass cousin of yours somehow got away from the two Garrison brothers."

"Got away, how the hell did that happen, Louie? First, that was yours and Cricket's job. You should have shot his ass when you found him on the side of the road up near the lake. I knew those two dimwit sons of bitches would screw this up. One with one eye and the other with no sense, hell they can hardy deliver drugs worth a shit."

"Well, I talked to Cricket and he said the Garrison brothers were on it. There is no way he is getting out of the National Park alive."

"You can say that again because when Cricket gets back here you two sons of a bitches are going back up there and finish the job I sent you two to do in the first place. Do you understand me?" As

Cecil grabbed Louie by his shirt, they suddenly heard noises of shouting and screaming coming from inside the van. "Damn it, those girls are awake." Cecil looked and saw the rocking movement of the vehicle and looked inside the window of the van. He saw that one was wide awake. Both men surrounded the van making sure they didn't lose another girl. Cecil grabbed the door and quickly opened it.

"Oh God what is going on? Where are we?" Melissa asked as she was waking up from the punch she received to the jaw.

Cecil tried to calm her down, speaking softly. "Now, now little girl you are alright. It's going to be OK; you come with me and uncle Louie. We'll take good care of you and your sister so don't you worry sweetheart," said Cecil.

Before she knew what was going on the sweet-talking man suddenly grabbed her. As she started screaming, Cecil placed his hand over her mouth, muffling the screams while Louie ran into the cabin and grabbed a bottle and a rag. Cecil swiftly moved her into the cabin, still kicking but now her screaming was more a sniffle as he handcuffed her to the bed and replaced his hand that was over her mouth with the rag Louie handed him. The rag was soaked in chloroform and Cecil pressed it to her face. Within seconds once again she was out like a light.

Both men stood for of a couple of seconds trying to catch their breath. “Damn she’s a screamer. Maybe we should charge extra.” They both laughed as they headed back to the van to retrieve the second girl. She was out cold so they would have to carry her. They wrestled with her to the cabin and handcuffed her to a bed. Cecil rapidly set up the IVs and in 20 minutes they had them ready for pick-up. Cecil thought the only problem was that they were a day early and had only two slaves. They were still missing the one girl. A beep, beep, beeping noise from one of the machines suddenly alarmed. It was the warning sounding from one of the heart monitors as lights flashed and beepers were going off. Louie turned around from the refrigerator full of all kinds of anesthetics. The second girl’s heart rate was deadly slow and slowing down even more as both men watched.

“What the fuck, Cecil! Is she going to die?” Louie nervously said as he kept watching the monitor’s levels dropping even lower.

“Those meds are too strong for this one,” Cecil said as he pulled the IV stand over to him. He looked at Louie. “Grab me a bag of saline out of the refrigerator, Louie.” He did and handed the bag over as Cecil then switched out the bags and replaced the strong anesthetic with a saline bag.

"She must be dehydrated. We will have to keep her fluids up and gag her when she comes to. She has been under too long. That dumb ass Todd would have killed her, damn him. We have got to get that prick." Cecil then looked at Louie. "Call up to the main house and get a couple of guys to come down here to watch these two. You and I are going to kill that cousin of mine," Cecil growled as he watched the IV bags, making sure they were dripping right. He then rechecked the girls' handcuffs, making sure they were securely fastened, and adjusted the chains, making sure they were secured around their ankles. He wanted to be sure before he left the room.

"They ain't going anywhere," he said as he turned out the lights to the room and locked the door from the outside.

Cecil's phone rang. It was Cricket.

"You better tell me he is dead."

"Cecil look, the Garrison brothers are on it. It's going to be OK. I'm almost at the house and we can talk when I get there, alright?"

"Hell no, it's not alright. I want you to turn that Hummer around right this second and you go find him. I want that cousin of mine dead. Do you understand me, dead? Not shot, not cut up, but dead as a doornail, gone from this earth!" he screamed into the phone.

Louie looked at Cecil. He was shaking just listening to the conversation.

Cricket allowed Cecil to let off his steam and waited a few seconds before answering. "Yes sir boss, I'm turning around as we speak. I'll call you when it's done."

"See that you do," Cecil replied, hanging up the phone.

Trying to calm him down Louie looked over at Cecil. "You know Cecil, you are the only one that knows all about those drugs. It's probably best that you do stay here. Cricket will make sure your cousin Todd is taking care of. I'm sure of it, sir."

Cecil knew he was right but was still pissed and looked Louie dead in his eyes. "Look here, Louie, I know you're right, and I know I need to stay here. But I don't need you or Cricket or anybody else telling me what to do and the next time I tell you boys to kill somebody you better fucking do it. Do you understand me?"

"Yes sir," said Louie as he looked down at the ground like he was dealing with a mad dog. He was too scared to look Cecil in the eye.

"Now grab this stuff out of the van. Let's go back up to the house. Do you want a cold beer? I've got a few in the refrigerator." Cecil put his arm around Louie's shoulder and they walked back up to the house. "You want some coke? I got some of that too."

Van Diversion

Chapter 27

THE HOTEL GUESTS WERE OVERFLOWING OUT OF THE LOBBY and into the streets and upset that they were kicked out of their rooms for no reason, as Connie and her crew made it back to the hotel. Police cars were everywhere. Rhys pushed Connie right up to the officer standing in the doorway of the Charleston Place Hotel.

"Who is in charge here? I need to speak to him. I'm agent Connie Womack," as she showed her papers, "and these are my men."

"Yes, Ms. Womack, right this way," as Connie, Rhys and Spider followed the police officer in the lobby and into a room off to the side. Officer Tandy was on the phone as Connie and the guys waited for him to hang up.

"Ms. Womack, sorry, that was the chief. He is on his way here now. We have every entrance covered, men on the roof and choppers in the air. I think we can start the room by room search anytime you give the order, and we are ready."

"Ms. Coleman? Who is watching her?" Connie asked.

"Ms. Womack, you don't know? She is gone, we can't find her. That's why we have all the security."

Connie looked up at Rhys then back to Officer Tandy. "OK, sounds good. I will be in the senator's suite when you start so give me a couple of minutes and I'll call you when I'm ready. I need to check if there are any clues left in her apartment. Does that sound OK to you?"

"That's fine with me. All right men; let's get back to our jobs."

Connie looked over at Spider. "If you need something get some help but get the computer stuff from the van and bring it upstairs too. I want you to start tonight. We have to find something on those girls."

"You got it Connie." Spider went back to the van to retrieve all the computers and other devices they had confiscated in the senator's house in Columbia. Rhys and Connie exited to the elevator and headed up to the presidential suite.

“You think they have her and they are still in the hotel, Connie?” Rhys asked as they started upward on the elevator and he turned her chair around enough so he could see her face’s reaction.

“I’m not sure, but I think so, who knows? If it was me, that’s what I would do. Most people would run but this guy is too smart. And if they are here I doubt we will find them, but maybe we’ll get lucky. We will know more when Spider gets up here with those computer files.”

“That’s it,” said Connie as she grabbed the cell phone out of her purse. “Oh man, Rhys that’s it, damn he is smart,” as she got her phone and tried to call Spider.

“What are you talking about Connie, who are you calling?”

“I’m trying to call Spider but no answer. Rhys, those files, that’s what they were after all along, and we brought those damn files straight to them Rhys.” Connie could not receive a signal on the phone in the elevator. Rhys, understanding the situation, quickly hit the emergency stop button on the elevator wall panel. “Damn this phone still has no signal in this blessed elevator.”

“I’ll call him, Connie.” Rhys kept hitting the open button and finally the doors opened and he stepped out. He turned to Connie. “Get up there and lock yourself in that apartment. You got your gun?" She patted her hip where she kept it.

"I'm good," she said as the elevator closed. Rhys then received a cell signal and quickly texted Spider the number 6. He would know what that meant, to check his ass, his 6, meaning something was up. Rhys ran to and entered the next elevator where the arrow was pointing down and hit the lobby button. He was on his way.

Spider was inside the back of the van grabbing the first computer on the stack. He had placed the hand truck outside where dozens of people were standing around on the sidewalk entrance to the lobby near the parking lot and all around the vehicle. Spider finally duckwalked out of the van to keep from hitting his head as he set down a few computers on the hand truck. A young man in pajamas and two others walked over from the crowd, approaching before Spider could turn and retrieve a few more computers.

"Hey, man, you need some help?" he questioned.

"No, Buddy, I'm good, but thanks anyway," said Spider, as he felt the buzz of his cell phone with Rhys' text message vibrating through his pants pocket.

"No really, I would be glad to help," said the

young guy standing behind Spider beside the van. Spider promptly looked down at his phone as he pulled it out of his pocket far enough to see the message from Rhys. He knew then something was up.

"Look guy I'm sorry, but I'm used to doing things by myself," as he reached inside the van hoping to find something to protect himself with and wishing he had his gun. The young man saw Spider fumbling around looking for something, and quickly stopped Spider's search by placing his gun into Spider's ribs.

"Hold it right there, hero, if you want to see those girls alive. I think I can handle it from here," said the young man as he grabbed the handle to the hand truck. "Now move away from the van, partner. I believe my friends and I will have that equipment you got there, if you don't mind."

"You really think so?" said Rhys as he walked up from behind him. "Now both you children drop your guns." The wave of people started to move uncontrollably as they shifted closer towards the van. Rhys could not determine who in the crowd were friends or foe as both hotel guests and attackers pushed their way closer to Rhys and the van.

"You ain't going to do anything big fella," said the one in the pajamas and pointed his gun at

Spider. "Move over there, pip-squeak, and you too big man. You two need to back the fuck up so we can get those computers and nobody gets hurt."

"Sure, junior, we'll stand right here," said Rhys as he waited a second for an opening and when it came he shouted, "The hell I will," as he quickly reached and grabbed one of the assailant's guns. He then, with one powerful right punch knocked the hell out of the guy. He watched him fall to the ground where he was out cold. Spider, on cue, kicked old pajama boy in the face, as he came around the side of the van where those two ended up fighting on the ground.

Rhys looked around checking out the situation as he stood his ground and was willing to take on all newcomers, fighting off several people to his left and right. Spider got the best of pajama boy but he still managed to get away when the fight was over. In the mix of it all were several other men who joined in but they were not there to fight. The fight was all a diversion. As several men divided, one man grabbed the hand truck and a couple of men went into the van and removed the rest of the cargo, which they came for in the first place. Once that was obtained, the fight was over. Police came out of the hotel and a couple of shots were fired and the crowd quickly thinned out. The guests ran into the hotel lobby and the half dozen assailants ran down the street into the alley and were gone.

Connie had searched the suite and Patty was not to be found. She had her cell phone in hand when she heard the shots fired and looked out her window from the suite. Her view was partially blocked but she could tell a mob was in the front of the hotel. She tried to call Spider and Rhys but they were busy at the time. By the time the Charleston police force came to the rescue, Rhys and Spider had fought off the crowd. Unfortunately old pajama boy and the rest got away before getting caught.

Rhys looked down and saw that neither the hand truck, nor the computers, was in sight. They were both taken during the so-called mob fight. Rhys looked over at Spider knowing that it was all a setup. "Tell me we didn't get suckered. And please tell me we have something worth a shit left in that van." Spider pointed to a couple of old flip phones sitting on the back seat, an old beat up Microsoft tablet that had no memory card in it, and an old monitor. "And of course, the four big desktop towers are gone. Isn't that grand," said Rhys.

"That's it Buddy." He looked over at Rhys and handed him the two flip phones, and the tablet.

"Looks like you have some work to do, Little Buddy. Can't wait to tell Connie our good fortune," as he pulled out his cell phone and called up to the presidential suite.

Spider answered back, "you can't make chicken salad out of chicken shit, Rhys."

"No, but we can go find that pajama wearing chicken son of a bitch and beat the shit out of him." Rhys turned his head and suddenly he saw something in the corner of his eye. It was over at the bushes that lined the driveway and the fountain in the hotel's circular driveway.

"Give me a hand, Spider," shouted Rhys as he ran over to the object he saw near the fountain. When he got closer he realized it was a person and that the person was Patty Coleman. Her mouth was taped closed and her hands were tied behind her back as she lay on her side on the ground, hoping someone would see her, and they finally did. "Help over here," Rhys shouted once again as Spider and two policemen came running.

Rhys speed-dialed Connie once again as Spider helped Patty sit up, removing the tape from her mouth. "Are you OK? We got you."

Rhys finally reached Connie on the phone. "Connie, you won't believe it, we have Patty!"

"Rhys, is she alright? Rhys?"

There was no reply. He had put the phone down to help Patty. She was a mess. Her hair was cut off, her clothes were torn to pieces and she had been badly beaten. Rhys looked over at one of the policemen. “Do I have to tell you to call a bus, an ambulance, damn it man?” The officer quickly responded and called one in. Both Spider and Rhys held to her as they waited for the ambulance. She tried to look at both of them through swollen eyes. Her bleeding lips were trembling and her hands were shaking as she sat there without saying a word. She was completely in shock. They wrapped a blanket around her to get her warm.

“Ms. Coleman, it’s Rhys Garret, can you hear me? You are going to be fine. We’ve got you now. Ms. Coleman can you hear me, Ms. Coleman?” She never said a word, just stared off in the dark of night. It would be a long time before she spoke again.

Sweet Dr. Shirley

Chapter 28

THE HOSPITAL HALL WAS QUIET. HARDLY anyone seemed to be there as Reese moved her arm coming out of her deep sleep, when all of a sudden the alarms started beeping on the IV machine, which sounded the switchboard alarms as well, awaking everyone at the nurses' station. Reese's eyes popped open as she quickly turned over in bed toward the machine with flashbacks of being back in the farmhouse basement, as the sound filled the room. Her eyes searched the room, making sure, as reality kicked in, that she was not in that hellhole. Her mind was completely in alert mode as she made sure she was in a safe location. Again her eyes were like a laser, scanning every nook and cranny of the room; after all, her going through a normal sleep routine was a new concept. She then flipped over in bed, expanding her search as her eyes followed the floral lines on the wallpaper till she came eye to eye with another person. She jumped a little when she saw her. She then watched in silence for a few minutes it seemed, as both she and the woman sat in the room with the curtains drawn closed without saying a word. The stalemate was soon over as the classy and very attractive lady spoke.

"Would you like for me to open the curtains a little bit?" said Kay Shirley, a nicely dressed lady sitting with her long shapely legs crossed at the foot of the bed with a clipboard on her knee. "How are you feeling young lady? I hope a little better now? You have been through a lot; I've been reading your record. It's quite unbelievable what you have endured."

Reese sat up in bed to see her better. She thought the lady was quite beautiful, and seemed to be a real nice and caring person. "How do you feel? Hot, cold, any headaches, stomachache, anything? Maybe frightened, upset, maybe even mad?"

"No, I'm OK, a little cold maybe, but it's a hospital. They always keep them too cold. But let me guess, you must be a shrink?"

Smart girl, she thought, and very cautious, still dealing on primal instincts and strong reaction to sounds, she wrote in her notes. “Reese, you are right, I am a shrink and my name is Kay Shirley. I'm a psychiatrist. Your uncle and a mutual friend of ours, a Ms. Connie Womack, asked for me to see you, and maybe I can help. Do you mind if I talk to you? I need to ask you some questions. Is that OK with you? If not, we can do it another time.”

“Yeah, I do mind. I already told the police, including my uncle who as you know is the chief of police in Charleston, everything.”

“Yes, I understand but there still are two girls missing, Reese. Your information is crucial if you saw them.”

“Yeah, I saw both of them. Both girls look a little younger than me. I think they were sisters, heck they looked like twins. So as far as talking, you know they came to kill me yesterday, so no thank you, I'm good.”

Kay understood Reese completely but she needed that information. “OK, I understand you are scared and frightened, but Reese you have the answers we need and you could be a big help. Those two girls might well die or be enslaved for the rest of their lives. And do you really want to live with that on your conscience?”

"Look, lady, I said no!" Reese pulled the covers over her head like a little girl. Kay got up and walked over to the head of her bed.

Kay pulled her cell phone out of her purse and started to press a few numbers on the phone. "Here's my cell phone. I'm calling Patty Coleman, the senator's wife. She's the mother of the missing girls. Here, you tell her no, here," as she tried to hand Reese her cell phone. Reese pulled back the cover and saw there was not a phone, as a smile appeared on her face.

"You got me," Reese said when she saw a little notebook in the lady's hand, not a phone.

Kay sat down on the edge of the bed. "You got away sweetie. Those girls are still living in that hell. Please help me help them and you too, Reese."

Reese knew the doctor was right, but she was scared and a little selfish to boot. "If you really think that what I know will help find the others I guess so, sure." She sat up a little more in the bed, as if she was going to take a test. "So what do you want to know, doc? How can I help you help me? Do you want to know how many times they fucked me, and how many guys at one time, is that it?"

The doctor placed her hand on Reese's but Reese quickly pulled it away. "No dear, what I want is for you to relax. No one will know anything you tell me. It's all confidential. It's part of my Hippocratic oath. I'm a doctor and not even the FBI can get this information. Now lay back in the bed and think of this as a journey unfolding. Just relax, close your eyes and think back. The person who you saw on the beach, the one that was so cute, do you remember his name or what he looked like? Or is there anything that stood out in your mind that night? Where you went when you left the beach? Was there anyone else you met? Please try to remember the night you were taken, and you and this boy sitting on the beach."

"I don't know if I can remember all of that," said Reese.

"OK, let's start slow. What was the boy's name, do you remember his name? Or maybe what he looked like?"

"I think his name was Kent or Kirk, no Curtis, that's it Curtis, and he was real nice at first, real polite and soft-spoken, a real gentleman, and you're right he was really cute you know, tall with long blonde hair. It was curly, past his shoulders. I was sitting on the beach. I went there to get away from everyone at the sleepover party a friend of mine was having, and I don't like a lot of those girls she invited. A sleepover at 17. Really, you think that's not lame, well I do."

"Did he ask you if you wanted to go somewhere

or do something fun?"

"He said all the right things and laughed at my jokes and yeah he invited me out. There was a party his friends were having down the street on Maybank Highway. They even had live music. I love music and he said a band would be there. To me it sounded great, plus he had a great looking red sports car and he was cute."

"Was he Hispanic, black or white?"

"He was white I think, but he had a great suntan. He looked more like a surfer dude. But to tell the truth I don't really know, but after we drove a few miles something didn't feel right. It was as if the second he got me in the car his charm was gone and he drove like he was late to somewhere. When we passed Maybank, I told him we were going the wrong way and he didn't say anything. He drove way out through the marshes. I thought he was going to surprise me and take me somewhere romantic. We then turned onto a dirt road out in nowhere, and then I knew something was really wrong and I told him so. It was then that he told me to shut the fuck up."

"He started to drive a lot faster, and I was scared. This was not the boy I met on the beach and he was going so fast. He pulled out his cell phone and hit speed dial, then he hit one button and put it down in his lap. I told him to please slow down. I was screaming at this point. He kept driving like a madman. I asked where he was taking me. I started to shout, stop the car and let me out, stop. That's when he hit me. He slapped me real hard. He yelled again to shut the fuck up. I don't remember much after that." Reese started to cry as she pulled her legs up to her chest and curled into a ball. Kay got up and put her hand on Reese's back and patted her a little, and touched her hair, like her mother used to do.

"It's OK, Reese, we got you," as she held Reese in her arms. "You are safe now," Kay quietly said. "It's OK, let's take a rest for now, and bless your heart." She stood there comforting her till Reese lay on her side and went back to sleep.

Kay went out into the hallway and said hello to the nurse on duty, and took a few minutes to regroup her thoughts.

"How's it going Doctor?" said the nurse. "She's a strong one, I can tell by just looking at that one."

"She's got a lot of her uncle Tommy in her. She will be fine. But I don't understand why her mother is not here."

"If it was me, I know I would be here, no question about that, unless?"

"Unless what? Unless you knew something

about this situation and you don't want your own kid to know about it?"

"You're pretty good, doc. What am I thinking now?" Kay turned away with a smile on her face and turned back. "Lunch."

"Man you are good!" laughed the nurse as Kay went back into the room and sat back down and waited till Reese woke up again.

"They raped me, you know that don't you?" Reese said as she was looking at Dr. Shirley. She cried a little more as she sat up in the bed and wiped the tears from her eyes as she spoke. "He finally stopped the car out near Bohicket Creek. I knew that place because my daddy, before he passed away, used to take me fishing down in there when I was a little girl. It's one big marsh. You really have to know where you are going or you can get lost pretty easy. It's over on the other side of John's Island off Highway 700 out in the grasses, low country." She then stopped talking and started to cry again. This time she covered her face in the bedsheet as she cried.

"Take your time, Reese, I understand how hard this is, but we need your help so we can find the others. Now you can do this, I know you can," the doctor said. Reese pulled down the bedsheet.

"As we pulled up I saw a group of guys

standing around a bonfire drinking and laughing. It all stopped when they saw me. There were several boys about my age out there and they were all drunk and smelled like booze. He got me out of the car and they all jumped on me like wild dogs. I tried to run but they grabbed me and started hitting and pushing and pulling my clothes off, till I was naked on the muddy wet ground." She stopped talking again and took several breaths and cried a little as she spoke.

"They raped me; they raped me over and over. They were taking turns; one after another they climbed on top of me. I kicked and screamed, but the others grabbed me and held my feet and hands so I could not move. I lay there as they pumped me like I was just a hole in the ground. It hurt so badly, as they drove me deeper into the marsh mud, crawling all over me, their fingers clawed into my skin as they rubbed all over me and between my legs. I can still smell their whiskey breath as they would try to kiss me, like that would turn me on. It was a nightmare. I shouted for them to stop and to leave me alone. They never did. One after another they held me down and climbed on top of me and had their way with me. They had sex with me on top, and in my backsides too. It seemed like it would never end. I could not move. My body could not fight back; I was a piece of meat laying in a field for the taking."

"After what seemed to be hours, I saw headlights. I was hoping the boys would run off but they didn't as the car pulled up. It was a van, a gray one, and two men got out. I could not lift my head but I saw they were wearing cowboy boots. I never saw their faces. I was too beaten up, too worn out, and too ashamed. I could hear them talking and one said, 'she will do, and the money will be sent to your bank account, Curtis.' One of their names was funny like a bug or something. I can't remember. All I know was that I lay in the mud with my face down and beat to a pulp, wishing I was dead before those two had their way with me as well."

"But they didn't. They grabbed me up out of the mud and sat me down in the doorway of the van. The one with a red baseball cap then tied me up and placed a pill of some kind in my mouth and stuck a beer bottle in my mouth and made me drink before placing tape across it. He had a black mark on one side of his face, I do remember that. They then put me in a large sack, a big bag of some kind, maybe a laundry bag and threw me in the back of the van. I could hear the cheers and shouts as we drove off. I knew they were going to kill me. I felt like I was dead already. They must have drugged me. I don't remember anything till I woke up." Reese suddenly stopped talking.

"Reese, we can stop anytime, you don't need to

finish. Let's take a break." Dr. Shirley stood up and watched as the young lady started to fight against her demons as the tears ran down her face. There was truly something that had scared her to death. Kay watched as Reese suddenly exploded out with screams. They could hear the shouts all the way down the hallway to the next wing of the hospital.

"It was so damn cold and dark!" she screamed. "Oh my God it was so cold and dark, no light at all, just black."

"Reese, it's OK, Reese I'm right here dear," Dr. Shirley said as she patted her hand to calm her down. But Reese did not stop. It was like water pouring down a water fall. You could not reverse it.

"The black space was so small, made of hard cold concrete, no light, nowhere to move. They just left me there to rot for days, lying naked on the wet, hard, cold concrete with no light. It was like a coffin. It was horrible. It was so cold and pitch black. Oh God, why did they do that to me? Who are these people?" she shouted.

"Now, now, it's OK, I'm right here Reese. It's OK," said the Dr. "It's OK dear. You did it. You are going to be OK," as she patted her back again. In a minute or two Reese calmed down and Dr. Shirley sat back down in her chair with her tape recorder still running. What a horrible and terrifying story, she thought, coming out of such a young and beautiful girl's mouth. "I'm so sorry," was all she could say as she tried to write down a few sentences for her report as Reese slept. It was over an hour or so before Dr. Shirley saw the bed move and she looked up and saw Reese sitting up again in the bed wide awake.

"I do remember," Reese said as she started back talking. "When they pulled me out of that so-called hellhole of some kind, it was more like a coffin. I don't know how long I was there, several days I guess, but I do remember the guys that pulled me out were not the same ones that put me in the van. I know that for sure now. The second group of guys seemed to care and worried if I was doing OK. They looked alike. They looked like brothers, I don't know, maybe. But the first group could give a shit that's for sure." She then looked straight at the doctor. "I think I killed him. I stuck a scalpel in his neck. It had to have killed him," she said as she pulled the covers up around her face again and lay back down in the bed.

"You are one strong girl, Miss Reese," said Kay as she walked over and touched Reese on the forehead. "When we get you back home, I would like very much to talk to you and your mother. Would that be alright with you?" she asked. Reese nodded her head yes and closed her eyes; she was worn out and needed to rest. "You sleep. I'm right here sweetheart. Nothing will happen to you while I'm here." She pulled the bedsheet up around the girl's neck. Kay collected her notes, checking the highlighted areas she wanted to discuss with Connie. She pulled out her phone and walked out of the room and started to close the door but stopped and took one more look at her patient. "What a brave girl. Bless you." With a tear in her eye she shut the door.

"Dirty Harry," Ward

Chapter 29

TODD LAY IN THE MIDDLE OF CATTAILS THAT GREW along the bank of the lake. He wondered if the coast was clear and if it was safe to retrieve his cell phone. It has to be only a mile or so from here, he thought, as his eyes searched the landscape for anything that looked familiar. The sun would be rising in a few hours. He had to get that phone. That was the only thing on his mind as he climbed out of the water and ran into the grove of pine trees. He sat down for a few minutes to rest after fighting to stay alive in that swamp water all night. He then lay back on a bed of pine needles to catch his breath after being chased by men, trucks and alligators, beat up and worn out. His skin was one big wrinkle as he rubbed his hands together for warmth. His eyes grew heavy. If I could sleep for just 15 minutes I will be OK, he thought. His eyes remained closed and would not open as his shallow breathing became long and deep. Within minutes his body stilled and he drifted off. The 15 minutes of slumber became more than an hour as now the sun was up and shining down on Todd's face. He blinked and squinted from the light and raised his hands over his eyes as he slowly opened them to the morning sunshine. He rolled over as his eyes adjusted and focused on an object, a black truck that was parked about 20 feet away. Before he could react the pain in his ribs hit him like a gunshot blast. Todd's eyes opened to the sight he did not want to believe and again the pain hit him in his ribs as he curled up in a ball.

"Get the fuck up asshole, we got you now." As the two men grabbed Todd, he tried the fight them off, kicking his legs and swinging his arms at them, but it was no good. They were too strong and too many as they picked him up like a rag doll and drug him to the truck. He could not believe it as the Garrison brothers were hauling him away, and thinking he was headed back to the trailer on the other side of the lake.

"Let me go!" Todd shouted as they were dragging him by his feet across the pine needles. Grabbing rocks and tree stumps, anything he could grab, he was doing all he could to slow down their effort. Then, out of nowhere, Todd heard a voice, and the brothers' advance was stopped dead in their tracks.

"Hold it right there fellows. Don't move," said Officer David Ward, a U.S. park ranger for the Francis Marion National Park, with his gun drawn. "Let that fella go and let's see your hands," he ordered both men, as Todd fell to the ground. "Son you want to get over here away from those two, please." Todd moved as fast as he could and crawled up next to the officer's legs. "Looks like you had been having a pretty tough night out here in the woods young man. I said keep your hands up sir, I would hate for this here gun to accidently go off in my hands."

"A park ranger, are you freaking kidding me, ain't no damn park ranger going to take me in," Eyepatch said as he raised his arms back in the air as ordered. As that was happening, the other Garrison brother pulled his knife out from under the back of his shirt and waited. Todd was getting stronger and stood up on his own power right beside the lawman.

"Sorry to disappoint you there handsome. Think of me as more like a Marshall Dillon on *Gunsmoke* or somebody like 'Dirty Harry' Callahan, anyone of those guys and I hope that takes the sting out, for you."

“Sir, these men were trying to kill me. They have been after me all night,” Todd said trying to catch his breath.

“I’ve been watching that truck of theirs driving around the lake all night, knowing they must have been looking for deer or somebody like you, but knowing they were hunting something. So I started to watch and follow,” said Officer Ward as he leaned over to check on Todd’s leg, and that’s when the brother made his move and tried to stab the officer in the back.

Todd shouted, “Watch out!” Office Ward quickly responded as shots rang throughout the woods. Officer Ward fired off four bullets, two apiece, hitting both the Garrison brothers, killing the one with the knife instantly and badly wounding Eyepatch, as he fell to the ground.

“Are you OK?” said Officer Ward to Todd.

“Yes sir, but he’s not,” as Todd walked over to Eyepatch, and he looked up at Todd. Blood was everywhere.

“I’m going to die over a lousy hundred bucks because of you.” That’s all he said as the life ran out of his body with his one eye still open. Todd just looked at him shaking his head.

“Come on son. I need to get you to a hospital

and report this crazy night," as he took a couple of pictures of the bodies with his cell phone. Todd wasn't about to tell him a thing as they both got in the park ranger's SUV and Officer Ward called into the ranger station.

"Station this is PR9 requesting help. We need an ambulance bus for two, sent to the south side of the lake near the boat ramp just off Highway 17. No need to hurry, over."

"Roger that PR9. Are you OK, over?"

Todd could not believe his eyes, as he looked over to the right and there it was. Here was where he had been headed all night. He did not realize it but he had made it to the phone. The car he was in was parked directly beside the boat ramp sign. His eyes quickly looked in search for the missing cell phone as the ranger talked to the tower. What should I do? he thought.

"Two down, third needs medical attention, over."

"Someone will be there soon. Do you need backup, over?" Officer Ward saw Todd start to get out of the car.

"I've got to pee," Todd said, as he walked a few feet and stood behind the boat ramp sign looking for his cell phone, pretending he was going to the bathroom.

"Negative on that station, we are all good here, over and out." As Officer Ward placed the microphone on the console he called out, "you OK out there?"

Todd knew he only had less than a minute or so. He did his search in a grid pattern starting at the sign and working his way out.

"You OK over there buddy?" called Officer Ward again.

Todd turned to say OK and that's when he saw it. His iPhone 5, it was lying beside the dirt road and without hesitation he scooped it up and placed it in his pocket. His body motion was that of relief as he walked back very nonchalantly and got back into the car. Officer Ward looked a little puzzled seeing a smile on Todd's face.

"OK, sir I'm good now. We can go," said Todd.

"Not so fast young man," said the officer as he started the car for some air-conditioning, as the heat of the morning sun started to get more intense. "We need to wait a few minutes till the ambulance and others get here. We gotta take care of your two buddies over there first," as he pointed to the Garrison brothers lying dead on the ground. "And there's always paperwork. I'll need to fill out some of that and then we will be on our way unless you'd rather take the bus, I mean an ambulance."

"No, that's fine but those two are no friends of mine. I don't know who the hell they are," Todd said loud and to the point. But the officer could feel something was up with this one. He would remain suspicious the whole trip to the hospital.

"PR9 this is headquarters, come in PR9, over," as the ranger's radio broke into their conversation.

The officer grabbed the microphone and replied. "Station this is PR-9, come in, over."

"Officer, after the bus arrives and the matters are in hand, proceed to North Myrtle Beach Hospital. The Myrtle Beach location cannot accommodate. You must proceed to NMB hospital, over."

"Right that, headquarters, NMB, will do, and over and out. Well, looks like our plans have changed a little bit but no problem. NMB is just as good, maybe better in my opinion." Todd was thinking that this might be his lucky day after all. If that girl is still there life is good, and her ass is mine, he thought.

Pleads the Fifth

Chapter 30

SENATOR WINN COLEMAN SAT IN HIS CELL AFTER HE WAS TAKEN TO the Charleston Police Station, not the Charleston jail off Leeds Street that houses well over 2,000 prisoners, but the smaller jail at the police station in town. Tommy John thought it looked better for his own political career, plus Coleman never was arrested. They were hoping that the kidnappers would try to contact them at the hotel and that part did come true. However, Coleman's assault on the police officer and the senator fleeing off to Columbia to hide evidence was not a part of Connie's plan, so they were holding him for questioning.

The senator sat in the makeshift visitors' room as the door opened and in walked a sharp looking young man in his 30s, wearing a $1,000 three-piece suit and $500 shoes. He laid his alligator skin briefcase on the table and shook Winn's hand.

"Well, counselor, it's good to see you again," said Winn as the lawyer took his seat.

"Likewise senator, how are you doing?"

"Well let's see Matthew, my children are gone, kidnapped I guess, I don't know. My wife thinks I did it or had a part in it, and she hates my guts right now. My run for governor is totally over and so is my political career. And oh yeah, I'm in jail; I guess you could say, not too good. What the fuck, Matthew, can't you get me out of here damn it? I sure pay you enough!"

Matthew Cohn was young but a very good attorney and worth every penny to Winn because he knew too much about Winn. "Now hold on senator, we are getting you out. They cannot hold you longer than 24 hours; you are here only for questioning. Heck, senator you have not been arrested, you'll be out in a few hours at the most.

Now here's the situation. As of right now, the children, the girls, are still missing and Patty is OK now."

"Now, what do you mean now, what happened to Patty?"

"Winn, she too was kidnapped, right there in her hotel room a few hours after you left Charleston, but they did find her and as far as I know she was not hurt too badly."

"I want to see her, I want to see her now!" he shouted.

"Now hold on senator. She is fine and you will get to see her soon. Now a Ms. Womack told me to tell you Patty is fine, and a few things have happened and they are getting closer in the case."

"Happened, what else has happened, Matthew?"

"One other girl that was missing from the Charleston area was found up in the Myrtle Beach area and she is doing well. So basically all you need to do is talk to the police and answer their questions. I will be here the whole time. If you don't feel like answering or you have a question about it, ask me first. Do not answer anything you do not want to answer, OK? After that we are out of here."

Winn relaxed in his chair after hearing all that

and knowing Matthew would be in the room with him. "Sounds good to me, but Matthew, my God, I hate that happened to my Patty. I should have been there. It's my fault."

There was a knock on the door and it opened, as Connie and Chief Parnell came into the room. "Good afternoon senator, I hope your night stay with us was favorable," said Chief Parnell.

"It was memorable I must say. Ms. Womack, you are looking lovely today. And by the way, this is my Attorney Matthew Cohn."

"Thank you, Winn, always a charmer. Mr. Cohn, it's nice to meet you in person," as they shook hands. Connie then turned back to Winn. "I spoke to the doctors and test results show no sign of a concussion and Mrs. Coleman is doing better today, a lot stronger."

Winn jumped up from his chair after hearing that news. "Better today? I was told she was alright."

Connie rounded her wheelchair closer to the desk they were sitting near. "Alright senator, your wife was kidnapped, forced from her apartment, beaten up, tied up and held against her will. We found her hog-tied out front of the hotel lying in the bushes beside the driveway. Not to alarm you sir, but she is far from alright. She is recovering and physically she is OK. But she was shaken up pretty badly. We would be glad to take you to her as soon as we are through with a few questions, if that is alright with you sir."

"I have a driver, thank you. I'll go see her by myself if you don't mind Ms. Womack. Now let's get this over with. I would like to see her as soon as possible."

"OK then," said Chief Parnell as he moved in a little closer to Winn's face. "Senator, tell me why you felt that you had to leave the hotel? Why did you feel so strongly about it that you knocked out one of my officers and fled to Columbia? Answer me that. By the way that's assault and that's why I can arrest you any damn time I want to. Hell, I should now."

"Yes, but we have this little agreement now don't we," said Matthew with a smile on his face as he looked over at Winn.

"I should kick your little ass out of here all together," said Chief Parnell.

"Please senator, answer the question. Why did you leave the apartment and run off to Columbia?" said Connie. "Was there something there in the house you wanted to find or was there something you wanted to hide, so no one could find it, maybe?"

Winn sat without a word being spoken; he moved his chair around a little and looked at his lawyer a lot. He drummed his fingers on the desk.

"Damn it man what is your answer?" shouted Chief Parnell as he pounded the desk with his fist. He then turned to Matthew. "Counselor you better talk to your boy or he is going to jail on assaulting a police officer, resisting arrest, and obstruction. Trust me; I have several more charges I could add. Your political career will be over, Senator Coleman, and I mean over."

The senator looked up at Matthew, and Matthew looked at Connie and Tommy John. "My client refuses to answer on the right that it may incriminate him. He pleads the fifth. This allows my client to decline to answer your question without having to suffer a penalty for not answering. Next question please."

"The damn fifth, are you kidding me, this ain't the *People's Court*, or *Judge Judy*. You are not on any trial senator," shouted Chief Tommy John. "We need some answers senator. We are trying to find you daughters. Now what do you say, sir? Why did you hit my officer and leave the hotel that night and run off to Columbia?"

Suddenly he spoke. "I want to see my wife now. If I don't see her you won't get your answers."

Connie looked over at the senator and asked the question herself. “Winn, was the information on your computers worth them killing your wife? And by the way they have those computers now. We don’t, but of course you knew that already didn’t you?”

“Look, why would they want to kill Patty? She doesn’t have anything to do with it, and those computers were not all mine either.”

“Do with what, sir?” Winn would not say a word more as he looked up at Matthew. Matthew then stopped the questioning.

“That’s it folks. Sorry, he is not going to answer any more questions till he can see his wife Patty and that is final. Winn shook his head in agreement to his lawyer.

Connie and Tommy John looked at each other and then Chief Tommy John spoke. “Here’s the deal, he rides with us and we will let the Colemans talk alone in private, but we will start back with the Q&A right then and there at the hospital. You got it senator?” Coleman shook his head in agreement once again. Then Connie looked over at the senator.

“Sir, I do have one more question,” as Winn looked at her. “Sir, why do your children hate you so much?” Again he was silent. Connie looked at him again. “Or maybe the question should be, why do they hate period?”

Troops Regroup

Chapter 31

CONNIE HAD EVERYONE MEET AT THE POLICE STATION before taking Winn to see Patty at the hospital. Rhys and Spider came over after trying to find something worth having in the van. They found hardly anything in the vehicle that would help and that's the answer they had for Connie when they met.

"Are you two sure that's all we have, a monitor and two flip phones?" Connie asked as they met in the chief's office in the police station.

Rhys and Spider shook their heads in agreement. "But Connie there is a lot of information you can find off those SIM cards out of a flip phone plus using the records from the cell phone provider," said Spider.

"Really, do you think we can stop a kidnapping ring with a flip phone?" Connie replied.

The office door opened and in walked a police officer looking for the chief. "Excuse me chief, what do you want me to do with the senator's personal effects? Is he free to go or not?" The officer stood at the door holding a plastic bag with the senator's smart phone inside. The chief got up from his chair and grabbed the bag.

"Thank you, officer, I'll take care of it. Thank you very much." With that he left the room as everyone else started looking at the bag.

"You are talking about luck," said Rhys.

"We don't know what we've got. Spider, I need for you to check it out," said Connie with a smile on her face as she gazed in the bag herself.

"Now hold it right there, ain't nobody going to look at that phone till I get the judge to issue a warrant. We can't open his private things; going through that phone is like breaking into a house without a warrant. Sorry, we will have to wait," said the chief as he put the bag in his desk drawer and locked it. "Now Connie you can start your meeting."

"Well then," she said as she looked disappointed on that situation but she went on. "OK guys, the case is pretty big at this point, so I wanted to brainstorm to keep our case fresh. Let's start with the white truck. The day before I got this case two men came to my house and tried to scare me off. They were driving a white Ford pickup truck. Was that just a coincidence? I don't know. But the vehicle that was involved with the hit-and-run in the Tony Hines case was a white Ford truck as well, and we have that truck on video, the same truck on the SC DOT camera disappearing off I-26 somewhere near Summerville on to Highway 17 Alternate, headed toward Monks Corner.

"Now we have a young girl, the chief's niece, Reese, that was found alive. She was found outside the North Myrtle Beach area, not far from Highway 17, the main road through town. She said that the two men who initially got her were not the same two men that kept her captive at the old farmhouse, but she could not identify the two men that tried to kill her in the hospital."

Connie turned her attention to the chief. "How about the chief, good shooting sir, heads up, good job," she said as Spider and Rhys clapped and gave the chief a thumbs-up. "By the way I did ID one of the men and yes, he was at my house, so we do have a small link," said Connie.

"Do we have any idea who those guys were and where they came from?" asked Spider.

"No," said Chief Parnell, "but we are in the middle of linking those folks with the owners of the cars found in the hospital parking lot, cell phones, along with the white Ford truck and the farmhouse. Something will stick and we have to find the main source of money. That's how we'll get them, you watch. As they say, follow the money."

"By the way, that farmhouse burned down the night Reese escaped. And a body, a very burned-up body, unrecognizable, was found at the site. The heat was so intense we couldn't use dental records. We believe it's the man Reese thinks she killed as she was running away. She also said those two men at the house looked like they maybe were kin, could be brothers. She also said there were two other girls there at the house; one was named Melissa, like the senator's daughter. She did not know the second girl's name, so we don't know for sure they are the senator's children or not. I sent Kay, my assistant, a picture of the Coleman's daughters so she can show Reese."

"Then we have the senator taking off to his house so you know something was or is still there. And a mob stealing those computers out of the van, really," she said as she looked at Rhys and Spider. "This thing is bigger than we thought. A group of boys or men rape Reese, sorry chief, and there is a group of boys, or men, that steal the computers. I say they are the same group of people. I bet you that the boy in pajamas is our guy Curtis, the young man that kidnapped Reese away from Folly Beach in the first place. How are all these people tied together? I don't know. But I can tell you this is no isolated incident." Connie looked at the chief as he started to talk.

"Well, Connie, that's pretty impressive. I see now why you get the big bucks. The information I have is from a park ranger out in the Francis Marion National Park off Highway 17 Alternate." Everyone looked up at the chief. "I know Highway 17 Alternate. It's out near Moncks Corner and Bonneau near Lake Moultrie. This morning a park ranger found a man that was being taken by two men. The ranger, in self-defense, shot and killed both men. The man they were after was sent to the hospital in Myrtle Beach."

"Myrtle Beach, is that not where your niece is located?" said Rhys.

"No, she's fine, she's in the North Myrtle Beach hospital. It's up the road a ways from the Myrtle hospital, about 20 miles or so."

Connie looked over at the chief. "I have an idea. Why don't we arrange a way that Reese gets a really good look at this guy. My friend Kay is there so Reese will be alright. And maybe I can make a trip up that way as well."

"Yeah, that's fine with me," said the chief. "I'll call Chief Johnson and have the boys in North Myrtle ready for his welcoming committee."

Rhys looked over at Connie. "Here's where I get lost; the Colemans, why? Why are they in this mess anyway? He's going to run for governor and all of a sudden his bodyguard gets killed, the wife gets abducted, and the senator himself runs from the cops to hide something, and of course the daughters are kidnapped. I don't buy it. Too much shit here, someone inside is pulling the strings, I call bullshit."

"This is not a game show, Rhys. I'll take how to solve a crime for two hundred, Alex. I know, their daughters being so-called 'kidnapped' doesn't add up to me either. But that is where we are, Rhys, until we can prove something different. And the chief's niece did say the girl in the farmhouse was named Melissa, just like one of the Coleman daughters."

"I agree with Rhys. Something about that senator, I believe he's in the center of this whole thing. I know it," said Spider. "I bet if we could link his ass with those stolen computer files we would have him dead to rights. And how much you want to bet he is hiding a copy of those files on something. I bet there's got to be a disk, or thumb drive hiding somewhere, and I bet your ass it's still in his house in Columbia. Want to bet on that?" Spider was standing in the corner of the room. His face was red he was so excited.

"Calm down, Monty Hall, let's make a deal before you blow up," said Rhys as he too was standing in the corner beside Spider. He looked over at Connie. "Well, what do you think girlfriend? Where are we in this thing?"

"I say we are about halfway. Chief, I need you to get someone you know and check out that farmhouse where they found Reese. There's got to be some good clues in and around that area."

"You got it," said the chief.

"Rhys, I need you to check the surveillance cameras at the hotel for a picture of pajama boy and send that to me, plus go to that area where Reese was repeatedly raped. The chief can tell you how to get in there. See if anyone knows anything down there. Spider, you and I are going back to Columbia and go through the Colemans' house one more time. Chief, I will need those warrants, one for the house and one for that phone. Can you get me that?"

"Will do, Connie, that's no problem."

“I’ll call Kay to check on Reese, and get her to look in on the man our park ranger friend found once he’s taken to the North Myrtle Beach hospital. Spider, if you are nice I might let you go work with her, she is real good looking.”

“I hope she doesn’t fall in love with me right away. I would hate being the heartbreaker.” As he laughed he noticed he was the only one that did.

“OK, Casanova, hold it down,” Connie said as she then laughed as well. “All right people let’s get going and remember that the main kingpin, maybe two, are still out there, so please be careful.”

“What about the Colemans? Are we just going to leave them alone?” asked the chief.

“You are welcome to put someone on them. I really don’t think they are going anywhere, but I would lock his butt back up for tonight. We can still hold him for 24 hours, right?”

The chief looked at Connie. “Yes, we can, plus if you guys find me some credible evidence that places him in the middle of things, we can hold that old boy for a while and who knows, maybe indict.”

Connie knew that was not going to happen. No, in her mind she knew there was someone they had not found yet. Someone bigger than a state senator, and she knew now this case covered a lot of people and several states. The bad news was she believed that the FBI would have to be called in sooner rather than later, and all their hard work would have to be handed over to the FBI. And if that saves a life, she thought, that will be OK with her, but it won't be today.

Someone To Answer Two

Chapter 32

THE PHONE RANG LATE AT NIGHT IN THE HOUSE beside the swamp. Cecil walked the floor back-and-forth till he started driving himself crazy, as his phone kept ringing. It's them, he thought. He cleared his throat and sat in his favorite leather chair. He looked at the phone, and indeed it was them. He took his time as he poured himself another glass of bourbon, cleared his throat for the second time and answered. "Hello?"

"Do you plan to lose any more girls tonight? We are starting to think that maybe you cannot handle this job. Do you think this is the case? And if so what do you think we should do about it, Mr. Cecil? Time is running out for you," said a man's voice with a French accent.

"Look here, I said I would have you three girls and I will, but I need more time. I lost two more men on this job tonight and the heat is coming down on me. Look, I have the two girls ready to go tonight. Tell your people they can pick them up anytime, they are ready now."

"That is incorrect, sir. You have three girls counting the young slave girl that we let you have that lives with you. She will do fine and is already broken in. You have done a nice job with her."

"How the hell do you know that, plus she is mine. She is not for sale."

"Everyone is for sale, Mr. Cecil, drug dealers like yourself, state officials, policemen, even the senator and of course her, unless you can find another one by tomorrow to take her place, but believe me, when they come they will receive three girls, do understand me you piece of shit, three girls." And then the phone went dead.

Cecil looked down at the phone and shouted, "Damn it!" He could not believe how messed up this whole thing had gotten. "Damn your time, Todd, I'm going to kill you, damn your ass." Cecil cut his phone back on and called another number. He could not believe this was happening.

"Hello Cecil, how are things going man!" answered the young man on the other end.

"Curtis, I need you and your boys to go back to

work. I need one more."

"No way man, this place is full of cops and army-looking dudes. Shit is messed up dude, totally messed up."

"Now you listen to me you little shit, I said I needed one more, so damn it I need you to get me one more girl or maybe they would want a pretty young college boy instead. Do you understand? My ass is in a sling, and I'm not asking, I'm telling you I need one now," he shouted. Curtis didn't know what to say and now he was really scared, knowing Cecil was crazy and was capable of doing anything.

"Look man, I'll see what I can do, but it's going to take a couple of days, maybe a week or two."

"Not good enough, tomorrow, I need one by tomorrow."

"No way dude, it ain't going to happen man. What do you want me to do, just grab someone off a school bus or something?"

Cecil thought for a minute and then answered. "That's not a bad idea; do you know any kid that drives a school bus?"

"I was kidding man. Are you crazy?"

"No, asshole, I'm desperate, so I want you to do me a favor. Think about how you are going to do it and call me back in an hour or so. We have to move fast, if something comes up I'll call you." Cecil ended the call.

He reached over and grabbed his glass of bourbon and patted his girl slave's head as she lay on the floor in front of him. She was there the whole time and overheard most of the two conversations. She looked up at him with sad eyes like an old Bluetick Coon hound dog. He kept patting her head as he drank his whiskey and thought about what he was going to do. He then thought, what the hell, and typed in the phone number for Todd and hit send.

Todd's pocket started to vibrate as his phone was on mute. The park ranger had no idea who Todd was or what was going on all night. Todd was not about to check and see who was calling but he had a pretty good idea. They were arriving at the North Myrtle Beach Hospital and soon he would be able to see her, the one that killed his brother. Then he could figure out what to do next as the vehicle came to a stop at the emergency entrance. Todd thought it was curious that not one time on the whole hour and a half trip had Officer Ward asked him one question. Not who are you? What's your name? Where are you from? He hadn't asked anything, that's not like a policeman or in this case, a park ranger. I guess park rangers are different than real cops, he thought. Or maybe he doesn't care; he was delivering the mail that's all.

"Well, here you go friend. Welcome to North Myrtle Beach Hospital. Here's the worst part, here is where we have to say goodbye," laughed Officer Ward as the doors to the emergency room opened and out came four policemen.

"What is this all about?" said Todd as the men opened the door and placed handcuffs on Todd's wrists and helped him out of the SUV. They then placed him in a wheelchair and wheeled him into the hospital and off down a hallway, not to the emergency room. They skipped that all together and went straight to the elevator.

"Hey where are you taking me?" he shouted. Todd had no idea where he was going until they got off the elevator and took him inside a small examination room that looked more like an interrogation room you see at a police station, with white halls and a large mirror, but it did have an examination table in the middle of the room and bright lights everywhere. Todd was inspecting his surroundings when in walked two doctors and two different policemen.

"Just relax, sir; we need to ask you a few questions."

The Worm Turns

Chapter 33

MUSC IS THE MEDICAL UNIVERSITY OF SOUTH CAROLINA and is located in downtown Charleston. It's where they had Patty under observation. Connie brought Winn up to see Patty after he found out she had been kidnapped, and he would not give the police any information till he got to see and talk to her. As they walked into her hospital room they found her asleep and hooked up to all kinds of machines and devices. Winn was shocked to see her this way; he could not believe it. This was not supposed to happen to his wife. Her hair looked like it was cut by a weed trimmer, all chopped up. Her face was badly bruised and swollen, so bad you could hardly see her eyes.

"Wake up sweetheart, it's me Winn, wake up Patty Lynn," he said as he patted her on the hand. She turned her head and slowly opened her eyes with a smile on her face, but it quickly vanished to a frown as she realized it was not her Tony who was trying to wake her by whispering sweet nothings, but her husband trying to talk to her. She started kicking and screaming. All she could see in her mind were all the other men and how they tortured and raped her as she kept on screaming.

"Get away from me," she said as she tried to push back his face from hers, the restraints attached to her wrist stopping her from doing so. Again she screamed, "Get him away from me, go away, quit, stop touching me, get away!" Winn then backed away as he stood up and watched his wife wrestle in the bed sheets with her eyes closed. "Go away, it's your fault he's dead. You killed him. Go to hell!" She curled up in a ball in the bed and sobbed.

"What the hell is wrong with her? Connie? Why is she acting like this? What have they done to her? She's not acting right at all. Is she drugged or something?" As Winn asked his questions the door opened and Doctor Benjamin Haney walked in the room.

"No sir senator, she is in shock," said the

doctor as he pulled out his stethoscope and checked her heart rate. She slowly started to calm down and he patted her arm at the same time. Once he had her at rest the doctor motioned to them both to go outside. The doctor turned from his patient and opened the door for the two of them to leave, as they walked out in the hallway. The doctor then turned to Winn, removed his glasses, and looked him straight in the eyes.

"Doctor, what is wrong with her? She's not acting right."

"Senator Coleman, I'm going to tell you straight up, there no other way to tell you, but your wife has had a nervous breakdown and there is no way to know the severity. There is no telling what all they did to her. We know she was repeatedly raped and beaten. To what extent and as far as how much torture she had to withstand, we don't know for sure. But when her vitals even out, like her heart rate and blood pressure, she will have to be transferred to a mental facility. I don't see her getting better here. She needs good mental help. If there is a facility you and your family prefer, let my staff know and we will do everything in our power to help. But at this point I'm afraid that type of facility would better serve her needs."

"Family, right now I'm the only family she's got," as the doctor helped Winn to a chair. "I can't believe this. It all happened so fast. She was not supposed to get hurt."

Connie quickly turned toward Winn when she heard that said. "What did you say senator?"

"They were going to leave her alone, oh my God," he said with his head in his hands. Tears appeared in his eyes.

Connie moved over closer to Winn to better hear him. "Senator, who was not going to hurt her? Please senator, what are the names? Where are these people?"

"All I know is one name."

"Yes, OK what is it, what's the name senator? Please do this for Patty."

"CECIL!"

Connie looked perplexed as she repeated the name, "Cecil? What or who is that?" she asked.

"He is a drug runner, and he also gets girls and trades them for money. He does that to help keep his drug business going. That is all I know. He said he was going to kidnap our two girls if I didn't get him some money."

"You knew about the kidnapping the entire time? Why didn't you tell us?"

"He knew Patty was having an affair with Tony, heck I knew it, but he was going to blackmail me and leak it to the press to ruin me. She had no idea; she did not know anything about it at all, that's the truth, Connie. I swear on my mother's grave." Connie could not believe her ears.

"Why did you go back to the house in Columbia?" Winn sat back up in the chair and took a breath.

"Because I have some information on a lot of folks dealing in sex trafficking. These are names of people in powerful positions throughout the state and a few other places. I thought I would use that as insurance to stop Cecil and get our children back," he said as he started crying. Connie watched as he sobbed, but her patience was running thin.

"Winn, listen to me, where is the information? We need that information. Now where is it?" The senator sat back up in the chair and straightened himself. Connie didn't let up. "Once again, senator, where is that information so we can find your children?"

Winn finally spoke. "It's in the cushion of a chair downstairs in the living room, the room you tried to interrogate me in the first time. Big leather chair with wings, you can't miss it. There's a thumb drive wedged in between the seat and the armrest. Now after all that I would like to see my lawyer.

After all, I'm a dead man now." As if on cue, walking off the elevator was Matthew Cohn, Winn's attorney. Connie looked over when she heard the elevator bell ding.

"My God, did you beam down from the stars? How did you know to come here at this time of day, Mr. Cohn? My goodness, do you have a sixth sense or something?"

"It's my job to know things, Ms. Womack."

"Well if that indeed is the case, we might need to take you in as well for questioning!"

"What are you talking about lady?"

"Your client here, Senator Winn Coleman, just confessed to knowing the kidnappers and the plot to take his daughters. Anyway, he is going jail tonight and will need a good lawyer. You know one?" She laughed and placed one handcuff to Winn's wrist and the other to the arm of the chair. "Chief Parnell will be here in a minute. He wouldn't want to miss this." Connie pulled out her cell phone and called the station.

Inside Job

Chapter 34

THEY LOOKED AT EACH OTHER IN THE DIMLY LIT HOTEL room as they both pulled out a cigarette. One lit the other's coffin nail and they both lay back on the bed and stared at the ceiling. Neither one said a word, knowing the sex was not that great this time. They both had more important things on their minds, one of which was how were they going to spend all that money once they got it, and second, were they going to leave the country together and to which destination? That was the verbal foreplay before their disappointing sexual performance took place. Could it be that the chase was better than the capture, once they had achieved their goal? Even sex lost its luster.

She reached over and grabbed a handful of vacation brochures. "I like Cancun or maybe

Belize," said Phyllis as she turned to her lover. Looking at a couple and throwing the rest on the floor, she explained, "they are both easy to get to by air or cruise ship, plus you can damn sure get lost among all the tourists down there. They would never find us even if they tried."

He didn't say a word as he got up to take a shower, rubbing his cigarette out in the ashtray on the nightstand. She sat up in bed, as she watched his nude silhouette walk out of the room, knowing he was having second thoughts. "Canada is nice too," she shouted to no reply as she heard the water in the shower turned on. She lay back in the bed thinking of her past and future as she thought of all the years she waited on those two like a slave, but no more. Not on Patty and Winn Coleman and certainly not him after all those thousands of hours she had to put up with those horrible children of theirs. Hell yeah, it's worth it, she thought, as she remembered back to all those times Winn would make her do all kinds of awful and hideous sex acts. That pervert screwed me in every way and in every room in that old house and Patty never knew it. And he was going to leave her for me, yeah right, that's what he said only 15 years ago, as she laughed out loud.

"Well, Senator Winn Coleman, looks like you're going to get what you and that stuck-up wife of yours deserves after all these damn years. I am through with having to put up with your shit!" Phyllis Grimes said aloud as she rolled over in the bed smiling. She, too, placed her cigarette in the ashtray and rubbed it out. "I say Cancun. It's warm and friendly and I love Mexican food," she shouted, not knowing if he was out of the shower and could hear her talking or not. She didn't care. She was so happy this thing was finally over. She didn't care where the hell they were going, be it Cancun or Kalamazoo. All she cared about was going and that was good enough for her as she rolled in the bed sheets full of travel brochures, smiling at the thought.

She never saw it coming; she had no idea that was going to be her last thought as he screwed on the silencer to his 9mm Beretta and stepped out from the bathroom doorway fully clothed with the shower water still running. She turned her head just in time to see him standing there. He pulled the trigger putting two bullets in her brain as she was thrown backwards with a thud into the headboard and onto the bloody bed sheets. Her body was still twitching as he walked over and pulled the sheets up and over her to cover her stare.

He unscrewed the silencer and placed both that and the gun in his case and placed that into a suitcase full of money. He turned on the lights and looked around the room as he gathered up his and her things. He started cleaning up the room, checking the drawers and the closet. He then pulled the travel brochures out from under and all around her lifeless body. He examined the situation, making sure he didn't miss the smallest of details before turning off the lights and leaving the room. As he shut the door a little too hard her arm fell out from under the bedsheet and her blood dripped onto the floor. She never made the flight to Cancun.

One Down

Chapter 35

TODD SAT IN THE SMALL BUT WELL-LIT ROOM with his hands handcuffed to a ring on the table in front of him just like at a police station. When he first arrived at the hospital they did perform a medical examination on him and let him clean up by taking a shower. But after that the policemen who brought him into this room read him his Miranda rights, and once again he felt like he was back in a police station. By now the strong lights beaded down on him so much he felt like he had been waiting for what seemed like hours till finally a woman wearing a white coat walked into the room and sat down in front of him. She has to be a doctor, he thought, as she looked down at her notes in her folder for a few seconds before she spoke.

"Mr. Todd Snyder, my name is Kay, Dr. Kay Shirley. I'm here to help you remember a few things and help with your transition back to normalcy after going through something as traumatic as what you have experienced in the last few days. Is that alright with you?"

"Yeah, but if you would like to show me normalcy, how about removing these damn cuffs," Todd said, and thinking to himself, you must be a shrink.

"It says here in my notes you were brought in by a park ranger, an Officer Ward, after being chased in the woods overnight at the Francis Marion Forest."

"That's right, I was just out for my nightly swim, lady," wondering where this was going.

"You were being chased by two gunmen who were killed by the ranger. How do you feel about that?"

"Lucky to be alive, just pure lucky, hell if Officer Ward had not shown up when he did, I would have been the one killed out there, and not those two good old boys."

Kay looked back down at her notes and wrote down a few words and looked back up at Todd.

"Why do you think they were after you, Mr. Snyder?"

Todd didn't say a word as he shrugged his shoulders as if to say he didn't know.

"What do you do for a living and do you have a family, are you married?"

Todd looked up at her. "What's with these questions lady? What's next, my favorite color, well its blue, OK?"

"Please, just answer my questions for me please."

"No, I'm not married. I'm a truck driver when there is something to haul. Work has been a little off with Obama running the world into the ground and all, and yes, I have a brother. His name is Raymond. OK, now can I go?"

Reese began crying even harder with tears rolling down her face when she heard the name Raymond. She knew that was the one she must have killed. And she knew right then the man she was watching through the two-way mirror was the one that had drugged her and imprisoned her for days in that hellhole of a farmhouse just outside of the North Myrtle Beach city limits. Connie sat beside her patting her on the hand, ensuring her it soon would be over now that they had their man and her world would slowly get better for her every day.

Kay then asked, “Have you ever been a part of or know anyone associated with a kidnapping ring, Mr. Snyder, and were you and your brother Raymond living here, right outside of town in that old abandoned farmhouse?”

Todd’s face turned white as the blood ran out. “Look I don’t know what you are talking about. I’m the one that was being hunted here. You need to ask the people that hired those two dead guys. I don’t know why you are still holding me. I want to go home. Lady, you have no right to keep me, no right at all.”

The door opened and in rolled Connie with Chief Parnell. The chief wanted to kill him right then as he pounded his fist on the table top in front of Todd. “Mr. Snyder, my name is Parnell, Chief of Police, Tommy John Parnell of Charleston, South Carolina, and this is Ms. Connie Womack, my associate.” He laid a picture of his niece on the table in front of Todd. “I have a question Mr. Snyder,” as he leaned over towards Todd’s face. “Have you ever seen this person before? Do you know her?”

“No sir, I have never seen her before. Who is she?” Todd asked, knowing full well it was the girl that got away after killing his brother Raymond.

“Did you not kidnap this young lady?” Parnell shouted as he pounded his fist several more times on the table. Todd was visibly shaking.

“No, I don’t know what you are talking about mister!”

Kay got up and stood between the two. “Hold on chief, this man is here to answer a few questions, not to be intimidated and frightened out of his mind.” She stood her ground, blocking the chief from getting any closer to Todd and to make sure Todd thought she was on his side of the situation.

“I don’t know the girl in the picture,” Todd shouted to Kay, “and I do not have to put up with this shit. I know my rights.”

Connie looked up at Todd from her wheelchair. “Mr. Snyder, Todd is it, I’m sorry if the chief’s actions upset you but the lady in question is a family member of his.” She pulled out Todd’s cell phone and held it up so he could observe that it indeed was his. “We have a lot of evidence proving contrary to what you are saying. Now before you leave this hospital you will receive an X-ray, CAT scan and a thorough physical to make sure you are in good health. You will then be expedited back to Charleston to the Al Cannon Detention Center or what we refer to as the jailhouse. That’s where you will face a couple of pages of charges ranging from first degree kidnapping, to maybe murder, who knows, unless you are willing to divulge anyone associated with the kidnapping of this girl in the picture. Do you understand me and the significance of what I am saying? Your testimony could save your life, Mr. Snyder. There are death penalty sentences for kidnapping in the state of South Carolina, much less torture and imprisoning somebody against their will. You are looking at a long time regardless what we make stick."

Todd didn't know what to do. Either the state was going to kill him or Cecil was going to. Not too many good choices to pick from. He didn't say a word as the beads of sweat popped out on his forehead.

"Now if you do decide to help us in our little investigation we will see to it that the judge will be gracious and more lenient on your sentencing Mr. Snyder, and Cecil will not touch you, that I can promise," said Chief Parnell.

Todd heard Cecil's name and could not believe it. They had him dead to rights and there was no denying it, he was caught.

"My brother and I did not mean to hurt anyone. We were supposed to just hold the girls till they called and transported them to wherever Cecil told us to, that's all." Todd pointed down at the picture of Reese with tears in his eyes. "We tried to help that girl." He looked up and stared right at Chief Parnell. "She killed my brother, chief, she killed him stone dead and I will never forgive her for that. He never hurt a soul his whole life. He was retarded, you know, a special needs person they call it now. He was all I had and she killed him." He then put his head down on the table top and started to cry. He was completely exhausted and drained to the point he was glad this nightmare was almost over, or was it?

Connie looked up at Tommy John. "One down, Tommy, that's a start."

He looked over at the two-way mirror. "I wish this nightmare never started for her," Tommy said, thinking of Reese. He knew she had to be upset after that statement from Todd that she had killed his brother.

Connie grabbed his hand. "You need to go comfort her Tommy. I'll finish up here."

Tommy walked outside. He saw Reese sitting on a bench crying. He sat down beside her and placed his arm around her shoulders. He kissed her on the top of her head as they embraced, all the while giving her the love she needed, and to make sure she knew this was not her fault.

Connie walked over to Todd and placed her hand on his shoulder. "This nightmare is not all your fault, Mr. Snyder, and I'm here to make sure this Cecil character gets what he deserves but I need your help." Todd knew then they had nothing on his cousin and he was not about to tell them any more than he already had, which was way too much.

"I don't know any Cecil," Todd replied as he looked over at Connie

"But in your statement you mentioned his name. You two would bring the girls to him. You said that in your own words."

"Sorry I can't help you lady," and that's all Todd would say as he turned his head away from her. Connie thought for a minute as she moved her wheelchair behind him and then motioned at the mirror to open the doors. She then rolled her chair around the table and unlocked the handcuffs. Todd began to rub his wrist.

"Alright Mr. Snyder, you are free to go. Sorry for the misunderstanding. Thank you for your time."

Todd looked over at her like she was crazy. Chief Parnell saw the door open and heard Connie's words and wondered what in the world she was doing.

"Leave, get out of here, Todd. It's over, you can

go anywhere you want to." He got up as if he was leaving and Connie grabbed the door handle. "But just remember one thing Mr. Snyder. That crazy Cecil character knows you were caught by the Federal Park Rangers and there is a great chance he knows you are here and I'm sure he can't wait to get his hands on you. I believe it was his men who were chasing after you in the first place, wasn't it? Now you run along."

Todd understood quickly what she was doing and she had him dead to rights. There was nothing he could do but sit back down. "Now wait a minute. You can't do this. He will kill me for sure and you know it. That's murder lady."

"You are a kidnapper. I don't give a shit. Where I'm from we call it justice."

"OK, OK, I'll tell my story, I'll tell you everything, just don't let him or his men get to me, please."

With that Connie had the doors closed and Todd confessed to his crime and told them all about Cecil's operation, or at least the parts he knew about. He told them about the hideout house in Sampit and the dozen or so men that worked for Cecil, and the white Ford truck and the fellow with the red baseball cap Cecil killed in the kitchen. He then looked at the two-way mirror and told Reese he was sorry. She was no longer sitting out there to hear, be he didn't know it. But he did feel better.

Bugging Out

Chapter 36

CRICKET SAT IN HIS VEHICLE BESIDE THE LAKE NEAR THE BOAT RAMP and watched as police cars after police cars drove in and out, along with a few ambulances thrown in, entering and exiting from the Francis Marion National Forest. The place was covered with official vans, cars and trucks. Cricket watched them as he quickly got his cell phone out of his pocket to notify Cecil of the news but as soon as he did a police car pulled up beside his car.

"Sir you can't park here, you're in the middle of a crime scene sir, and you must move this vehicle now please."

Cricket leaned out his window and spoke to the officer. “Excuse me sir, is everything all right? My friends and I were coming to go camping in here. Is it safe, will we be OK here?”

“Oh sure, yes sir, everything is fine. We had some business to attend to, looks like some fellow was being hunted down by a couple of bad guys but one of our park rangers finished them off. Yeah, he shot and killed them both. Crazy world we live in these days, crazy world.”

“That fella they were hunting, is he OK? I guess he got hurt too?”

“No, I think he’s fine but they did take him up to Myrtle Beach Hospital or North Myrtle, I can’t remember, but yeah he’s OK.”

“Well thank you sir. I’ll come back in a couple of hours. I guess things will be clear by then?”

“Should be clear soon. I thank you for being so understanding.” The cop tipped his hat and drove off.

Cricket could not wait to tell Cecil what he had learned. He picked up the phone off the seat again and pressed dial. He moved the car out of the crime area and pulled off down an old dirt road as Cecil answered.

“Yeah, Cricket, what’s up?”

“Cecil, Cecil, you won’t believe it! They shot em! They killed them both! They are both dead,” he shouted into the phone as soon as Cecil answered.

“What the fuck, Cricket? I can’t understand you. Who shot who? Slow down. Now who and what are you shouting about?”

Cricket took a breath and slowed down. “The park rangers, here in the campground, the park ranger shot and killed both Garrison brothers and they sent Todd up to Myrtle. You need to get the hell out of there Cecil. You know that sorry cousin of yours will tell them everything.”

“Where did they take him, Cricket? Where in Myrtle did they take him? Think.”

“The policeman told me the Myrtle Beach Hospital or North Myrtle Hospital. He didn’t know for sure.”

“Good, they must have shot his ass!”

“No, I don’t think so Cecil. One of the policemen said he believed the fella was alright. It sounded like they just took him in for a checkup I guess.”

“Shut the hell up and get your ass to Myrtle now and check on both hospitals and all the clinics if you have to. He has to be at one of them and when you find him call me back. I’ll move the girls to the cabin at Awendaw on Sewee Bay out down by Anderson Creek. You know the place. It's where we drowned those two pimps from Ohio."

"I know exactly where you're talking about, yes sir, I know the place."

"Good, then hurry up and call me as soon as you find out something."

"Will do boss." Having his new orders, Cricket turned off the phone and headed up Highway 17 to Myrtle Beach.

Cecil turned and walked down the hall to the kitchen where a couple of his men were playing cards. "Alright boys, everyone off your asses. We are bugging out of here. You guys know the drill. Everything needs to be gone before the cops get here! Tiny, you need to make sure we have all the computers in the van."

"But boss we have everything on our phones."

"Shut up and do what I tell you. We don't want to leave any evidence behind, dumb ass. Blaine, I need you to gather up the boxes of drugs and medical supplies in here and the cabin. Get Skeeter and his little brother Bo to help. Be sure to get anything you think we will need like extra guns and ammo. Roscoe, get enough food to last for a couple of days and grab a couple of coolers with ice.

I'll call everybody else and tell them that we are bugging out to the cabin at Anderson Creek. Screwy Louie, you come with me. I need you to help me get the new girls out of the cabin. Now we need to be out of here like yesterday so move your asses!" he shouted. Everyone took to their task at hand. Cecil was not about to call his associates. The delivery of the three girls would have to wait. Saving his own ass was all Cecil had on his mind and he wasn't about to wait on anyone, much less the cops.

In 20 minutes the place looked like a ghost town. The girls, plus Cecil's slave girl, were all handcuffed and placed in a large panel truck along with beds and all the medical supplies they would need for weeks. They placed all the supplies in their cars, trucks and vans, but before they left Cecil wanted to make sure that the cause of the fire would look like a meth-lab exploding. He got several bottles of hypophosphorous acid and a few bottles of red phosphorous and stood in the doorway and threw them in the fireplace.

And that was exactly what they thought as the police and fire trucks arrived at the Sampit location. All four buildings were burning, lighting up the low country sky for miles, as the caravan of vehicles made its way down the old swamp road.

Cecil sat up front in the truck while Skeeter

drove, but all Cecil was thinking of was Todd. He had just lost everything and in his mind it was all because of Todd. "I'm going to kill that son of bitch if it's the last thing I do," Cecil cursed as he and his men headed southeast along the marsh and coastline. Suddenly his phone beeped from receiving a text message. Cecil pulled the phone out of his pocket. It was from Cricket. "I FOUND HIM IN NORTH MYRTLE BEACH." Cecil laughed; he could not wait to see his long-lost cousin.

"I'll see you soon cousin," he said out loud. "I'll see you soon!"

It's That Easy

Chapter 37

CURTIS WALKED UP AND DOWN IN FRONT OF THE ROW of mail boxes, pacing back and forth waiting on the school bus. He could not believe he was doing this for Cecil, but this kid, she was the one. He had done his homework and had studied both her and this bus route. He had checked everything. The one thing he could not believe was that there were kids at that age that still rode the school bus. But he could understand that with both parents working she had no choice. After all, he was in a rural part of the county south of Charleston in an area called Ravenel on Highway 17, not far from where he took Reese the night he caught her.

With no more time than he had he was feeling pretty confident, but he had to work fast and with only a one-day window to boot. With the pressure coming from crazy Cecil he went ahead with it and got up his team of guys. He then had them watch the bus routes a day before and follow several buses on their routes all day long; checking to see whose parents or friends did or didn't wait on their kids to be dropped off. Out in the country those kids who were not picked up by a friend or family member still had a pretty good ways to walk. Curtis took notes of the ones that had nobody around waiting on them, and of course no high school kid would be caught dead with a parent walking them home. He wanted to make sure no smaller kids got off at the same stop, scared their parents could be there waiting on them. After he gathered the information he checked through it all from his guys and it just so happened that the one kid he followed fit his specifications to a tee.

This stop was as perfect as it was going to get, on short notice anyway. Curtis stood, ready to hunt and catch his prey as the school bus finally arrived at its destination, the air brakes signaling the stop. Curtis stood beside the mail boxes like he was supposed to walk her home or something. He watched as the young girl that looked to be 14, maybe 15, stepped down off the bus platform onto the dirt road. She looked like she was dreading the hike; it was a long way to walk to her house that was at the end of a mile-long road. She smiled as she walked by Curtis and he smiled back. She thought he was cute.

"Hey, you going to walk by yourself?" he called out to her.

She turned, as if he was talking to someone else, and then she spoke. "I sure am," she replied as she blushed.

"Want some company? I'm going to see my Aunt. She lives down the road there too."

"Sure, we're going the same way, but why are you walking? Isn't that your car over there?" as she gazed over at his little red sports car shining in the sunlight, sitting beside the dirt road. She could only dream of such a ride. At the same time, the school bus driver drove off not suspecting a thing, as she waved goodbye.

"Yeah but on a pretty day like today I like to walk, plus walking is healthy. Don't you think so?" He said that knowing she walked this trek everyday both ways and would love to ride in a sports car like the one he had.

"Yeah, but you have a nice car. Let's drive down this time, what do you say? By the way, my name is Megan, what's yours?"

"Oh, its Curtis, my Aunt is Mrs. Peterson, third house from the end." From his research using the white pages he knew it was the residence of someone with the name Peterson. Curtis was in luck because Megan knew and loved Mrs. Peterson. She was a sweet old lady. And that last bit of information made Megan feel a little more at ease. The more she talked to him the easier it got, plus he was cute. "You know you are not supposed to ride with strangers."

"But you're not a stranger now, you're Mrs. Peterson's nephew, Curtis," and she laughed.

"Well then come on, we'll ride in my car." That's all it took to get her inside that vehicle with a total stranger. Curtis started the car and headed down the dirt road toward her house.

"Go faster," she shouted and he responded by double clutching the pedals and shifting into high gear. They were moving pretty good, but too fast for him because they were quickly approaching her house. Suddenly things got better when she shouted, "Let's do it again!" So Curtis turned the car around and headed back towards the highway. He then reached over to the glove box and removed the chloroform-soaked rag that was in a ziplock bag. She never noticed what he was doing. She was enjoying the ride too much.

"Here, hold the wheel," he said to her as she grabbed the steering wheel. She never saw it coming as he applied the rag to her face. She put up a short fight and kicked a couple of times but then collapsed like a rag doll in the front seat, still holding onto the wheel. "That makes three," he said out loud. The tires screeched when the rubber hit the asphalt coming off the dirt road at a high speed. He was headed back up Highway 17, but this time he was making sure nothing would go wrong and decided he was going to hand-deliver this one straight to Cecil in person.

Curtis pulled out his phone and called him, knowing Cecil would be pleased. What he didn't know about was everything Cecil had been through in the last few hours with the cops breathing down his neck.

Cecil was standing at the cabin off Anderson Creek. He had just arrived as he answered his phone. "Cecil, I got number three with me in the car and I'm headed up your way now!"

"What, you are bringing her to me now?"

"Yeah man, you said you had to have one more and if I didn't get you one you would have my ass. Damn dude, is everything OK? I'm on my way to Sampit right now!"

"No it ain't OK, dude. It's all fucked up, and we ain't in Sampit. Don't go to Sampit. The cops are all over the place there. We moved operations to the cabin near Awendaw off Anderson Creek. Do you know the place?"

Curtis pulled the car over to the side of the road after hearing the word cops. "Hell no, and I don't know where the hell you are, and here's a news flash, I don't need to be driving all over hell and back with a girl passed out in the front seat of my car with cops all over the damn place either. Now what the fuck, Cecil! You should have called me man."

"Call you! I was a little busy, dude. Sorry but I was thinking about my own ass at the time. Now look calm down and take her to Bulls Island, you know where that is, right? There's a gas station on the right at the caution light, there on 17. The boys will be there in a gray van. Call me when you get close and we will pick up the package. Does that sound cool to you?"

"OK, man, I'm turning around now and I should be there is less than an hour, but you better be right, man," he said as he hung up the phone. Curtis was scared to death knowing the chloroform would not last forever. He had no choice but to exit off I-26 and steer the car on the off ramp down into North Charleston to turn around and head over the Wando River Bridge. "This is so messed up," he shouted as he hit the steering wheel and set his new course. He then looked over in the intersection and saw a cop car at the red light. In his paranoid state he did not come to a complete stop and turned quickly back on the on ramp as he decided to go back over the bridge he hated. He never noticed the Amber Alert sign flashing as he merged into the right lane.

The bridge was its usual busy thoroughfare, and in hindsight it was not the best time for him to reach over with one hand and try to move her a little more upright, trying to make her look awake or a little more normal anyway. At least she was not laid out on the seat passed out on chloroform looking like she had been shot. The horns of the passing trucks and cars startled him as he ran the car's right tire into the curbing on the Wando River Bridge causing him to quickly jerk the steering wheel to the left and back in his lane, making him pay more attention to the road.

"Straighten up, damn it," he commanded himself, knowing that the bridge was notorious for bad wrecks, six lanes of traffic hauling ass up or down hill all the time. He was very aware of cops monitoring the traffic as well and was on the lookout as the little sports car eased down the downhill side of the bridge now entering Daniel Island, the new upscale area where the new money lived. He caught a glimpse of the grandstands as he passed the Family Circle Tennis Center complex, which annually held the Volvo Car Open women's tennis championship. Big deal, he thought, as he passed by and saw the banners flying.

Not much farther now, only about five more miles to go before turning right on to Highway 17 and no more than 30 minutes before he would be at Cecil's, he thought. That's when the first kick in the ribs shot pain to his right side, then again another. She's awake alright, he realized, as the noise of her screaming got his attention real fast. He fought both her and the steering wheel at the same time. The car was all over the road as sounds of tires screeching and horns sounding could be heard all around him.

"Let me out you son of a bitch! Help! Let me out asshole!" she shouted. He pulled the car off on the shoulder of the road without hesitation, fighting to get into the glove compartment as the volley of kicks and screaming kept coming at him with no letting up. That's when he first heard the sirens of the two police cars behind him. It was over and he knew it. He stopped his fight and placed his hands on the steering wheel while her kicks never stopped. The police circled and pinned his little red sports car on the side of the road.

"Sir, get out of the vehicle with your hands up on top of your head," he heard over the loud speakers of the police car. The young girl opened her door and fell on the ground. The policemen ran to her defense with their guns drawn. Curtis sat quietly as the cops surrounded his car, knowing his little day trip to Cecil's was over!

The Backside Blues

Chapter 38

CONNIE LOOKED THROUGH THE TWO-WAY MIRROR surmising the demeanor of her subject before entering the room.

"He looks sweet enough don't you think?" She looked over at Rhys. He watched and wished he was somewhere else.

"Yeah, that's the little sweet pajama-wearing son of bitch that kidnapped at least four girls, put Ms. Coleman in the loony bin and tried to kill me over a damn computer! Yeah, he's a sweetheart alright. Why don't you let me interrogate him?"

Connie's lips made a smile as she thought he might be right this time. "You know Spider is right. You do come up with some great ideas. So here's the drill, you go in there first and scare the hell out of him and I'll come in and make him feel better."

"Works for me, here give me that," as he grabbed her note pad and gave her a wink before he walked into the room. She hastily moved over to the mirror and watched as Rhys went to work on their subject.

Curtis's head popped up as he saw Rhys walk into the room. He remembered the scuffle they had the first time they met in the parking lot of the Charleston Place Hotel. Still a little afraid of his size, Curtis carefully watched Rhys as he sat down in front of him.

Rhys read his name off the notepad. "Afternoon Mr. Curtis T. Morning, have you had a nice stay so far in these lovely accommodations they have in this fine city jail?"

"Fuck you, cop, and I ain't telling you shit!" Curtis shouted and Rhys knew right off he was scared to death of him.

Rhys didn't flinch. He kept looking down at Connie's notes and turned a couple of pages back and forth. "Calm down handsome. I'm not going to hurt you, not yet anyway." Curtis turned his face away.

"It says here you are 24 years old. Pretty old to

be dating teenage girls, isn't it?" Parents live in West Ashley and have a beach house on Sullivan's Island. Father's a contractor, mother's a school teacher, and I wonder if they know about your extracurricular activities. Let's see here, so far we have you on embezzling money, gang rape, kidnapping and sex trafficking and that's the first paper, wow! What a great career for a good-looking kid that graduated top ten in his class at the Citadel. Your parents are going to be so proud of you. They must be proud of your older brother too. He graduated from MIT. What's he do, kill people, or something?"

"You shut the fuck up about my family. You don't know anything about living with those people. They go through their lives doing what they think you're supposed to do, like you and everybody else. They don't know shit about having a real life."

"Oh you do, you know everything about life at 24 years of age. Damn you are smart, but are you bulletproof?"

"You can't shoot me!"

"Don't push me, I don't want too yet, but I bet old Cecil does, and I bet he will, soon as he finds out you're in here. I'm sure he has his folks in here, and I bet they are just waiting to rape your pretty ass. After that you will wish you were dead. They don't take too kindly to rapists in here buddy boy.

Heck, Cecil could have you killed anytime he wanted."

"You're just trying to get to me." Curtis was physically shaking.

"Get to you, hell I'm the only one keeping Cecil away from you now. You see, Curtis, all I'm doing is my job, and that is to get information out of you. After that I really don't give a shit. And if you do make it out of jail alive, being a pretty boy, it won't be long before you will be someone's bitch. And pretty boy that's something you'll have to deal with, not me, not your parents, but you and you alone smart ass. And son that's some real-life shit to deal with." Curtis didn't say a word. "Now you give me a call when you are ready to talk." Rhys stood up and looked back down. "You better watch your ass!" he said as he left the room.

Connie gave Rhys a high five as he walked back into the surveillance room. He promptly turned around to see what effect he had on young Curtis, who was face down on the desk.

"Looks like it's my turn now," said Connie. Rhys grabbed her wheelchair handle.

"No, let's wait, give him some time to think about this situation. If I were you I would call his folks. Let them see him."

“I’ll wait a few hours but I’ll let the real cops do the family thing. I don’t know if I’ll do that right now. I’d rather have Kay come down from Myrtle and have her give him a shot. The ride takes about two hours from Myrtle Beach to here, and that will be about perfect.”

“So we just wait?”

“Heck no, handsome. We have lunch, my treat,” Connie said.

“Now you’re talking!”

“Connie looked over at the police officer standing beside her. “Officer, please escort the prisoner back to the holding cell. We are done with him for now. We’ll be back in about two hours.” Connie grabbed her phone and called Kay.

Morning: A New Dawn

Chapter 39

CURTIS WAS BROUGHT BACK TO THE INTERROGATION ROOM. Connie and Rhys sat and watched through the mirror as Kay walked into the room to ask Curtis a few questions. Enjoying his view, Curtis watched her every move.

"Mr. Morning, I'm Doctor Kay Shirley and I have a few questions to ask. Is that OK with you?"

"Well hello, good looking, I've never had a doctor that looked like you before. And as far as questions, go ahead. It's not like I can stop you."

She looked at him over her glasses and decided to go straight to the heart of her questions. "What is your reason for these kidnappings?" she asked as she wrote in her notebook.

"Pretty lady, I don't know anything about any kidnapping. Heck, that girl picked me up, and get this, at a bus stop of all places."

"Sir there was a girl found kicking and screaming in your car. When the police arrived she said she was kidnapped and that you drugged her. Chloroform was found in the car, OK." He didn't say a word.

She then looked at him and sat down as she read more of her notes before she asked, "You like to control everything don't you? The intoxication of power is very addictive. Some people like you, they have to hide their insecurities; you've got it pretty bad. The part I don't understand is where do you get this hate for women? Did your mother treat you badly, or do you have a hard time enjoying sex with a woman? I don't get it, Mr. Morning. You are very good looking and you know it. Matter-of-fact you seem to use it like a gun, to shoot down your victims, don't you? And again that's powerful, having the control over young and impressionable girls. Again I believe it goes back to your mother, now doesn't it?"

"You leave my mother out of this, you hear me

lady!" he shouted as he looked up and pointed his finger at her. She knew then she had touched a nerve.

"Kidnapping, would you say it's more about the money than your hatred of women? Or about the same, sort of a 50-50 deal in your mind," she said as he squirmed in his chair.

"Look, lady, I don't know anything about kidnapping and I don't hate girls, women or any bitches, OK. Now leave me alone," he shouted as the door opened and Rhys and Connie came inside.

"Well, Mr. Morning, looks like you have met my associate, Doctor Shirley. Are you ready to help us save several young girls' lives from your associates, like Mr. Cecil?"

"No, I'm not ready, lady, and you can take your handicapped ass and that gorilla of yours the hell out of here, I ain't telling you a thing."

Rhys walked over and grabbed his shirt and with one hand picked him up off the chair he was sitting on. "Then come on sweetheart, you're going to jail."

"Hey! Hey man, stop! OK, I said OK, let go of me!" Curtis shouted, as Rhys dropped him back in his seat. "You've got to promise me immunity and relocation, that's the only way I'll talk. Like you said, they will kill me if I stay in here and that's the truth and we both know it."

"Mr. Morning, we have two women that will identify you as the kidnapper. We have cell phone records plus a couple of cell phones like yours to identify your association with Cecil. The bus driver, plus several neighbors identified you as the man that drove off with the young girl today. In other words, Mr. Curtis T. Morning, we have your ass. Now if you would like to lessen your time in jail, we might be able to work out some kind of immunity to some of those charges. You will still need to cooperate with my old handicapped ass and the big gorilla over there," as she pointed to Rhys. "Do you understand me? Everything, your friends' names, dates you kidnapped the girls, places you took them, addresses of your whole gang that you hang out with, plus Cecil and his boss's name. I mean everything."

"Yes, I understand," he sighed as he looked up at Kay. "I would like to give my statement to her."

"That will be fine. We do appreciate your help. Those girls' lives are in your hands, Curtis. Please help them," Connie said as she and Rhys once again left the room.

Connie looked over at Rhys. "We need to round up some of those guys who are on his phone. See if Spider can get enough audio of Curtis's voice off our interview to use so they will think it's him and we can tell them to meet him somewhere. And you'll just happen to be the one there."

"That sounds good to me. How about that thumb drive? You still want me to go to Columbia and get it?"

"No, that's taken care of; I had a Columbia police officer retrieve it and he is on the way with it as we speak. It was right there in that leather chair like Winn said it was."

"I told you that you can always trust him," as they both laughed. "Yeah right."

Say Winn

Chapter 40

WINN COLEMAN LOOKED OUT THE WINDOW of his jail cell that was down the hallway from Chief Parnell's office in the police station. The chief had him there rather than have him placed in general population at the county jail. That's about the only nice thing that Chief Tommy John did, Winn thought. Winn figured the honor of the office was enough to grant him that, at least that, plus all his years of service. "Hell, I deserve that much," as he talked to himself and stared out at the pretty grass lawn and trees. Nice landscape for a police station.

"Thinking about escaping?" he heard a voice with a French accent say as he turned around and saw a man looking through the bars of his cell.

"Sure is a pretty day. Don't you hate being all cooped up in here, Monsieur?"

"Excuse me, do I know you?" Winn replied with a puzzled look on his face, as he walked closer to the bars to better see this stranger who had popped in.

"No, friend, you don't know me but you have dealings with my people or let's say my boss's people. I am only a pawn in this game, no big fish here, only a messenger, friend."

"Well, friend, who is your boss?"

"That you will never know, but his associate in this affair," as he stopped and looked both ways up and down the hallway before speaking, "is Mr. Cecil. I believe you do know him, right?"

Winn's face turned white with shock at this news. He didn't know what to do as he tried to talk. "How did you, I mean who sent you? What do your people want now, my children? Hell, you have them I guess. My wife is a basket case and I'm in here. Damn it man, what else do you want?"

"Our money, senator, we told you that you had 24 hours and that was two days ago. Time's up, sir."

"What about my daughters?"

"Oh Monsieur, I'm so sorry but they're gone."

"Gone, what the hell do you mean, you son of a bitch!" Winn shouted.

"Please, sir, your voice," said the mystery visitor in a very calm tone. "Please be quiet. We don't want to alarm anyone, now do we?"

"I did send you over half of the money the first time you asked for it."

"No, Monsieur, we did not receive anything close to that amount of payment. That small amount only inflamed the situation if you know what I mean?"

"I don't care if I pissed someone off. Hell man, how could I do anything? I've been under arrest after the first day and I did send you a lot of money. Where did that go? Does it not count?"

"You might want to take that up with your man, Monsieur Miller, your new bodyguard. It seems that he has suddenly taken a trip, a long trip out of the country."

"What do you mean, out of the country? He left?"

"Yes, and I believe your nanny wanted to leave with him as well but she apparently didn't make the trip. Must have been a lover's quarrel, I believe they must have broken up. Police found her lifeless body in an old hourly hotel outside of town. I believe it's one you had visited on several occasions."

"Phyllis is dead too?" Winn turned away from the visitor and looked again out the window at the freshly mowed grass. "Looks like my time will soon be up at this rate," he said.

"They don't want to kill you right away! But I digress, like I was saying, we did promise that you and your wife would have 24 more hours. How did you repay our kindness? All you did was run away to Columbia to cover your own ass. In doing so you left your wife helpless, and that's how she was taken and abused by many men for hours. It was entirely your fault, senator, but you see after all of that Monsieur, we still want our money."

"Well, you are just going to have to kill me. I don't give a shit anymore. If my children are dead and my wife is damaged I just don't care anymore."

The stranger held up his hand and stopped Winn in midsentence. "No, Monsieur, they are not dead, not yet. They are gone from here, living a different life. But without the rest of the money—well, I'm afraid slavery will be their future and destitution will be yours, Monsieur."

"You go to hell, Monsieur! I'll kill you, you son

of a bitch! Guard," he shouted. "Guard!"

"Where I stand that looks very unlikely. Good day, senator." With that the mystery visitor was gone, disappearing down the hall and out through the doorway behind the back stairway.

The guard walked right by him as he was making his way to the cell. "Yes sir, senator, is there something you want? Are you OK?"

Winn collapsed on the foot of the bed still holding onto the bars as he looked up at the cop. He had nothing say to him. Winn knew there was nothing anyone could do and that his life, as he knew it, was over.

The Call

Chapter 41

THE CABIN BESIDE ANDERSON CREEK WAS VERY small. There was hardly enough room for both the girls and Cecil. The men would have to sleep in their cars and trucks or on the ground, Cecil thought, as he sat on the back porch in his favorite chair, a La-Z-Boy they had brought from the old house. He watched the birds fly in and out of the tall green grasses of the low-country marshes. His mind was whirling with all kinds of thoughts, wondering what had happened to Curtis. He should have been there hours ago. And then there was Todd, his cousin. Todd sure as hell hadn't done Cecil any favors, causing the whole gang to leave Sampit, his home, and come here out in the middle of nowhere. But how could Todd know anything about Curtis and his operation? This thing was getting out of hand, he thought, as he wondered what to do next. His phone rang. It was an unknown number. Do I answer it or not? he thought. "No," he said out loud, listening to it continue to ring. His curiosity got the best of him and he couldn't stand it any longer.

Oh hell, "hello, who's this?" he asked.

"Cecil, I was . . . call and instruct . . . to have . . . girls . . . tonight. Cecil's cell phone was breaking up. The reception was terrible. I . . . you back . . . eight o'clock . . . Do . . . understand?"

"Yes, but we can't, not tonight. We had to," and the phone call ended. That was them, he thought. "Not tonight, damn it!" he shouted out into the marshland, causing the birds to take flight. Cecil stood up and stretched his long arms out in the air and cupped his hands around his mouth. "Louie," he called out.

"Yes sir, Boss," he said, as he threw down his axe beside the stack of wood and walked from the other side of the cabin where he had been chopping firewood for the stove.

"It's game time, Louie; let's get the girls ready.

We are going to try to have a delivery tonight so call everybody and have them ready to go. I want about five guys to help you escort the girls up to the highway around eight o'clock, and another thing, see if you can find out anything on Curtis. He's real late getting here. I'm worried about that boy."

"Got it, Boss." Louie pulled out his cell phone and went to work trying to call his men.

All three girls were lying in one small bed. They heard the conversation between the two men. Their legs were chained to the bedposts and all they could do was wonder where they are going and when. All three started to cry.

Cecil wondered what he was thinking. There was no way he could deliver the goods tonight, not with all the cops combing the area and no cell signal. And where the hell was Curtis with the third girl? It was so messed up, he thought. But what if he was to leave, just he and the three girls, take off to a new location that no one would think of? Now that might work, he thought, as he pulled out his phone and texted a message to one of his men. "Yep that's the plan," Cecil said as he pressed the send button on his phone. He then pulled a joint out of his shirt pocket and lit up. His chest swelled as he took a big inhale as the smoke filled his lungs to their maximum capacity. He held his breath for a few seconds and then he let out a large exhale as a flume of smoke filled the air. After three or four more tokes life started to look a little better now. Cecil sat on the porch feeling no pain, oblivious to the marsh birds flying and landing close to the cabin.

One Bad Man

Chapter 42

CONNIE LOOKED OVER AT KAY AS SHE WAS FINISHING her notes on her interviews and interrogations of both Curtis Morning and Todd Snyder. She was in an office down the hall from Chief Parnell, waiting and drumming her fingers on the handrest to her wheelchair. Connie hated to wait on anything and Kay knew that she had no patience, as she looked over at her tapping her fingers.

"Hold your water lady. I'll be through in two minutes."

"You'll be through now. You're not writing a novel here, Anne Rice. What's the verdict, who are we dealing with in this Cecil character?"

Kay stopped writing and placed her pen down beside her notebook on the table, looking up at Connie with a real concerned look on her face. "Connie, this is one bad man. His name is Cecil B. Locklear. He's half Lumbee Indian from around the Pembroke, North Carolina, area, and is Todd Snyder's first cousin on his mother's side. Old Cecil makes his money mainly in drugs, deals in heroin, crack cocaine and marijuana by the boatloads, but lately he's been on the FBI's radar with sex trafficking. The FBI believes there's a new syndicate organization made up of businessmen and state officials right here in South Carolina."

Connie interrupted. "Yeah, but why did this group of folks pick this guy since he is only a drug dealer?"

"Yes, but if you dig a little deeper he turns out to be a little more than that. His story starts when he somehow managed to fool Uncle Sam long enough to do two tours in Somalia. His last tour was in Iraq before they kicked him out for insubordination and threatening to kill his superior officer and second-degree murder. He did 10 years for that in the military prison in Fort Leavenworth, Kansas."

"Great, he's ex-military and nuts?"

"Yes, but it gets worse. Check this out," as she slid her notes from his military and mental assessment records over so Connie could read them. Connie looked over the notes then quickly looked back up at Kay.

"He's ex- Army Ranger Special Forces; in August 1990 he was under Commander Jackson Randall Womack, head of Seals Team Four out of Little Creek, Virginia. What! He was in Jack's outfit; I can't believe that!" Connie read more. "His expertise is psychological warfare, are you kidding me, where he specialized in extreme interrogation techniques. Well that's great. He probably did stuff like waterboarding, and Chinese water torture. I'm sure he knows all the other wonderful ways to maim and kill someone as well!" She looked back up at Kay.

"Connie, it was Jack's direct testimony, saying that Cecil went rogue, killing one of his men during a special operation is what landed him in Leavenworth."

"No, he put himself there when he disobeyed authority and helped kill somebody. That's what got him time in Leavenworth, not Jack."

"You don't think he had anything to do with Jack's death, do you?"

Connie turned her head without saying a word as she thought of Jack.

"Anyway, Todd believes that's how he is able to break down these women in such a short period of time. It's easy for him. Heck he was trained by the best of the best. It's like he can put people under his spell. Todd said the people that work for him do anything and everything he tells them to do."

"Yeah, because they are scared to death of him, that's why."

"Well maybe, but when I say everybody, we're talking a small army here, Connie. From both Todd's and Curtis's testimony he has somewhere between 30 to 40 bad men, maybe more, working for him. The size and scope of his drug empire is huge. He owns most of the low country all the way up to Wilmington, North Carolina, and down to parts of Georgia and maybe Florida. And I'm afraid he has the same territory in the sex trade as well."

"Maybe so, but I bet money is the reason for the sex trade. It takes a lot addicts and cash to run a drug empire on the scale of Cecil's, plus brains, and I don't believe old Cecil has that much of either. He looks more like a puppet to me, so we will definitely need to do some more homework on this so-called sex organization. We do that and we'll find out who makes up the cast of all these influential men. Then we'll find the big banana who is pulling all the strings on old mister Cecil. And trust me, Kay, we'll find him. And by the way that's great work getting all that information Kay, good job."

"Oh, and by the way there is another thing, he's not only a bipolar drug addict, he is a complete sociopath. With that warped mind of his, killing is nothing to him, and he will show no remorse. Connie trust me, he won't hesitate. You've got yourself a full-blown Rambo nut job, right here girlfriend," as she tapped her finger down on Cecil's dossier. "You better be real damn careful with this one, I mean it."

"Thanks for caring mother hen, but I'm going to get those girls back. It's more than my job. I promised those families. We have got to find them, Kay."

"I think I already have, well, to a point."

"What, you know where they are? Why didn't you tell me sooner, Kay? Where are they?"

"Hold on, Connie, they aren't going anywhere till those girls get delivered to somebody. Curtis said they had to move from their Sampit location to somewhere in the Awendaw area near Bull Island. He was on his way there when the police stopped him but he didn't know exactly where they were. Cecil was sending someone to get him, so maybe we can use that to our advantage. I should have told you sooner but I had to explain who you are dealing with. He is very dangerous."

"Thanks for the love, girl, but I'll be careful." She then turned out of the room into the hallway where Rhys and Spider were talking. She looked up at Rhys. "We need to talk."

"Sure what's up? Are we going after this Cecil guy or not?" said Rhys as he went to grab her wheelchair and Connie stopped him.

"Why didn't you tell me you knew him, this Cecil Locklear character? Damn, Rhys, he was in your unit and worked beside you and Jack and you didn't tell me anything about it, why?"

"Well, first of all I was not sure it was the same guy. It was a long time ago, Connie. He was in our unit for only one mission and he screwed that up royally. He's straight-up nuts, hell he killed one of my brothers-in-arms."

"How does that happen? He was an army ranger for Christ's sake!" she shouted.

"The guy was OK at first, or at least he acted like it. But as time went by, for some reason he snapped, and by the way he hated Jack. I wouldn't be surprised if he had something to do with Jack's death, but hell he hated any kind of authority.

Damn, I'm sorry Connie. I thought this guy was still in Leavenworth or in some mental hospital. I didn't know Chief was anywhere near here."

"Chief?" she said repeating Rhys.

"Yeah, that's what we called him in the unit. Being an Lumbee Indian he liked to be called "Chief" I guess." Connie didn't ask any more about him as she then looked over at Spider.

"Don't look at me. I didn't know the guy."

"Well enough of that, come on, let's go see Tommy John," she said as they headed down the hallway toward the chief's office. Rhys grabbed the handles to the wheelchair and headed Connie in the right direction, so they could all muster in Chief Parnell's office.

Chief Parnell was on the phone as he looked up and saw Connie and her posse waiting for his attention. "OK that's great. I'll see you—" he stopped talking as the door suddenly opened with Connie leading the way. "Wait one second Connie. I'll be right with you guys," as he held the phone covering the receiver. He then went back to the first conversation he was having on the phone. "Yes, sorry, yes sir we'll be there. I'll call you when we are in route. Yes sir, always willing to work with the FBI, thanks again," he said as he hung up the phone. "OK Connie, what is it? What is so damn important you could not wait till I got off the phone?"

"We found him. We have the general location of Cecil. He's the head man in this case, chief," said Connie as she rolled up closer to his desk. Chief Parnell stood up at his desk and looked over at the trio.

"Would it happen to be in the area of Bulls Island near Awendaw, up near Anderson Creek?"

"How did you know? We just found out ourselves."

The chief sat down of the edge of the desk and looked over at their surprised faces. "One word, people, drone."

Connie and Rhys did not understand what the chief was talking about, when Spider spoke up. "Of course, the Unmanned Aircraft System, or UAS. The U.S. Forest Service has adopted that policy and has been using drones to manage the forest fires and logging, which covers hundreds if not thousands of acres of land. They found our man using a drone, now that's cool."

"Hold on, Spiderman. That's the easy part. Now we have to come up with a plan to get those girls without someone getting hurt," said Rhys as he looked over at Connie. "Got any ideas, lady?"

"Well you guys might want to wait a minute." Everyone focused on the chief as the room became quiet. The chief walked back to his desk and sat down. Rhys and Connie looked at each other, but said nothing.

Spider had a look on his face and stood up. "I know . . . what if I drive Curtis's sports car. He was supposed to meet with them in Awendaw with the girl. If you don't think it's too late, maybe we can surprise them by using me as a decoy. All we need now is someone to play the girl." At that exact moment Kay walked into the chief's office, not knowing what they were cooking up.

"Chief I need you to sign off on this paperwork, sorry to interrupt, right here if you don't mind." She pointed to the place on the paper for him to autograph.

"She's our girl. Don't you think she would do fine? What do you guys think?" said Spider. Kay looked around the room at everyone looking at her.

"What are you all looking at me for?" she asked as everyone sat there gawking.

"She'd be great, she's small and cute," said Rhys.

Connie was not as sure, as she answered with opposition. "I don't know about Kay's helping. It is real dangerous, too dangerous for someone who does not work in the field. I'm sure the chief has someone, a policewoman that can fit the bill."

"I'm afraid not, Connie. With the cutback on our yearly budget, this last year we were cut pretty thin. I don't have anyone to spare, maybe the FBI or SBI, but not here."

"We don't have time for all this. Kay, do you want to help save those girls?" Connie asked.

"Well, of course, but what can I do?"

"All you got to do is take a ride with me baby, that's all," said Spider as he put his arm around Kay and gave her a little squeeze. Connie was still hesitant on the idea.

"Kay, you ride with me, I'll have to think a little more on this one, OK?"

"We will need everyone working together on this one. Do you know where the FBI and the SBI want to meet with us?" said Rhys.

"Just outside Mt. Pleasant about 30 minutes from here," said the chief as he was rifling through his desk. He stopped when he found what he was looking for and pulled out his .44 Magnum revolver. "Better safe than sorry."

Spider watched as the chief pulled the big gun

out from the desk drawer. "Damn, I guess so, Dirty Harry Callahan."

The chief gave the gun that had been in that drawer for years a quick look-over and cleaning. "That should that care of Cecil's ass and anybody else that gets in my way." He replaced his .38 with the .44 Magnum in his holster and tied it down to his leg like in the old western movies. "Connie, I need to talk to you while your guys get ready," said the chief.

"Sure, chief. Rhys you get everything we got and I will meet you guys outside in 10 minutes, is that good?"

"Sounds good boss, we'll see you then," said Rhys as he, Kay and Spider left the room.

"What is it, Tommy John?" Connie said as she looked up at the police chief.

"That was the FBI on the phone earlier. I'm afraid they want you to sit this one out and, in their words, let the big boys handle it. This Cecil character has been on their radar for a long time and they feel it's their baby. You know we talked about this earlier, once the Fed's get involved they won't let go."

"But chief, we handed it to them. We did all the work. Shit on them, we are entitled to this case and you know it!"

"Well we are, well I mean, at least the Charleston Police Department is, not you and your guys."

"What?" Connie shouted as she pounded her fist on the chief's desk. "I have two men in there that have seen more combat than 20 of those pencil-neck geeks put together. And a far as I'm concerned we are going with or without the FBI's permission. My people and I will be outside in a few minutes."

"Connie, it's not my call. You understand that don't you? There is no way we would be this far along on this case if it were not because of you and your group's hard work. I would be the first to tell anyone in the FBI that. And as far as I'm concerned you can work with me anytime."

"Does that mean we can go? We will not get in the way, I promise, just let us help."

The chief thought for a second and then answered, "OK then, but you just show up. Don't tell anybody I sent you and we'll meet you outside in a few."

"Thanks Tommy, you will not regret it," she said as they shook hands.

Tommy then looked puzzled at Connie. "But

are you sure we have all the information from the sorry senator? Is there anything more you think you could get from him? I would hate to walk into a trap with that Cecil character."

Connie saw where this was going and agreed to go see the senator before they left. "OK, I'll go check on the senator, and see if I can squeeze out a little more information from him, and meet you as soon as I get through. Does that sound good to you?"

"That sounds great, Connie," the chief said as he stood up from his desk.

She then turned her wheelchair to go out the office doorway knowing full well he was going to leave her. She tried, but the good-old-boys' system was too strong and she knew it. But as she left the room the only thing on her mind was Jack. She still could not believe that someone like Cecil was in her Jack's unit. Jack was too good not to thoroughly vet someone before letting them become a part of his team, plus Cecil was Army Ranger and Jack was Navy. It did not make sense. She shook her head knowing something did not feel right, but right now she had this case to work and she was off to see the senator, as she pushed her wheels forward down the hall.

Getting Ready To Leave

Chapter 43

ALL THREE GIRLS DID NOT DARE MOVE AS CRICKET tried to dress them up a little, getting them ready for the big delivery as Cecil demanded. He tried to brush their hair and straighten up their clothes some, but the more he tried the worse they looked. He wasn't used to doing this kind of girl thing and he obviously didn't know what the hell he was doing, so after a few frustrating minutes and his patience shot, he simply handed the hairbrush over to Cecil's slave girl, U.

"Here U, you give it a try," as he handed over the hairbrush. That was her name to everyone that worked for Cecil. He always called out "hey you come here" and it stuck.

"What the hell, Cricket get in here." Cricket knew to quickly stop whatever he was doing when the boss called.

"Make sure the other two look good. I'll be right back," Cricket said as he ran off to attend to Cecil's needs. Cricket certainly did not want to make Cecil any madder than he already was, not today. Cricket knew Cecil was already on edge, so he got up and left as quickly as he could.

"Be right there Boss, I'm coming," he shouted.

U moved over on the bed closer to Melissa and started to untangle her long curly red hair, as she was instructed to do and while her sister watched.

"Why do you do everything they tell you to do? Ouch," Melissa shouted as her hair was being pulled and brushed. The pretty young girl with the shaved head did not say a word. Instead U turned Melissa's head around so she could see U place a finger to her lips as to say, be quiet. The sister asked the same question and again no answer. Both girls couldn't understand U's silence, and again she was asked.

"Why do you do everything Cecil says? Hell, you lay around here most of the time naked, like his lapdog ready to serve his master," Melissa questioned, while U kept brushing and brushing harder till the hairbrush became entangled in the long red hair. Mad and frustrated on both fronts, one with the hair and the other with the two girls questioning her loyalty to Cecil, U suddenly reached her breaking point. She quickly got their attention by throwing the brush across the bedroom floor and proceeded to walk around in front of Melissa so they both could see her face. U did the only thing she knew to do to shut both of them up.

The two girls were startled as she belted out with a loud sound of "Aaaarraaaggg," as she opened her mouth and tried to yell. Both girls jumped back in horror as U's growling made her sound more like a bear than the pretty young teenager she was. Sadly that was the only noise that could come out of her mouth as she showed them the hideous truth— she had no tongue. She then turned her head away in shame as if it was her fault that it had been removed for not being more obedient to Cecil's needs. Cecil's own hand had cut out her tongue. The shock was too much to bear. The two girls, in horror, closed their eyes and covered their own mouths with their hands so their screams would not be heard. It made them both sick to their stomachs at the ghastly sight.

"Oh my God! I'm so sorry. We did not know," Melissa said.

"Oh heavens, you poor girl," the other girl said." They both hugged her and cried at the same time, as they tried to comfort their new-found friend.

Cecil and Louie were standing on the front porch as Cricket arrived. Cecil looked down at his watch, then back up at Cricket and Louie. "That boy Curtis should have called me by now, something is bad wrong. I want you and Screwy Louie here to take the van and go check out the Sewee Restaurant, but get on Highway 17 around Milcrest Drive. That way ya'll be able to ease up on the parking lot and see if Curtis and his red sports car are there and not the cops. Better still, call me when you get to the blacktop road."

"Yeah, that ain't no problem Cecil, will do boss," answered Cricket.

"No problem, right, like you taking care of my cousin Todd up in North Myrtle."

"Now Cecil you know the police were all over him. I couldn't get within a city block of that hospital, you knew that."

"I know that's what you told me," Cecil said as

he turned and looked out over the marsh and watched a few birds fly out over the horizon. "That's alright. His ass will be mine one day. He'll be easier to get to in jail anyway. Now back to the situation with Curtis. Again, are there any questions or any problems you can think of?"

"Just one, how do we know it's him? I don't know what the guy looks like." Cricket and Louie waited for Cecil to enlighten them.

Cecil's personality quickly changed as he shouted out to his two servants. "Well Einstein, I imagine he'll be the one that says 'hey, I'm Curtis,' and he'll be driving a damn red sports car like I said with a passed-out girl in the freaking passenger's seat, dumb asses! Now get the hell out of here and call me when you and Screwy get there."

"Will do boss, I'll call you, no problem, you got it." The two ran off the porch and got in the gray van and drove off. Cecil watched as the van vanished out of sight down the dirt road headed towards the small village. It was hardly a crossroad, if you could even call it that.

Cecil never saw or heard the drone circling way above high in the sky. The FBI watched as the van left the cabin and monitored their every move. The time for the raid was close at hand and Cecil had no idea what was about to happen.

Cecil knew he had to act fast as he watched the vehicle drive off but the drugs he had taken earlier were kicking in. He quickly started daydreaming and once again his mood changed back to being mellower as he relaxed when he turned to look back out across the marsh, watching more birds. His thoughts began to turn to memories and remembering when he was a kid. He and his parents would camp out here on this very spot and fish all week to fill the oak barrels of salt with the fish they caught, so they could survive the winter.

"Damn it boy, hurry up and get those fish in those barrels, don't make me beat the shit out of you again. Pick the damn thing up, we ain't got all day you little shit, you are just like your dumb ass mom! God, do I have to do everything around here?"

Cecil shook away the memories and focused again on the marshland as he pulled out a cigarette and lit it. I damn sure hated that son of a bitch died of cancer I could kill him my damn self, Cecil thought as he took a big long draw of the Winston Light. But on the other hand that nephew of his, Todd, I can damn sure kill his little ass, he thought. He took one more drag as he threw the cigarette butt into the marsh water and headed up to the cabin to retrieve the girls and to get the hell out of this place and all its memories.

No Winn For FBI

Chapter 44

CONNIE NERVOUSLY MOVED HER WHEELCHAIR AS SHE WAITED on the guard to bring Winn inside the visitor's room of the jail. Connie knew the stuff was about to hit the fan and she wanted to pick Winn's brain one last time in hopes of finding something, anything that might help with the rescue attempt before they left.

Winn, Todd, and Curtis were all three being held in the same jail but in separate cells at the police station down the hall from Chief Parnell's office, not with the general population at the Charleston Correctional jail in North Charleston off

Leeds Street. Chief Parnell did not want anyone to be able to get to these three. Plus it was handy to have them close by for interrogation. Connie's patience was about to run out when the door finally opened and in walked the senator wearing handcuffs.

"Do you really think that's necessary?" She looked at the guard and then down at the handcuffs. The guard pulled out his keys and she watched as he removed them. "Please senator have a seat. I just have a few questions. This won't take long."

Winn rubbed his wrists as they were granted their freedom and sat down at the table between him and Connie. "Well what brings you back to me Ms. Womack? Do you need some more information before you guys try your hand at big bad Cecil and his little army?"

Connie moved her wheelchair closer to the table. "It would look very favorable on your records if you did cooperate; we all need a little help at some point in time senator."

Winn sat back in his chair. "There's no need to rush out there Connie. He's not your man. There are a lot bigger fish to fry than that nut job." He leaned over closer to Connie so the guard could not hear. "Did you get the thumb drive or not?"

“No, Chief Mannes in Columbia said he would get one of his officers to bring it but so far he has not shown up yet. He must be running late. I guess he’ll be here in a few hours or so.”

“No, he won’t, and he’s not going to be here by tomorrow. Connie, that guy is gone. They would not let him get to you with that thumb drive no more than they would let me be governor. Hell, they didn’t even let me run for the damn office. Winn Coleman and his one-day campaign, that’s got to be a record,” said Winn as he laughed.

“Are you telling me this is what this whole thing is about? Your run for the governorship, and what about the girls, don’t you want them back?”

“Don’t you understand Connie? If they don’t want you to have it you’re not going to get it. Be it my girls, the thumb drive, or anybody or anything, you are not going to get anything without their permission, and sweetheart, that’s the end of the story. These are powerful people. Don’t you think if I know you are going after Cecil those people whose names are on that thumb drive know it too? Trust me Connie, it’s a setup and remember I know some of those folks. So there’s a good chance I won’t be around much longer either.”

“Winn, you are a state senator. Nobody is just going to get rid of you.”

"No, then ask Vince Foster, hell, ask President John F. Kennedy. They both pissed a bigger stream than me by a long shot. I'm telling you, Connie, you have no idea who you are dealing with. And not giving you any of those names is probably the only thing keeping me alive, believe me on that."

"Well regardless of Freemasons, right-wing Tea-Partiers or whatever conspiracy groups are out there, we are going to get those girls. We got one of them and we will get the others. I promised your wife and by God that's what I'm going to do, with or without your help, Winn. My team is going to do it."

Suddenly Winn stood up and motioned towards the guard. "We're done here. Guard, isn't my time up? I need to go back to my cell now," as Winn looked back at Connie as he was walking off. "You be careful, Ms. Womack. That Cecil is one mean son of a bitch, not to mention he's smart as hell too. Just ask your boy Rhys! He can tell you all about Mr. Locklear and your husband back in the day."

"Yeah, I hear you, but I have one last question senator. Why did the organization let you out of their so-called secret society in the first place, or did they?"

Winn, not answering the question, looked at Connie, realizing she was a lot smarter than he had thought.

"I'll see you when I get back senator." Connie rolled her wheelchair out the door and down the hall a few feet and stopped. She sat there in the hallway for a couple of minutes thinking back on that visit. All of a sudden she heard her name being shouted down the hall.

"Connie, Ms. Womack," shouted Carol Spoon the chief's secretary. "I'm glad I caught you. Chief Parnell has already left. He said if he could they would meet up with you and your guys outside of Mt. Pleasant near Boone Hall Plantation. He was going to call you later. He said not to tell you now but I couldn't just let you wait for him to call. He also said something about they were on the move in a van moving towards Awendaw. He thinks the girls are in the vehicle. He and the FBI are going to head that way. I'm so sorry, Connie."

"Don't you worry, Carol. I'll call Tommy John back and see what's going on, and again thank you." Connie rolled her chair back down the hall to her office where everyone was waiting.

"Spider, you need to scrap that idea with you and Kay. It looks like Chief Parnell and the FBI are going it on their own. It doesn't look like we were invited to the party."

Rhys was standing by the window watching

the rain fall outside. He turned back around towards Connie. "The hell with the FBI! Why don't we come up with our own plan to help? Spider, is there any way you can patch into that drone feed so we can see what they are seeing?"

"Sure but you need to give me some time," as he moved his chair over to his computer and started his magic. Connie went over to her own computer and looked up Google Earth and started pulling up maps and images of the area where they thought Cecil was hiding. After a few minutes she turned back around toward Rhys.

"Rhys, look at this," as she pointed to the computer screen. "If you were here," as she pointed at Bulls Bay and the islands surrounding that area near Awendaw, "would you be planning an escape by car, with only one major highway which is 17 and not an interstate?"

Rhys took one quick look and realized there was no way anybody would try that. "No, I would have a boat handy for sure, maybe two. Those creeks are real shallow. You would need something like a flat-bottom johnboat maybe, but once you are clear of the shoals and sandbars I would want something that goes fast," as he looked back up at Connie.

"Or maybe something nobody would think twice about, like maybe a commercial fishing boat," said Connie as she looked at the fishing village of McClellanville up the river only a few miles from this area. She then turned to Kay. “Kay why don’t you check to see if there’s anything in Cecil’s past that would link him to the town of McClellanville.”

Kay stood up and moved towards the door. “Better still why don’t I go ask Todd? He’s right here in the jail. That’s why they are here, so we can interrogate them, right?” and out the door she went.

“Damn I love that girl,” Spider said as he looked up from his computer.

Rhys and Connie both looked over at Spider and at the same time shouted, “Shut up Romeo and get back to work.” Rhys’ laughter was quickly ended as he thought of Cecil and how he would love to meet up with him for one last time.

Connie noticed the expression on his face. “What is it Rhys, what’s wrong?”

“I can’t believe we got kicked out of our own party, Connie. Damn I would love to catch that Cecil with my bare hands.” Connie pointed to the computer. “Don’t you worry big man. We will do the next best thing. His ass will be ours. Now let’s get back to work and catch this son of a bitch.”

Tried and True Escape

Chapter 45

CECIL WASTED NO TIME AS HE WATCHED Cricket and Louie drive off in the van headed northwest to Awendaw. Without hesitation he went straight to work getting the old inflatable boat out from beneath the cabin, lying under a few blue tarps. With an air hose and foot pump in hand within minutes he had her ready to go. Cecil pulled the small boat across the sandy ground and started the inspection, checking to see if the dinghy was seaworthy or not as he placed her in the water. He first looked for cuts and scars on the outer rubber lining and of course checked for air leaks as he thought of what essentials he might need to fill the dinghy. The trip would be an ambitious one heading straight out Anderson Creek to Bird Island, a small piece of land out in the middle of Bulls Bay in big water, where he planned to meet up with his shrimp boat and crew, but right now she was still docked at Cape Romain Harbor near McClellanville. He went back to his truck and removed the boat motor, a 9.9 horsepower Evinrude. Not built for speed, it was a good old engine he had kept forever and she was tried and true and always performed excellently in time of need, like now. He fastened the Evinrude to the wooden board on the fantail of the rubber boat and went back to the cabin to get his supplies. It took several trips back and forth from the boat and cabin to gather all he would need before he retrieved all three girls. Once he packed the small boat with all the essentials he pulled out his cell phone and began texting.

SKEETER R U @ THE BOAT? DID U GET EVERYBODY? Cecil texted as he walked once again up to the cabin but this would be his last and final time. He heard the phone ding in reply.

NOT YET BUT SOON EVERYONE HERE BUT 2!

CRICKET & LOUIE LATER GO WITHOUT U NEED TO LEAVE ASAP!!!

WILL BE @ ISLAND SAME TIME IN 2 HOURS

GOOD C U THEN, Cecil wrote as he pressed send and cut off his phone, hoping everything would work to plan and knowing he would not get much of a cell signal out on the water to call or text Skeeter again if he needed help.

"OK everyone, listen up," he shouted as he walked into the room where the girls were huddled together on the one bed. "Change of plans. We are fixing to leave this place and we are going to take a little boat ride. Now, time is of the essence so we need to be quick about it and go straight to the boat. Don't try to run away. That will only make me hurt you," as he showed them his gun. "Do you understand me?" All three shook their heads in agreement as he then unlocked them from their chains. They all rubbed their sore wrists as he hurried the girls up and marched them down to the water.

"You call this a boat?" said one of the girls, and Cecil did not respond. One by one each girl made her way into the small rubber boat and sat down, but Melissa, who complained the first time, stopped before getting in and complained again.

"We can't all fit in that little thing," said Melissa as she pulled against Cecil's hold. He quickly pulled out his large knife and placed it up against her neck.

"Bitch, don't make me cut out your tongue too," he shouted as he pushed her backwards causing her to fall into the boat. The others quickly helped her up to her seat which was nothing more than a small piece of board. Cecil then ran a chain through all three pairs of handcuffs. The girls had to slide over as close as they could so the chain would fit as he locked the three together. He gave them all a don't-mess-with-me look, then placed his knife back into its leather sheath and rearranged his supplies that the girl had knocked over, making room for himself to step in the fantail section of his vessel. He pulled the rope on the outboard once, and then twice as blue smoke poured out the exhaust as the tried and true marine motor sprung to life starting right up. Cecil looked up at the cabin for the last time, then pushed off with one foot and stepped in the rubber dinghy with the other, easing their way off shore and away from the cabin.

Cecil had a little smile on his face knowing that Cricket and Louie had made a great diversion when they drove the van up to Awendaw. He knew that if the cops were watching, and he knew they probably were, he'd be home free once he made it to Bird Island and met up with his fishing boat and crew, as the small rubber dinghy made its escape through the backwaters of Anderson Creek. All kinds of beautiful waterfowl like blue heron and egrets sat along the water's edge as they meandered through the still waters headed to Bird Island in Bulls Bay. "Skeeter better make it or this will be a short trip," Cecil thought, as the little dinghy wound its way through the shallow waters and disappeared from the cabin view among the tall and thick marsh grasses of Anderson Creek. The girls didn't say a word in fear of retaliation from Cecil's hand as they huddled close together shaking as if they were freezing. All was quiet except the putt-putt sound of the outboard Evinrude as they slowly made their escape from Tommy John and the FBI who were patiently waiting at the Sewee Restaurant for someone who would never arrive.

Cricket slowed the van down as he approached Highway 17 and surveyed the landscape looking in both directions before merging onto the thoroughfare with his hands at ten and two on the steering wheel like he was taught in drivers ed. To the naked eye the road looked like any other country road but to hardened criminals like Cricket and Louie it looked like the entrance to a Bruce Springsteen concert. Cops were everywhere. The road was dotted with big black SUVs and plain-colored Lincoln Town Cars with no markings, all along the quiet highway.

"Look there's another," Louie pointed and without a question they both knew they had spotted another cop car. The closer they got to the Sewee Restaurant the more intense the mob of cops became. Cricket soon realized there was no way they were going to meet with Curtis or anyone else at that location as they kept driving north, headed to the shrimp boat in McClellanville, hoping it was still there.

Suddenly blue lights lit up the front grill of the black SUV that had been following them, and before they knew it five or six vehicles had surrounded them, as sirens and blue lights filled the low country air. Cricket pulled the van over to the side of the road and waited for the welcoming committee of the FBI.

"Well, ain't this some shit," he said as he lit up a cigarette and waited.

Cabin Fever

Chapter 46

SPIDER WORKED FEVERISHLY AT HIS COMPUTER DESK TILL the screen flickered and he shouted, “I’ve got it, we’re in.” The rest of the team moved in closer to get a better view of what was on the computer’s monitor as the video images came across showing the overhead view of the low country marshlands. Looking more like an old Disney nature film than a reconnaissance mission, the video they all watched showed the area as far as the eye could see. They saw nothing but miles and miles of marsh grasses and low-country wetlands. Suddenly there it was, a small house sitting on the banks of Anderson Creek, but it looked more like a fishing shack as the drone got closer and the cabin came into view. Connie watched as she saw the drone pass over the white

Ford truck which was parked out front of the cabin. She could see where several tire tracks had marked up the sandy ground. The freshly made ruts proved that more vehicles had recently been there as well. Supply boxes were stacked up all around the cabin, some covered with blue tarps but most were just lying on the ground as if they were placed there in a hurry.

"There sure as hell have been a lot of folks there and they don't appear to be on a fishing trip. That's got to be it. Can you circle back around, Spider, and move in closer on that," said Rhys as he pointed to an object on the screen.

"No Rhys, I can't. I told you I can't do anything but watch. We have no way in controlling the drone. Unfortunately someone else is doing the piloting thing so all we can do is look at the same things they are looking at."

Connie looked disgusted as the drone flew straight over the cabin and kept going off in a different locale viewing more marsh grasses. "They don't have a clue on what they are looking at," she said under her breath. She quickly picked up the phone and called Tommy John's secretary, Carol, on the intercom.

"That's it. I'm calling somebody. We need some help with this. Those guys wouldn't know what to look for if they saw it. Hello Carol, it's Connie. I need your help. I need for you to call someone dealing with the National Parks and Forests now. I don't know who to call or what department but we need help with someone who is in charge of working with drones. Do you know who we need to talk to, Carol? We don't have any idea."

"No, but I'll find out, give me a minute. I'll call you right back, Connie," and she hung up the phone.

Connie next pulled out her cell phone and called Chief Parnell. "Tommy needs to know he's at the wrong place."

"Hello, Chief Parnell here."

"Tommy it's me, Connie. Where are you? I think we found Cecil's hideout."

"Connie, I'm up at the Sewee Restaurant outside Awendaw. What's going on? By the way I'm sorry about leaving you guys like that. I felt like I had to go, I hope you understand."

"Sure, but listen Tommy, it's about Cecil."

"Cecil, yeah what is it about Cecil?" He sounded puzzled with Connie calling him in the first place.

"Tommy, I need you to get someone in the FBI to get them to turn that drone of theirs around. I think we found Cecil's hideout. It's down on one of the backwater creeks in the wetlands. I don't think it's too far from where you are right now."

"Drone, that thing spotted Cecil's place? That's great. They can replay that tape if they missed it and we can find out where he is. Let me check on that and I'll call you right back. Thanks, Connie, great work!"

Connie turned off her phone and looked over at Rhys at the computer. "Rhys do we have everything ready to go, weapons and supplies?" He nodded his head yes. "Good, show me a map of this area that the drone is in."

"Sure." He stood up and moved over the large map on the table in the back of the room. "Right here," as he took his finger and circled the area he thought was right.

Connie studied the map in relation to everything around and thought she may have discovered Cecil's plan. "I think we might have to sit this one out but we need to call the coast guard and send them to check these three islands right here," pointing to Bird Island, White Island and another smaller one. "If I'm right this is where Cecil will meet his crew. He's a drug dealer, you know, so he must have a fishing boat or something and when they come to get him we'll pick him up and catch the whole lot."

"Now, Connie, with all due respect, we don't know if he has a boat, much less know where or if his crew is going to rescue him somewhere on Bird Island, or Gilligan's Island. How can you be so sure?"

"Well, Rhys, you tell me what big-time drug dealer and sex trafficker these days doesn't have a boat that lives near the third largest seaport on the east coast?"

"Sorry to interrupt you guys from arguing," said Kay Shirley as the door opened and she rushed into the room. She began to lay several papers down on Connie's desk and then grabbed one of the papers and handed it to her. "Look right here," as she showed Connie the piece of paper. "The *High C,* that's it, that's Cecil's shrimp boat or trawler, or whatever it's called. Its port is out of McClellanville alright, listed as a commercial fishing vessel owned by, now get this, Roy Mannes."

Connie looked up at Kay in disbelief. "Are you talking about the Columbia Police Chief?"

"Yeah, and there is a number of other names on the list too, one of which you know pretty well." She pointed to it and looked down at Connie to see her expression when she read the name.

Connie couldn't believe her eyes as she dropped the paper on the floor, saying the name aloud. "Winn Coleman, that son of a bitch!"

The office phone rang and Connie answered.

"Connie, Carol here, I have U.S. Forest Ranger DeWayne Allred on the phone. He said he is in charge of the U.S. parks and forest drone program here in South Carolina, but he said that we have no authority to tell him where they can fly their drone."

"Sorry Carol, but please tell Mr. Allred we'll get back with him later. We are right in the middle of something. I can't talk to him right now so please thank him for his time, OK?"

"Yes, Ms. Womack will do, is there anything wrong in there, and are you guys OK?"

"Yes dear, we're fine, thank you for asking. We are just real busy." She hung up.

Spider sat watching all of this going on, and remarked, "Man this place is jumping now," as Connie's cell phone started ringing again.

"Yes, Tommy, what do you have for me?" Connie grabbed the backside of the paper Kay gave her and started to take notes on it.

"OK, Connie, a Lieutenant Dan is going to call you. He is the one in charge of the national drone program in conjunction with the U.S. Park

Service."

"Lieutenant Dan, really, you have got to be kidding me."

"No, Forest, I'm not, you get it, Forest, U.S. National Park Service," as he laughed. "Sorry, anyway he has been told to fly that thing anywhere you say so."

"Great, but you guys are at the wrong place. You need to split up. Send half your men to a fish cabin at Anderson Creek and you need to head to McClellanville's marina right now to catch a shrimp boat."

"A shrimp boat? What the heck are you talking about, whose boat?"

"Cecil's, Tommy, we think that's the way he is planning on getting away with those girls, by boat. And here's one thing about that boat Tommy. It turns out that a couple of our friends are owners in the boat. One is your friend, Chief Roy Mannes, and another is everyone's favorite senator and your buddy and mine, Winn Coleman."

"You're shitting me, damn and the surprises just keep on coming! You're sure, Roy Mannes? I've known him for years."

"Oh there's one more thing Tommy. We need to call the coast guard. I think Cecil is headed to

Bird Island. It's off the coast in Bulls Bay."

"I know where Bird Island is. I tell you what Connie, I'll call the coast guard. You wait for a call from Lieutenant Dan, run Forest run, ha, ha," as he laughed while hanging up the phone.

Connie liked how it was going down. The case was coming to a head. If everything went as she thought, those girls could be rescued by tonight. But in all her years at this game the one thing she knew too well is that it never goes as you plan, never.

Big Water

Chapter 47

LIFE ON THE WATER FOR SHRIMPERS AND FISHERMEN is a hard one to say the least and a damn tough way to make a living. It takes years of experience in reading charts and tide tables and knowing how to navigate through the shoals and jetties. It's not only hard but very dangerous for the well-trained and seasoned old salts, much less to a novice seaman and full-time drug dealer. But even with all that experience, a good fisherman knows you still need good luck and good weather.

That's the one thing Cecil never took into consideration in his haste. The weather can change in a second on the big water. Cecil kept his eye on the skies above as he watched the ominous black clouds roll in, quickly darkening the skies. They had made it as far as the mouth of Anderson Creek, which at that point was the size of the great Mississippi, but they still had time to turn inland and hit the beach to wait out bad weather if need be. The only thing between them and the open ocean of the bay were the jetties. And seeing they were in a small overloaded rubber boat with a 10-horsepower motor in bad weather, that task seemed pretty tall for even the most seasoned seaman, let alone an inexperienced drug dealer.

"We need to go in, put this thing into shore. We can't make it out there. Man you are crazy," Melissa shouted as the rest of the girls closed their eyes and prayed.

"I told you to shut the hell up, girl, and I'm not going to tell you again. Do you understand me?" as Cecil shook his fist at her. "Now be quiet girl and let me study on this, jetty."

Cecil turned his focus back to the water as he watched and counted each wave of the brackish water colliding with the salt water crashing onto the boat and causing hard work for the small engine which was laboring under the strain of the strong currents and rip tides. The dinghy rocked back and forth against the powerful waves, causing the water to start crawling over the balloon-sided boat. The water was rushing in on all sides now as the girls' screams were muffled by the roaring waters. Still Cecil would not quit; there was no turning back now as they found themselves dead in the middle of the jetties. Wave upon wave hit the boat and were getting larger and stronger with each passing new one. Cecil and his crew were being tossed and pulled like a fishing cork bobbing up and down with every new wave as if the movement was the rhythm of Poseidon's heartbeat, steadily getting stronger as his anger got more intent with each beat. Cecil held to the throttle of the Evinrude for dear life, hoping he was steering their way through this aquatic gauntlet. The spray of water hit their faces hard as the boat rocked back and forth, so hard at one point Cecil knew for sure they were going to capsize. But the small dinghy endured and steadily they kept making headway.

Wave after wave hit the boat and the thought of how much more could they take crept into their minds as time ticked by. Slowly and surely they made their way. The waves now did not seem as strong, as each wave that hit seemed to be less than the last one. The small boat made it through the rough waves of the jetties and now they were just riding big ones. Larger, slow rolling waves greeted them as they made it to the other side and now it was ocean water beneath them and they could not help but feel anything but small. The waves were so large that their view of land would disappear completely till they made it to the top of another and with each roll of a wave the girls' moans were getting louder. They all felt sicker as both the waters and their stomachs churned with each new mound of water.

The *High C*

Chapter 48

THE RUST COVERED OVER THE FADED WHITE PAINT WITH MORE RUST on the *High C*, an old 75-feet long shrimp trawler built in Biloxi, Mississippi, in the Steiner Shipyards over a half a century ago. But the old girl still made good steam and was still considered one of the fastest ships of her class. This made her very desirable and pleasing to folks in the drug and now sex trade. Her captain was Theodore James Jolly, an unkempt old salt with the appearance of an unclean Santa Claus but a seasoned sailor and navigator of these waters off the South Carolina coast. After the death of his wife Captain Jolly lost his moral compass with his descent into the bottle. The old captain set his prices to the highest drug dealer. In this case it was Cecil and his gang that acquired his services for the last few years. Deep down he was a good man who had wished on several occasions he had never come across the likes of Cecil. After the phone call from Skeeter he wondered what criminal adventure he would be on this time as he sat in his captain's chair chewing on the end of a two-inch cigar.

He watched the cloud of dust rise as the three vehicles drove through the unpaved parking lot of the marina on their way to his ship. He watched their approach as he looked through the dirty glass windows of the forecastle, the front section of the ship. The two trucks and one car pulled up alongside of the *High C* and stopped. Nine men got out of the vehicles and started unloading their gear. Skeeter threw his hand up in the air to say hello and Captain Jolly returned the welcome.

"Hey, asshole," the captain whispered under his breath as he took his last swallow of Old Crow whiskey and wiped his hand on his dirty beard. His demeanor quickly changed once he noticed Cecil was not among the gang of men. A smile came across his face and he let out a loud and strong, "hello, welcome aboard mates, come aboard," as the men formed a single line, carrying guns and supplies as they started their way up the gangplank. Suddenly they heard a loud crack as one of the men's foot broke through an old rotten board. A couple of guys stopped what they were carrying and quickly grabbed their comrade before he fell into the water. The captain just laughed a little to himself.

"Oh, by the way, I'd be careful of the gangway. She's got a broken board or three there." Again the old man laughed.

"Damn, Captain J, you need to fix that before someone could get hurt," said Skeeter as he watched his man Biscuit pull his leg out of the hole. "Looks like you do need to lose a few pounds there, Biscuit." The man quickly recovered as he pulled his foot back through the missing board and walked onto the ship with a slight limp. "We need to get underway ASAP captain. We're on a rescue mission."

"Rescue? What the hell are we saving, a drowning kilo of heroin, or a lost cargo container of hash pipes? I didn't know a boatload of missionaries just boarded my vessel. You boys don't look like the lifesaving type to me. Where's your Bible?"

"Shut up old man and get this bucket of rust underway. Cecil is out there somewhere and we got to find him."

“You want me to take the *High C* out in this weather?”

Skeeter looked all around and there was nothing but clear blue sky. “What are you talking about old man? The weather is fine. There ain’t a cloud in the sky.”

“That’s why you are not the ship’s captain and I am. Trust me, the weather is bad out there and I’m not going to risk my life or the life of my ship on that Cecil character. He is rotten to the core and I hope the son of a bitch drowns.”

“Now listen here you old piece of shark bait, you might have been around since the Dead Sea was sick and know all there is to know ‘bout ships and stuff, but you are going to take us out there and take us now,” said Skeeter as he grabbed the old salt by his arm and pulled him up close to his face. “Now get this tub of shit moving, and do it now, do you understand me old man?”

“Sure, sure thing, Skeeter, no problem. You get your men to man the rail and start casting off the mooring lines.” The captain stood there like a rock, his eyes not blinking as he rubbed his whiskers and stared with his cold steel eyes. Skeeter knew not to piss off the captain but he was left with no choice. He had a deadline to keep and he wasn’t about to piss off Cecil either. He’d rather take his chances pissing off the captain with his idle threats, than being killed by Cecil if their plan failed, plus he worked for Cecil and not Captain Jolly. The men quickly stowed their gear and soon took on the role as a seafaring crew as they had done many times before on their drug-running adventures in the past.

Skeeter made his way back up to the bridge after stowing his belongings down below. He looked out the windows and watched as the ship slipped down the waterway. Walking over to the large table full of charts and maps he pointed to the map. “Here, right here, this is where we are going,” Skeeter said to the captain as he pointed to Bird Island on the map.

“What, you boys going on a picnic, going to do a little shell hunting? Are you like all the rest of the tourists that want to go out to that big bucket of a sandbar?”

“Not today, captain, we’re going to Bird Island because that’s where Cecil and our precious cargo will be. Now you just steer this boat where I tell you. That’s all you need to do and you will get your money, OK old man?”

“Sure, Skeeter, I’ll drive the boat where you tell me, sure thing young man, sure thing.” The captain then turned his attention back to navigating and putting the ship on course to Bird Island as he watched the weather start to turn. The clouds grew darker and the ship rocked a little more. Captain Jolly didn't say a word as he obeyed his orders and stayed on course like he was told to do. He retrieved a full bottle of Old Crow and took a quick snort and placed it back in his secret compartment beside his gun. He kept telling himself it's a short trip and quick money, as he steered his vessel through the narrow shoals of Cape Romain Harbor into the waters of Muddy Bay as the clouds kept building, still growing darker.

Weather Or Not

Chapter 49

THE LONG PROCESSION OF BLACK SUVS FILLED THE PARKING LOT of the old marina. Chief Tommy John Parnell stood at the empty slip that once housed the shrimp boat the *High C* that was now vacant of her mooring lines. FBI Special Agent Lawrence Talbert stood beside him as he too stared at the empty slip.

"How about it now, Larry, can we get the use of that drone and maybe a boat or two, now?"

"I don't see why not chief, plus I'll call the coast guard; they need to get involved as soon as possible. I'm sorry Tommy, you and Connie were right the whole time. I'll call and wake my people up on this matter right away. Don't you worry if those girls are out there we'll get them," he said as he walked back to his SUV to call his superiors for authorization.

The small rubber boat was now alone in the great landscape of the ocean. As far as Cecil and the girls could see there was nothing but water and lots of it. The small motor still kept its strength as it puttered along. The waves would once in a while crawl over the sides and sneak into the boat but for the most part the worst thing they had to endure was the sheer size of the waves and constant up and down movement which never seemed to slow down much less ever stop. This motion really got to the girls, whereas in the beginning they were fighting against getting sick and now they found themselves battling against throwing up, and at this point they were well past being sick. Cecil wanted to use his cell phone so bad, but was afraid that if the cops were around they could lock in on his signal. He wasn't seasick but he was sick of the whole thing and he had endured enough of this voyage as he started to second-guess his decision. He could not believe the difference between riding in a small dinghy compared to the hundreds of boat rides he had taken out to Bird Island back and forth in a ski boat. Maybe Bird Island was too far or maybe they missed it to the south, the tide was stronger than he first thought. His mind was already playing tricks and they had been out at sea less than two hours he thought, and that's when he felt his first rain drop, then another. All four passengers looked skyward as the black clouds let go their moisture and the rain came pouring down. Their only thoughts were what else could go wrong.

The rain was pounding down on the *High C* as Captain Jolly had warned the crew beforehand as the shrimp trawler made its way out of the shallow tributaries to the rolling waves of the big water. The trip should be a short one but in this weather no one knows for sure as the seas grew stronger. The door to the bridge started to open but quickly slammed shut as Skeeter slipped on the wet steps and reached for the rail as the captain grabbed Skeeter by his arm to steady his footing from the rolling movement of the ship. "What part of the island are we going to," he asked.

"Part, hell I don't know captain, Cecil just said to meet him there on the island. Why?"

"Why, because that's a pretty big piece of land, we will have to circle till we see them I guess?" We'll start on the north side that's where most folks go to party. The captain then went back inside the bridge to navigate but to mainly get out of the rain, and to take another shot of whiskey, knowing that it was going to be a longer voyage then he first thought.

Cecil looked down again at his compass, still showing due east. “That island should be here,” he said out loud, and the girls looked up, now knowing they were truly lost.

“How did you lose a whole island there, Captain Kirk, asked Melissa? Everybody knows you follow the flight of birds. It is called Bird Island, right.”

Cecil didn’t know whether to hit her or kiss her as he turned the dinghy slightly to the north, knowing that before the rain when he watched the sky earlier he had seen the birds, and sure enough the birds were flying in their new direction. But still the rain, the wind, and the sea had the best of the small rubber dinghy as they fought their way through each wave. They also noticed the rain or the lack of it as it began to slacken off to a mere sprinkle as the clouds started to break-up as well. Another hour passed and the small crew looked as if they had been beaten. They were waterlogged, seasick and tired of being a captive to Cecil and the ocean, and even Cecil was ready to leave his watery prison. Then suddenly Melissa started moaning, as she shouted out and started frantically waving her arms for attention as she pointed and cried out “Land.” Cecil too turned and saw what caught her eye over the horizon and they all breathed a sigh of relief as the tiny ship headed to the beach and partial freedom.

The *High C* was on its second attempt of navigating the complete circumference of the large land mass of Bird Island. Skeeter and his crew were getting anxious as time was slipping away. They did see a few pockets of people shell hunting and partying even in the rain, but no sign of Cecil and the girls as they passed by the Island for the second time. A U.S. Coast Guard helicopter then came into view as it appeared to be circling as well. Captain Jolly's gut feelings were telling him that something had to be up. He just smiled and waved to the helicopter crew as he watched them pass overhead.

"Don't worry, Skeeter, you can tell your men this happens all the time it a very common scene when there has been a shark attack or a drowning has occurred. It's summer time and it happens all the time, it's OK."

"You drive the boat, old man, Cecil is out there somewhere and we'll find him soon I know it, just drive the boat." Then a text message came over Skeeter's phone.

"WRONG ISLAND…THINK WE R NORTH OF BIRD"

"Captain, turn this ship around, we're at the

wrong damn island, Cecil said he is north of here."

"He must be at White Island we passed that on the way here, and hell that's a tiny piece of land, lucky he found that one or he could have been lost at sea for sure," as the captain went back inside and changed course as the ship listed hard to port and headed due north.

Cutter Makes Waves

Chapter 50

ALL 111 MEN ON THE COAST GUARD CUTTER *Hamilton* were ready as it pulled out of her home port of North Charleston once they got the call from the FBI. The cutter received more information after the shrimp trawler, the *High C*, was spotted in those same waters off Bird Island by the coast guard helicopter that saw her earlier. Whatever Cecil and his men had to defend themselves, it would not be enough to combat the 418-feet-long *Hamilton* and her 57-millimeter gunfire control system, much less her four .50 caliber machine guns.

As Skeeter's cell phone rang once more he answered. "Man, Skeeter, you better get the hell out of there! I got word that a damn coast guard cutter is headed your way." It was Cricket on the other end shouting.

"What are you talking about, Cricket? We haven't seen anything out here."

"I'm telling you that my cousin, you know the one who works at the shipyard. Well he has a brother-in-law that works for the coast guard. You know the same one that got us that Mexican heroin deal last mouth. Well, he said they are headed out your way bro, you better tell Captain Jolly before all hell rains down on you boys."

"We haven't found Cecil yet and we can't and won't leave until we find him."

"Cecil, he can take care of himself and besides, they can't get you boys for anything yet, but soon as you pick up Cecil, well that's a different matter altogether. I'm just letting you know about the cutter." Cricket said good luck and ended the call.

Captain Albright stood beside the radioman as they both listened to the transmission they intercepted. He then pushed a button on the control panel to talk to his command center. "Sir, did you get all of that?"

"Roger that *Hamilton* we sure did." The captain smiled and replied to command. "Please send that transmission to the FBI. That might be something they need and want for evidence."

"Roger that sir," said Captain Albright of the *Hamilton* as he turned to his helmsman. "Alright Pete, let's get out there and be ready to intercept that trawler as soon as they retrieve their cargo. Now all ahead full."

"Yes sir, captain, all ahead full," said Petty Officer Pete Newland, the sailor manning the helm, and the cutter sprang to life as she headed to Bulls Bay and somewhere near Bird Island.

"Radioman contact Hilo one with the coordinates and tell them to be on the lookout for any small vessel. If they're out here we'll find them."

"Roger that sir."

Damn Those Tourists

Chapter 51

CECIL TOOK A LITTLE TIME TO REST AS HE LOOKED at his dead cell phone. He watched the water pouring out of it and threw it down on the sand in disgust. He quickly got the girls up off the beach and started looking in the waters for any sign of Captain Jolly and the *High C*. Cecil looked at the strange sight of standing dead oaks trees and eroded roots, which had been bleached white by the salt and sunshine, standing in the sand as if they were alive. He knew then where he was. They were not on White Island at all. No, they were on Bulls Island and they were standing on Boneyard Beach where tourists come to see endangered animals like the wood stork and where the loggerhead turtles inhabit along with egrets, herons and pelicans. They were in the Cape Romain National Wildlife Refuge, a refuge for migratory birds. Cecil realized that they must have traveled in circles because Bulls Island was south of and right beside where they had started out in the first place, Anderson Creek.

"We are at the damn bird watchers island! We have to get off this beach," Cecil announced. "We have to get out of here before more tourists show up." He turned and sure enough he saw a couple walking hand in hand along the beach. And the more he stared across the sand, the more people he noticed. They were everywhere.

"Hey buddy, you guys need some help?" Another couple was eyeing the shipwrecked crew of Cecil and the girls. Cecil didn't respond as he motioned to the girls to get in the boat. The girls did not move, which prompted Cecil to pull his gun out far enough for them to see it. In a defiant move all three girls continued to sit on the beach and refused to move. As more people walked up they realized they were looking at emaciated girls handcuffed to each other. Cell phones started filming as others started calling 9-1-1. The numbers of people grew like a flock of seagulls sighting popcorn lying on the beach. More and more tourists walked over to the crowd to investigate. Cecil walked up shouting at a man filming. “Give me that phone,” he shouted as he pulled it away from the onlooker. Before he could attempt to call Skeeter the crowd of people began to close in on him and the girls. Feeling he had no choice Cecil pulled out his gun and fired into the air.

“Get back damn it,” shouted Cecil as he fired a second round, and everyone dived to the ground as fear overcame the brave crowd of bird watchers. They quickly realized this was not a part of the tour. Cecil once again tried to retrieve the girls as he pulled on their arms, but they had had enough and would not budge as they anchored themselves to the sand. Death would be a relief to them at this point and they stood fast in their convictions. Even in the face of death people kept filming, texting and calling on their cell phones. Cecil knew he could not overcome this obstacle and retreated back to his rubber dinghy with his gun blazing as he fired two more warning shots into the air. “Don’t you move! Stay back,” Cecil shouted, but a few men started to feel brave once again, standing up as their own sign of defiance. Little did Cecil know that the word was out to the Awendaw-Bulls Island ferry captain and everyone else as social media exploded with images and messages. From Facebook, Twitter, Snapchat, to YouTube, it was all over the Internet.

“Holy shit, look at this,” Spider shouted in the office as Connie and Rhys quickly moved over to his computer monitor. Connie looked on in disbelief.

"Is this live?" Connie asked Spider as he nodded yes. Connie looked at Rhys and before she could say anything Rhys already had his cell phone out calling Chief Parnell. Connie looked back at the screen and watched as the Internet captured this surreal reality TV show playing out in real time.

"Now I said get back," shouted Cecil again as he made his way closer to his dinghy but this time without the girls. Dozens of women were running to their aid. The rest of the crowd, mostly men, was slowly advancing on Cecil's position, getting closer with every step. The tourists, now turned heroes, would not be easily frightened or scared off by Cecil's threats. Once again a shot was fired but this time not by Cecil's hand but that of U.S. Park Ranger David Ward. He was the same ranger that had helped Todd escape from the Garrison brothers at the lake. He quickly approached, but his SUV was cut off from Cecil and the rest by the rushing water of Price Creek. Seeing an opportunity as Cecil was distracted by the shot, several men tried to overtake him. They jumped on Cecil, grabbing his arms and tackling his legs but the group was no match against a hardened veteran, much less an army ranger. Again gunfire rang out as one man fell, then another. Cecil managed to fight off his bird-watcher assailants as a woman who was helping the young girls screamed. One of the wayward bullets had found its target. Her lifeless body fell over beside the girls. U's blood trickled down the front of her T-shirt as her ordeal was now finally over after months of pure torture. She now could rest. Her head fell over facing the girls as she died peacefully with a slight smile on her face. Melissa helped close U's eyes as both girls cried.

Cecil tried to fire his gun once more but was out of bullets. The courageous group of men, were not about to stop because there was no giving up at this point. He began to fight his way back to his boat, hitting one man with a powerful right cross, knocking him out with one punch. He quickly pulled out his knife and cut another man, giving Cecil more time as he tried to start the boat motor. He pulled and pulled on the starter cord but even his trusty Evinrude let him down, as it too refused to obey his command. Cecil frantically tried again but the motor refused to start. Looking up, he could see the group of men totally surrounding him. Cecil's world as he knew it was about to come to an end. The entire national refuge area was cut off. The sky was full of helicopters, police and park officials heading to the ferry landing. The coast guard cutter *Hamilton* could be seen entering the bay.

In one last stand of defiance Cecil quickly reloaded his gun with a couple of bullets. He steadied the rubber boat, trying to get off one more shot into the innocent crowd or to shoot another one of his girls. Park Ranger David Ward's .30-06 Springfield zeroed in on Cecil. The fatal shot to the head found its target and Cecil's body fell out of the dinghy face first into the waters of Bulls Bay.

The crowd of birdwatchers and the whole Internet audience cheered as Cecil Locklear's reign of terror was finally over. The two sisters held each other and cried with tears of joy. Cheers could also be heard throughout the offices in the police station. Rhys stared at the monitor, watching the lifeless body in the water, thinking, Bye you son of a bitch, that one's for Jack. Connie said nothing, shaking her head up and down yes, we got him! The drone circled overhead as it captured Cecil's body floating face down in the water on video tape, for the Internet world to see.

The news traveled quickly as word of Cecil's demise reached Skeeter. He knew with Cecil's death he was now in charge of Cecil's operation and his men. He turned to Captain Jolly who knew something was up. "Looks like you got your wish there, captain. It doesn't look like old Cecil is going to make it to the *High C* this trip."

"He's gone?"

Thomas "Skeeter" Wise turned away to hide his emotions from the captain and faced the open ocean waters. "Here is to you, Chief," as he placed his hand to the brim of his cap and saluted his fallen comrade. From Iraq to Fort Leavenworth and now here at Bird Island those two had been through a lot together. Through all those years somehow the road got twisted along their way. They both had started together at Fort Benning Georgia, as elite army rangers and now they both had ended up outlaws of the worst kind.

Captain Jolly watched Skeeter and started thinking of his wife who died a few years back. He tried to console Skeeter by saying something nice, but all that would come out was, "well, alright then, looks like I'll head us back to port." As Jolly retreated back to the helm Skeeter stood looking toward the clouds. He watched the skies as the helicopters and even the drone broke off their circling. Both the coast guard cutter and the *High C* set course to cruise back to their home ports but this time without their precious cargo.

Day of Reckoning

Chapter 52

TODD SNYDER SAT IN HIS CELL WAITING TO BE TRANSFERRED to the regular jail in North Charleston, but in Connie's eyes he showed true remorse, as he kept apologizing for his involvement. To her he seemed truly hurt, not only for the loss of his brother, but that he had anything to do with the kidnapping. And in her opinion, in the eyes of the court that would go a long way.

Curtis, on the other hand, was just plain scared of prison and was still willing to testify against anyone if it would lessen his sentence. He knew a guy like him would not make it very long in jail. Connie couldn't help but feel the same way and deep down she was hoping he wouldn't make it either.

As for Winn Coleman, he was through talking to the police or anybody else. Connie tried to give him some information about the girls but he would not listen. He had lost everything and everyone he cared about and in his opinion his life was over. He was fed up and completely tired of being used and forsaken by his friends, colleagues and especially tired of the lies and conceit of the children. Connie tried to feel a little sorry for him but deep down she couldn't. He was so corrupt and a South Carolina senator at that, she thought, as she turned to leave the visitor's room. She wanted to see all three one last time before they were sent off in different directions throughout the criminal justice system. Once out in the hallway she noticed Winn's attorney Matthew Cohn sitting in a chair outside the visitor's room. He too had been denied visitation rights and was waiting on Connie to exit.

"Hello again Ms. Womack. How are you today?"

She did not like him one little bit and felt pretty disgusted having to talk to him about the whole situation. "Well hello counselor, what brings you back here? I see your client won't talk to you either, so why don't you just slither off like a nice reptile."

"Well here's the thing, Ms. Womack. I have other clients that are involved in this matter that would like to stay anonymous. The information that the senator possesses could be a plus or a grave hindrance to his being safe."

"You are talking about the list of names that participated in that organization which deals in illegal sex trafficking and kidnapping and extortion and in some cases murder. Are those the clients you are speaking of, counselor?"

"Well, you can't say all of that about my clients; these are very prominent people in high places Ms. Womack, very powerful people."

"You sure keep a good list of high-quality clientele I must say, Matthew. And your list of clients will be the first place I'm going to look so I can take down that kidnapping organization. No wonder people place lawyers in such high regards; you are one sorry piece of shit."

"You can't talk to me that way."

"So you came down here to see if he told me who these people were, for what? So you could scare me or maybe to blackmail me, is that it!"

"If those names get out Winn Coleman dies."

"Well mister smartass you can tell your clients to hold their breath, because without his wife, his children and his career, he is dead already, and this case is resolved and about to be closed. And by the way counselor, I didn't go back there because I needed any more of his testimony or a list of your precious clients' names. I went back there out of courtesy to his office as a state senator and gave him an update on his daughters' well-being, thank you very much."

In the middle of the exchange between Connie and the lawyer, Rhys came walking down the hall checking on Connie. She had been in the jail a pretty good while. Plus he had some news to give her from the chief as they were wrapping up things on Bird Island.

The chief wanted Connie's help in doing a background check and finding out the identity of the poor girl Cecil had shot so they could contact the parents but there was also another reason. The big surprise he could not wait to tell Connie was the news that the girls found there were not the Coleman daughters, but were twin sisters from New Jersey, Melissa and Emily McMullen, two runaways who came down to Myrtle Beach for spring break and fun. As he walked around the corner he saw her sitting with the lawyer.

"Hey, Connie, I just got off the phone with the chief." He suddenly stopped, noticing that Connie was upset. "Are you all right?" He then looked over at the lawyer, and asked again, "are you OK, Connie?"

"Yes, I am, Mr. Garrett, thanks for asking but if you could be so kind, could you please throw this piece of shit out of this police station. He has tried to bribe an officer of the state."

Without hesitation Rhys responded, "With pleasure, Ms. Womack!"

"Now wait a minute, I didn't do any such thing, Connie. You know that's not true!" he shouted as six foot five inches and 240 pounds of all muscle grabbed him by the shirt like a bag of laundry and pulled him through the exit door. The lawyer tried to fight back and shouted, "Let go of me, let go you big gorilla!" Rhys then opened the door with one hand and gave one last push with the other, and through the doorway Cohn flew as he landed in the grass with the sprinkler system on full blast. Rhys just laughed as he watched Cohn slip and fall several times before he managed to get up and get out of the raining sprinklers. Rhys locked the door behind him. He looked and waved good-bye through the small windowpane, watching Cohn standing there mad and soaking wet. Rhys laughed once again. "That guy is an asshole." He turned back to Connie who was also laughing as she looked out the window.

"You can say that again."

"That guy is an asshole," and they both started laughing. Connie reached up and held his hand as if to say thank you, and Rhys bent down and gave her a good long kiss on the lips. "You are welcome."

She leaned upward and kissed him again, this time longer and harder. "I've been waiting years for that," she said as Rhys stepped back and grabbed the handles to her wheelchair and with a little smile on his face pushed her back up the hall.

"Let's go home. I need to feed Tricks," said Connie, wearing a smile.

"Is that what they call it these days?" as they both laughed.

Skeeter Shakedown

Chapter 53

THE RINGING OF THE BELL SOUNDED AS THE DOOR to the Early Bird Diner opened and Rhys Garret walked inside. He stopped to take a quick look around through the crowded group of hungry folks till he found his target. He slowly worked his way around the traffic of incoming and outgoing customers and finally found an opening as he looked down the long row of bar stools and took his seat next to the end of the lunch counter. The short-order cook was hard at it, and the waitress was chomping on that piece of Juicy Fruit gum she was chewing in her mouth.

"Can I get a black cup?" Rhys asked as the

waitress came whizzing by him. He slowly turned his stool to the left and glanced at the customer eating his breakfast.

"Sure hon, coming right up," as she stopped dead in her tracks so she could give Rhys a slow, long look-over. She appreciatively gazed at him, not seeing many customers looking quite that handsome, not in this joint anyway.

"Hey Wanda, how's about some more coffee down at this end," shouted a customer and breaking the spell Rhys had on her as she hurried to the hot pot of coffee.

"How's the job promotion going there, Skeeter, pretty big step-up I guess?" Rhys questioned the customer to his left. Without looking directly at Rhys the patron nonchalantly finished his last bite of breakfast and took his time drinking the rest of his coffee. He slowly wiped his mouth with his napkin as he was thinking what to say before he spoke. He then turned toward Rhys.

"Well, I'm surprised it took you this long to show up lieutenant, long time no see, Garret. What brings you to this lovely establishment? Is it the ambience or maybe it's Wanda? No, I'm thinking it's because you were scared, that's it, scared old Cecil would pull another fast one on you again like in Bagdad, or are you here in town because you are still trying to get in the pants of Commander

Womack's old lady?" Rhys quickly grabbed Skeeter by the shirt with his left hand and pulled him straight off his stool, having his right hand cocked back and ready to strike. At the same time three men who were sitting in the booth behind him jumped up and surrounded Rhys.

Skeeter laughed out loud. "Lieutenant, may I introduce three of my associates, Wynken, Blynken and Nod," as he pointed to Cricket, Biscuit and Screwy Louie. Rhys didn't move as he tightened his fist causing Skeeter to choke as he began to squirm. In a hoarse voice Skeeter tried to talk. "Now get your hands off of me you son of a bitch."

"Here's your coffee hon," and right on cue Rhys reached out and grabbed the whole pot out of the waitress's hands.

"Thanks, sweetheart." He then pointed the pot of hot scalding coffee at Skeeter's crotch. "I got a better idea, dickhead. Let's have your boys back up a little or the temperature in this place is fixing to rise. Now move!"

"Hold it big man, now wait one minute." Skeeter quickly turned to his men. "You heard the man, back up damn it! Back up! Now what do you want from me, Rhys? You guys got Cecil. He's dead. I don't have any beef with you."

"The only thing I want from you is for you and

your men to know that I'll be watching your ass. If you or anyone that works for you like these three here try to mess with Ms. Connie Womack again, I'll be all over your ass, do you understand me?"

"Look man, we just sell a little drug in this town, that's all, and believe me, I don't want any part of that crazy kidnapping business. I'm out. You can trust me on that."

"I said do you understand," as Rhys pulled harder on his shirt.

"Yes, I understand man. She is off-limits, yes I understand!" he shouted. Rhys let go and placed the pot down on the counter and then poured himself a cup.

Skeeter looked at Rhys as he straightened up his shirt. "I must say before we kill you, Rhys, you got a set of balls on you son, coming in here and threatening me, knowing I would have a few men with me. Yes sir, you are one dead, but brave, son of a bitch."

"He's pretty smart too, Mr. Skeeter Wise." Suddenly Chief Tommy John and Spider stood up in the booth behind Skeeter and his men. They had been there the entire time and Skeeter never saw them. Rhys had once again got the drop on old Skeeter and there was nothing he could do about it. "If I were you, I believe now would be a good time to leave before I have this entire restaurant surrounded by Charleston's finest. And yeah, I'll overlook that little idle threat of killing my good friend here. Oh, by the way I'm Chief Tommy John Parnell at you service," as he showed him his badge and his gun.

Skeeter and his men got up and moved over to the exit sign. He then turned back toward Rhys as they stepped out through the doorway to the parking lot and looked back over his shoulder.

"This ain't over, I'll see you again, Lieutenant."

"I'm counting on it, Skeeter, and you can bet I'll be ready."

Epilogue

EDDIE MILLER SAT COUNTING HIS BLOOD MONEY making sure it was all there and was exactly the amount he was due as the Caribbean breeze blew through the open windows of their cabana. The girls sat in front of the television oblivious to reality as they worked on their nails and makeup. Not truly understanding nor wanting to deal with the whole situation of what had occurred in the last few days, all they cared about was that they were free.

To their cold and calculating hearts the loss of their parents meant basically nothing to them, to them, their parents had it coming. For one thing Winn was not their real father, at least that was the way they looked at it. And using the other girls the way they did, well that was just part of playing the game of revenge to them. Their whole life was a game of charades which was made up of a long list of consequences for lots of people. To them it was a game of childish revenge but to everyone else it was life-changing. It started with their father, or stepfather Winn, who for years mentally and sexually abused them. Once they discovered his secret society of sex trafficking they were out to get him and they had succeeded. Ironically, he would be serving years in prison for something he didn't do. The icing on the cake was that his political career was totally ruined.

In their eyes Patty, their mother, was never there for them. She was a senator's wife, caring more about climbing the social ladder than showing her family the love and respect they wanted and needed. Her marriage was a sham for years and after a time she didn't care. She was too busy living her own life and enjoying her sexual escapades with her boyfriends. Winn could do as he pleased and the girls saw that side too.

But Patty's biggest mistake was that, when in one of her many drunken confessions, she revealed to her daughters the identity of their biological fathers. After all those years of pain and hell the girls had to endure at the hands of Winn Coleman, Patty picked that time for them to find out that Winn was not their real father. One father was not a senator at all but a half-breed Lumbee Indian, turned drug dealer and sex trafficker named Cecil Locklear. The second was a good man, a loyal and obedient servant, ex-military man and family bodyguard to the senator, Tony Hines. They were decimated to learn that their lives were a lie, as hate and pure embarrassment fanned the flames of revenge and set the whole fiasco in motion. Their mother would be institutionalized for years, if not for the rest of her life, after the dramatic events of the last few days, and especially after losing her true love Tony, Melissa's biological father. The girls saw the consequences as payback.

Both girls took no blame for the events that happened. After all, it wasn't their fault that years of bad parenting or the absence of parenting all together, with only nannies and bodyguards, showed them no love. Their lives were full of lies and deceit, not to mention the nights of rape and mental cruelty, and a mother who turned a blind eye to it. This was the environment that created them, and how they became monsters themselves.

But now they had their freedom and all the riches they needed, knowing the passwords to Winn's hidden bank accounts and offshore money. An added bonus was having the list of names on Winn's thumb drive, the names of all the people in the sex-trafficking organization. No one was going the mess with them now. They were free to travel the world, and to do whatever they wished.

Now the only question, as their twisted brains

went to work, was what to do with Eddie.

Eddie then shouted, “Come on girls, you guys ready to go out on the town? We’re going to have some fun tonight.” They both turned toward each other and smiled.

The End

From the Author:

I want to thank each and every one of you for choosing to read my book. I truly hope that you enjoyed the journey that Connie and the gang took you on. And stay tuned, I'm excited to say that I have already started a new book with Connie Womack which will be coming out soon. I do ask that you please take the time and write a review, or give it a star rating. Again thank you and please tell a friend about my work. It would be greatly appreciated.

William Brent Hensley

As I worked on this novel my research suddenly opened my eyes to a world most of us cannot imagine even exists. It's a world where thousands of exploited kids are being sold like cattle and living in hellacious conditions, lost and scared and feeling it's impossible to escape. Even here in my hometown of Myrtle Beach we see hundreds of lost souls every season and even though it is heartbreaking as we watch them walk aimlessly down the beaches and streets, most of us do nothing to help. Whatever their situation and regardless how they got to this point, whether a lost teen that started as a runaway, or as a foster child who grew up in a broken home, their lives are important. We must not turn our backs to this situation any longer. I am simply asking that if you see anyone that may be in need of help or if you have information on a missing child, please contact the **National Center for Missing & Exploited Children** by calling **1-800-The-Lost**. That number is 1-800-843-5678. Your act may just save a life.

Thank you

Wm. Brent Hensley